Readers love
the Copper Point Medical series
by HEIDI CULLINAN

The Doctor's Secret

"Cullinan weaves themes of racism and Asian culture, family pressures, and the value of friends, home, and love into a deeply satisfying romance."

—*Publishers Weekly*, Starred Review

"If you like slow, trope-filled romances with high stakes and happy endings (and a side of codes and gurneys), this is a must-read. Cullinan knows how to keep her readers hooked!"

—Love Bytes

"I stayed up past my bed time to finish this book and it was totally worth it."

—Two Chicks Obsessed

The Doctor's Date

"…the story's magic is in how their affection for each other helps them individually achieve self-confidence and self-love. This tear-jerker is a captivating winner."

—*Publishers Weekly*, Starred Review

By HEIDI CULLINAN

With Marie Sexton
Family Man

COPPER POINT: MAIN STREET
The Bookseller's Boyfriend

COPPER POINT MEDICAL
The Doctor's Secret
The Doctor's Date
The Doctor's Orders

DREAMSPUN DESIRES
The Professor's Green Card Marriage

TUCKER SPRINGS
With Marie Sexton: Second Hand
Dirty Laundry

Published by DREAMSPINNER PRESS
www.dreamspinnerpress.com

THE BOOKSELLER'S BOYFRIEND

HEIDI CULLINAN

Published by
DREAMSPINNER PRESS

5032 Capital Circle SW, Suite 2, PMB# 279, Tallahassee, FL 32305-7886 USA
www.dreamspinnerpress.com

The Bookseller's Boyfriend
© 2021 Heidi Cullinan

Cover Art
© 2021 Paul Richmond
http://www.paulrichmondstudio.com
Cover content is for illustrative purposes only and any person depicted on the cover is a model.

Mass Market Paperback ISBN: 978-1-64405-858-9
Trade Paperback ISBN: 978-1-64405-857-2
Digital ISBN: 978-1-64405-856-5
Library of Congress Control Number: 2020944386
Trade Paperback published January 2021
First Edition
v. 1.0

Printed in the United States of America
∞
This paper meets the requirements of
ANSI/NISO Z39.48-1992 (Permanence of Paper).

For Shawn and Holly
who already know how to get there

Chapter One

RASUL YOUSSEF knew he'd gone a bridge too far when his literary agent said, "Either throw away your phone, or consider our relationship terminated."

Rasul smiled even though Elizabeth couldn't see him. "You want me to throw away a brand-new fifteen-hundred-dollar phone? While I'm talking to you on it?"

He'd been trying to charm her into calming down, but Elizabeth wasn't playing. "You're getting a burner that can't do anything but text and make or receive calls." He heard clicking in the background. "There's a store in campus town, four blocks from you."

Rasul sobered. "I'm not going to throw away my phone."

"I busted my ass to get you this gig at the university."

"It has seven thousand students. It's hardly a university."

"Quit trying to get out of this through semantics. This is the end of the line for you in every way, which you well know. It's taken every ounce of my leverage to get your publishing house to give you a *fourth* extension instead of insisting on the repayment of your advance."

He truly hated being reminded of this. "I spent that a long time ago."

"You think I don't know that? You're on the hook for a staggering chunk of change if you don't provide them with something to publish. You're out of options. You either write this book, or you're heading toward an end I will not, and I say this with love, follow you down."

Rasul sat on the couch that came with the furnished apartment. A cloud of dust rose around him.

Elizabeth kept delivering the hits. "I wish I could say I'm *surprised* you'd try to sandbag yourself when you're this far against the ropes, but sadly I've come to know you too well for that. This is it, kid. I'm done watching you let that two-bit model stand on your back to get herself a better patch of mud in the gutter. I'm done explaining away the wild parties and Instagram stories when you should be working. And I'm *absolutely* done running damage control on paparazzi spreads of you and your damn ex partying so hard you missed your flight to Wisconsin."

His flight had been to Minnesota, with a two-hour drive *into* Wisconsin, but he had enough self-preservation instinct not to point that out. "That wasn't planned. Adina called me when I was low, and she was low too, and so…. Anyway. I'm in Copper Point now. I'll send you pictures. It's ridiculously small. And Bayview University is a joke."

"The university, with its stipend, furnished apartment, and cushy teaching schedule, is your last chance at a career. You're lucky the president is an eccentric old man who doesn't read gossip magazines but did see your book in an airport once."

Rasul couldn't argue with this, which he hated. He still stung from his damn alma mater turning down his request to be visiting faculty. They bragged about him and his awards on their website, but they couldn't let him come back and coast through some seminars while he finished his work?

Elizabeth kept going. "You're an amazing writer, and you could be an excellent teacher. Yes, you received international acclaim for your freshman and sophomore novels. But your last work was out six years ago, and your third book is long overdue. As far as everyone else is concerned, you've been whoring around the globe instead of working. You and I know it's more complicated than that, and I've done my best to be patient. At the same time, your decisions affect my career. If you can't show me you're serious, we're going to part ways. This is our last conversation on the phone in your hand. It's up to you whether or not we reset on another device. What will it be?"

Rasul ran a hand through his hair, letting his fingers tangle in the long curls. "I can't go on a boozy bender with Adina while I'm in northern Wisconsin. There's no need to get rid of my phone."

"But you can get drunk and sext her, and you'll put it on Instagram the same as last time."

"I'll uninstall Instagram and delete her number."

"As if that will stop you when you hit a low. That woman is worse than any drug for you. She manipulates you, you know it, and you let her."

He desperately wanted to argue that wasn't true, but he was done lying to Elizabeth. He grunted noncommittally instead.

"Besides, you told me three times already you deleted her number. Either you're lying, or you have it memorized."

Best to get her away from this line of conversation where he had no chance of calming her down. "I need to be able to do research. Take photos. Look things up on the fly."

"Last I checked, your book wasn't set in Wisconsin, so the photo argument is bunk. As for research, you can use your laptop. You can go to the library. There's no argument you can make that will change this condition. And as a bit of warning, if you try to tell me you need social media to promote yourself, I'll hang up and send you the papers breaking our partnership immediately."

He *had* considered that argument. She'd been frustrated with him for years for his inconsistent, unremarkable presence on social media, except for when he got drunk or angry with the state of American politics. His Twitter was him yelling at trolls. His Instagram was filled with drunken party photos. He'd cameoed on Adina's YouTube channel, letting her put him in makeup, endured getting quizzed by her fans, and so on.

God, he'd put Elizabeth through the wringer. Maybe he should just let her go now and be done with it.

Except if he did that, he'd truly be out to sea. Even he could acknowledge he was on thin ice, career-wise and… well, in every manner possible.

But damn, his *brand-new phone*.

He leaned his forehead against the window of his apartment, staring at a group of leggy college girls as they sauntered by. They were hot. So was the guy with them. So young, though.

Probably he shouldn't let himself think things like that—they could be his students.

Man, but they were young. Little babies starting out in the world. They had no idea what hell waited for them.

Sighing, Rasul shut his eyes. "How about a compromise? I'll mail you my phone."

More clicking. "There's a post office a block south of the cellular store. Seal your phone in an envelope, take it with you to the cellular shop. I'll call ahead and arrange everything. You have forty minutes to comply. Call me on the new phone."

She hung up.

For five minutes Rasul grumbled around the apartment. It was sterile and unwelcoming in the extreme—he'd never write a word here. It smelled funny, like the previous resident had cooked nothing but hamburgers and french fries, and the decor was abysmal. Why couldn't Elizabeth have put him up in some quaint waterfront cabin?

Because you don't have the money for that, and thanks to you, neither does she or her agency. No one else is going to bail you out either. You've spent the last few years subliminally sabotaging your career and all your connections. She's the last person willing to stand by you, and she's about to walk out the door. Get your ass out of this apartment and to the post office.

His first instinct was to defy that chiding voice, to go find a bar and get wasted. It was difficult to turn away from that impulse, but he had enough self-preservation left to understand this was his last shot. Time to commit to a career and a liver and a chance at happiness that lasted beyond a drink, a joint, or the hit of a pill. This was his final opportunity to stop disappointing his friends, his family, and himself.

It was humiliating as hell, and he hated it with every fiber of his being, but Rasul grabbed his keys and wallet—and phone—and headed out the door, ready to do as Elizabeth told him.

The one consolation was that it was nice outside, and while the apartment complex left a lot to be desired, the neighborhood was quaint, charming even. The walk to the post office was tree-lined, and amazingly, some of the leaves had already started to turn. To be expected, he supposed, since he was so far north. The post office itself was a combination of ancient and clumsy modern renovation that amused him. He did have to fight the clerk when he said he wanted to take the envelope with him unsealed.

"They're real strict about you taking metered postage out of here." The clerk, a pretty woman in her twenties, regarded Rasul with apology. "You can't add any weight to it at all, and it has to go out today or it'll be a mess."

Rasul had no idea this was a thing. Frowning, he tried to decide what to do. "Do I have to buy different postage, then?"

"It'll be tricky with the insurance. Sorry." Tapping a manicured nail against her cheek, she considered the metered envelope between them. Coming to some kind of decision, she leaned forward and spoke in low tones. "Tell you what. You go ahead and take it with you. But you gotta promise you'll mail it today, and don't tell anybody else I did it."

"You're an angel. Thank you so much." He picked up the envelope and tucked it into his shoulder bag. "Should I bring it back here to be mailed?"

She waved a hand. "Nah, just take it into any mailbox by five."

After thanking her again, he headed back to the street to head to the cellular store. Strolling beneath the tree canopy again, he followed his phone's GPS to the mobile phone retailer on University Avenue. Damn, but *that* was actually going to be a problem. He could get lost in a paper bag.

He received a few long stares as he meandered. A couple of people seemed to know him on sight, which wasn't surprising. He'd been in the scandal junket a lot during the year with Adina, and of course there was the news fresh off the presses from last night. Elizabeth hadn't called him because she'd been trolling his 'gram. He was wearing his "disguise" outfit—sunglasses, hair pulled back in a ponytail, grungy clothes—but since that's what he kept getting photographed in, it was more advertisement than camouflage.

Man, but he really didn't want to give out any autographs right now, or field any curious questions. He double-timed it for the cellular store.

The place was busy as he entered, but a manager came from behind the counter, smiling. "Mr. Youssef, this way, please. I already spoke to your agent and have your purchase waiting, and I'll be mailing her your phone."

Several people watched him, a few only perking up at his Arabian surname. Rasul did his best to ignore them. "I need to transfer a few numbers before I hand over my other phone, though."

"She already gave me the numbers she says you'll need and had me preprogram them. Would you like to check them to verify?"

Goddamn it. Yes, he would, but he knew better than to try. Odds were good she'd ask the manager if he added any. "No, it's fine. Thanks."

If the manager caught the annoyance in his tone, he ignored it. "Very good." He handed a small black object to Rasul. "Here you are."

A flip phone. An actual flip phone, as if it were 2007. To send a text, he'd have to fumble through the dial pad. *Seriously*, she couldn't even let him text? He wanted to toss the phone and storm out.

Instead he opened it, verified the only numbers listed were Elizabeth's, his parents', and the dean of Bayview University. He pocketed the device. "Thanks."

The manager's smile didn't dim. "And your envelope for me?"

With a heavy sigh, Rasul passed over the envelope and his smartphone. "The woman at the post office was incredibly insistent this had to go out today with the postage I put on it with no weight added."

The manager took it. "Thank you. I'll get this out right away, as is." He hesitated, and Rasul knew what was coming before the man spoke. "Would it be rude of me to ask for your autograph?"

Oh, but it would have been satisfying to snarl and refuse. Instead Rasul inclined his head and waited as the man scrambled for pen and paper. The people who'd seemed concerned at his surname now looked vaguely interested. Rasul didn't stick around to let them query him.

As soon as he was out of the building, he called Elizabeth on the new, terrible phone.

"Well done," she said, not even bothering with a greeting. "You still had fifteen minutes to spare."

"How much did you pay that guy to do your bidding?"

"Hmm, let's see. I can't remember, but it was less than the amount of money I've lost trying to prop up a selfish playboy, so it seems an investment well made."

Touché. "Just don't take my laptop, all right? Otherwise you'll never get a novel."

"Oh, if I don't get a satisfying update within the next ten days, I'll have the campus tech guys restrict your search ability so narrowly you'll be using the card catalog to look things up."

"I don't think they actually have those anymore."

"It's interesting how you'd rather argue about these conditions instead of work."

"Look, you know damn well creativity isn't a tap you turn on and off. I can't just suffer this kind of humiliation and then cavalierly whip out another chapter."

"I've been an agent for twenty-three years, and my wife is a painter. I understand the whims of creativity painfully well. But you've proven partying and destroying your image online isn't giving you the pump-priming you need. My gift to you is a new source of potential inspiration. Take walks. People-watch. Pick up a new hobby. Make friends who don't want to use you. Go find something new to read. I hear they have a lovely bookstore there."

Rasul pinched the bridge of his nose. It wasn't as simple as a lack of inspiration, not at all, but he wasn't going to bring that up. In fact, the one thing he'd figured out was all the partying was an effort to keep from thinking about the problem. Giving Elizabeth the corner of his mental carpet meant she'd wrench it up with one yank, leaving him no choice but to examine the mold and writhing insects beneath.

"Ten days," she said. "I'm going to contact you in ten days, and you're going to tell me about your progress. I won't tell you what that has to look like except that you'll have to convince me you're moving forward enough for this to continue. It goes without saying that if I see a single social media post from you or about you, it's over."

That made him panic. "Look, I can't help it if other people talk about me."

"Let me rephrase: if I see a post that makes me think you've end-run me, we'll have a problem."

He didn't relax. "Adina has a lot of photos. A lot." And a few naughty videos, some of which made him sweat at night.

"Oh, trust me, she's receiving a similar call from her agent, though I think that relationship is beyond saving. If I see any photos from her, I'll do my own investigations. Don't worry about her or anyone else. Do whatever you have to in order to finish this book."

With that, she hung up on him.

Grimacing, Rasul pocketed the phone and stuffed his hands in his pockets, no longer interested in the quaint scenery. Which direction was his apartment? Of course, he didn't want to go there anyway. He had some welcome gala for new faculty that night, but that wasn't until eight. It was four in the afternoon now. Way too many hours to kill.

He started wandering.

There were a lot of shops on University Avenue. An Indian restaurant, Italian restaurant, a Wiccan shop, comics store, art gallery… huh. This place had a little more culture than he would have suspected. There were a lot of bars, and they were tempting, but going there was a step backward, not forward. He considered Café Sól, a charming, understatedly elegant coffee shop, but it looked more crowded than he was ready for right now.

University Avenue eventually led to a small highway, and after crossing at the light, Rasul noticed the street name had changed, as had the businesses dotting it. Main Street Copper Point was more what he'd expected to see in this one-horse town. A community center, Lutheran Church, library, tae kwon do club, and Christian book and supply store. He wondered what the people who shopped there thought of the Wiccan store on the other end of the street.

There was also a bookstore, as Elizabeth had suggested, and the name made him laugh. Moore Books. Twenty dollars said the owner's last name was Moore, and what a quaint but understated pun. It was a proper ramshackle bookstore too, the towering, overcrowded shelves visible through the tall antique windows. As Rasul approached, he saw that though it was clearly a historic building, the stairs had been replaced with a sloping ramp to the side with a reasonable gradient.

Rasul ascended the ramp and pushed open the door, his heart sighing with a sense of rightness as a slightly discordant bell announced his arrival and the scent of old paper hit him in the face. The floors creaked too, a well-polished but ancient hardwood, and the ceiling above him was made out of legitimate tin. The shelves were packed with books, but they were well-organized and clearly labeled. A small front-facing shelf boasted new releases, but also store favorites and local interest titles.

Both of Rasul's books were included, with prominence, in the store favorites section.

Only a handful of patrons were visible in the maze of shelving, and the few in his line of sight barely spared him a glance before resuming browsing. The middle-aged woman in one of the armchairs near the front window regarded him slightly longer, but even she soon returned to her own business.

This bookstore, Rasul decided, feeling the truth ring in his soul, was a good place.

"Hi. Welcome to Moore Books. Can I help you find anything?"

Rasul turned to the speaker, a white man about his age wearing a button-down blue shirt and a tan cardigan. Except for his light brown hair, he looked like a young Fred Rogers, down to the navy sneakers.

"Just browsing, thanks." Rasul ran a hand through his hair and tugged at his ponytail. "Nice store."

Mr. Rogers's doppelgänger brightened slightly. "Thank you. I'll let you wander around, but if you decide you need any assistance, find me at the checkout desk."

The man turned and disappeared into the stacks. Rasul watched him go.

He certainly acted like the owner, but if this was who'd listed *both* of Rasul's books as his favorites, he'd given no indication he knew who Rasul was.

Whatever. He was grateful for the privacy, however he got there.

Rasul wandered, taking everything in. The whole first floor was fiction, broken into genre: general fiction, mystery, science fiction/ fantasy, romance, horror/thriller. It was a large area, both in width and length, running all the way to the back of the building. The upstairs, however—accessible via some deliciously creaking and curving stairs or a sleek, modern elevator—was all nonfiction and children's books. The children's area was charming and quite full of people. Another large recommendation area was on full display here, though these suggested reads were provided by the town's librarian.

There were also two cats, a prim gray tabby with a white tuxedo belly, judging Rasul severely as he passed by its perch on top of a low shelf in the general fiction section, and a longhair gray tortoiseshell nested in the middle of an educational toys display upstairs. He also encountered a teenager in a store apron shelving titles, and when she saw him, she squealed and dropped everything in her hands.

"Ohmygod, you're Rasul Youssef."

He smiled his patented smile for fans: welcoming, charming, but not exceptionally inviting. "Hi. Sorry to make you drop your things. Can I help you—"

But she'd already run off, disappearing into an area marked STAFF ONLY.

Rasul picked up the books from the floor, slid them into the appropriate places on the shelf, and gave the cat a hesitant pat. The cat meowed at him, rubbed his hand, and burrowed back into the toys.

After this Rasul meandered to the first floor again, trying to decide what he wanted to browse first. The general fiction section mostly gave him angst at the moment, so he wandered into the genre shelves. He lingered over a book by Lois McMaster Bujold he hadn't even known was out, set it aside to purchase, and picked up another title by an author he hadn't heard of. He was leafing through it when Mr. Rogers reappeared, smiling in that helpful way bookstore owners had.

Rasul waved the book in the air between them. "You read this one, or hear about it? Any good?"

Rogers came over, focusing on the cover, then brightening. "Oh, yes. It's excellent. Highly thought-provoking, but not at all heavy. I believe they were nominated for a Hugo."

Good enough for him. Rasul put the book on his pile. "Any other recs?"

"Of course. Are you looking exclusively for science fiction and fantasy?"

"No, no. Thought-provoking but still fun and in no way pedantic is the mood I'm here for."

"Hmm." Rogers tapped a finger against his lips as he perused the shelves. "How about *Here and Now and Then*? Have you read Chen yet?"

Rasul hadn't. "What's it about?"

"Oh, it's excellent. A time-traveling secret agent struggling to maintain a relationship with his daughter gets stranded in the past for eighteen years, though when his rescue team comes, he finds out it's only been a few weeks in his proper timeline. And also he can't remember his family."

Rasul's eyebrows rose. "That sounds perfect."

"From what I know of your tastes, and given what you said you were after, I think it will fit the bill perfectly."

So the man *did* know who he was, but he was playing it cool. God, Rasul wanted to *live* in this bookshop.

He did a quick perusal of the man beside him once again, but nothing lit up. Mr. Rogers chic just didn't do it for Rasul.

The man missed Rasul's cruise, too busy wandering to the opposite shelves. "Hmm. Please don't be offended by my question, but have you read *I Capture the Castle*?"

Rasul's heart instantly filled with longing. "Forty-five times, I think, but back when I was young. Put it on the pile. It's time for a reread." It would smart a little to have too much in common with James Mortmain, but perhaps that would be good for him.

Good God, was that why Mr. Rogers recommended it?

Before he could figure out how to ask, the bookseller had another volume, this one taken from the manga section Rasul had somehow completely overlooked. "This is a bit off the beaten path, but I honestly think you'd like *My Brother's Husband*. I have both volume one and two in stock, but feel free to start with the first one to see if I guessed right or not."

"You picked up my favorite childhood novel. I trust your judgment. Put both on."

Rogers nodded. "I'll keep these at the front desk and wait for you when you're finished shopping."

Rasul lingered with the manga, picking up some volumes of series he'd forgotten to finish and starting another pile nearly as big as the one Mr. Rogers had taken away. This was going to get expensive, but he would rather eat ramen than have nothing to read. Plus this entire bookstore felt like church for authors. This was practically writing, shopping here.

He was pondering whether he could afford to buy the entire *Fullmetal Alchemist* series when a commotion at the front of the store drew his attention. The bell jangled constant peals of warning as the sound of many feet and an eerie chorus of feminine giggles filled the bookstore.

"Oh my God, do you think he's still here?"

"I'm gonna get my picture with him."

"I'm gonna make him sign my *chest*."

"*Sick*. Get him to sign your tit and I'll give you twenty bucks."

Rasul's stomach plummeted to his feet as he scanned frantically for an emergency exit. No question but this crew was here for him. The next thing he heard froze him cold, however.

"Don't forget to tag Adina so we get the shout-out."

No way. *No way*, this couldn't be happening, not when Elizabeth had just handed him his ass.

Before he could spiral into a deeper wave of panic, Mr. Rogers appeared. He no longer looked like a demure children's show host, however. His lips were in a thin line, and it was clear someone was about to get an earful.

Rogers nodded curtly to the front of the store. "My apologies, Mr. Youssef. It seems some young people in Copper Point don't know how to behave. With your permission, I'll help you leave the store undetected."

Though Rasul nodded in relief, he also cast a sad glance of longing at his books.

Rogers swept them up at once. "I'll get your books for you. Come, follow me up these back stairs. The first-floor rear door is alarmed, but I live above the shop and have my own entrance." Rogers was already unlocking an unassuming green door with a sign reading PRIVATE, KEEP OUT. The door also had a small cat door at the bottom.

Once Rogers had the door open, he ushered Rasul ahead of him. "Up the stairs and to the right. I'll take you out through the kitchen and get you to your car."

"I don't have a car—" Rasul broke off and swore as he tripped over something on the stairs. It yowled. A black cat swiped at his leg, then darted up the stairs and into the shadows.

Rogers sighed. "Moriarty likes to hide on the top stair. I swear one day he'll be the death of me."

He named his cat Moriarty. Rasul considered reevaluating his rescuer's hotness potential once again, but then he remembered the sweater. Nope.

Rogers led Rasul into the kitchen, sat him down, and pulled up his pant leg with the no-nonsense composure of a kindergarten teacher. "I'm so sorry, he drew blood. He's had all his shots, though. Let me get you some disinfectant." He hurried away before Rasul could say anything, then returned with a tidy plastic box full of first-aid supplies, which he set down beside Rasul. "I'm going to run downstairs quick and sort things out. Please make yourself at home. There are glasses in the cupboard, as well as mugs for tea. I'll be back as soon as I can."

Without waiting for Rasul to say a word, Rogers was gone.

After staring for several seconds at the place where the bookseller had disappeared, Rasul fished through the first-aid kit, put some alcohol on a pad, and cleaned the cut with a soft hiss. After he put a bandage on the cut, he collected his garbage and stood to search for a trash can.

The apartment was the complete opposite of Rasul's. It overflowed with things in a way that made Rasul feel comforted and safe while also being absolutely neat and clean. As he wandered from room to room, he saw the whole place was much like the main body of the bookstore, old but well-maintained and in several aspects modernized. The kitchen had a pokey feel to it, but the appliances were all sleek and modern, the countertops granite. The living room creaked as Rasul crossed it, and the overstuffed sofa came complete with a knitted afghan right out of the 1970s, but a small television mounted on the wall was the latest brand and connected to a Blu-ray player. The bathroom was the best, full of old white tile with an actual iron claw-foot tub, but also an impressive rainfall shower and a modern sink. It was as clean as the rest of the apartment, not so much as a hair on the floor.

He hurried back to the kitchen, where the black cat had taken up the observation point on the top of the fridge and growled at him when he came too close. He didn't want to get caught snooping when Rogers returned, but it was taking forever, so he took the man up on his offer and made himself some tea—a loose-leaf Earl Grey. He'd just finished steeping it and was having a sip when the door from the first floor opened and smart footsteps double-timed up the stairs.

Rogers wiped the residual look of murder off his face, but he was still stern as he entered the kitchen. "My apologies for taking so long. It seems my part-timer alerted her friends that you were here, and those friends told their friends, and the end result was a swarm of sixteen-year-olds. A friend of mine came over to mind the shop for a few minutes, and another is en route to escort you home." He passed a sturdy polyurethane bag with MOORE BOOKS printed on the front and overflowing with books. "Please accept your selected titles gratis as an expression of my apology."

"I can't possibly take so many books for free," Rasul said as the bookseller pressed the bag into his arms. The thought of having more money for food was tempting, but this was a bridge too far. These were the man's livelihood. "I'm more than happy to pay."

"I'm afraid I can't accept your money today, but we welcome you back when you next need something to read, at which time I can assure you no one will harass you while you shop." His expression suggested he might stand guard on the ramp with a shotgun, but then it softened slightly. "Both your novels are in my top-ten favorite titles. Please consider the books a gift from a well-contented reader as well."

This guy was going to give Rasul a huge head. Damn shame about the sweater. "Can I sign your copies, then?" It didn't feel presumptive to assume the man had his books in the apartment.

For the first time, the man's demeanor cracked, and the fissure of delight and eagerness on Rogers's face made something surprising curl in Rasul's belly. The spark was gone as soon as it came, however. "I wouldn't dream of imposing."

"It'd be my pleasure, seriously. You have no idea how much you saved me there. My agent is *not* in the mood to see me splashed all over social media with a bunch of teenage girls. Please, let me sign them."

The longing crept back in, and Rogers sighed. "If you insist." His cheeks flushed adorably as he gestured to the living room. "They're… in here."

Rasul's books had, in fact, pride of place on the top of a small bookshelf, both of them nestled next to works by Sir Terry Pratchett, Neil Gaiman, Sarah Waters, and—

Rasul grinned as he pulled out the volume. "*I Capture the Castle.*" He whistled and handled it more carefully as he felt the plastic cover and saw the faded landscape splashed across the spine and front. "First edition. Impressive."

Rogers blushed like a proud parent. "A gift from my mom and dad when I graduated high school. They wrote supportive notes in the front panels, which scandalized me at the time, but I'm incredibly grateful for them now." Before Rasul could ask what he meant by that, he took the book from Rasul, slid it reverently back into place, and withdrew *The Sword Dancer's Daughter* and *Carnivale*, placing them in Rasul's hands.

Rasul was patting his pockets when Rogers gave him a beautiful fountain pen he immediately wished he could ask for instead of the books. He didn't, though, only cracked open *The Sword Dancer's Daughter* and went into author mode. "How shall I make it out?"

"To Jacob, please."

Rasul dutifully inscribed each copy: *To Jacob, who has the loveliest bookstore I've ever seen, Rasul Youssef* in *Dancer*; and in *Carnivale* he wrote *To Jacob, my hero, Love, Rasul.* He worried that might be a bit too familiar, but he did feel significant affection toward the man right now, for the rescue, the books, and the tea.

Jacob—though honestly, Rasul was going to think of him as Mr. Rogers forever—took a moment to blow across each inked page before whipping out an *actual blotter* to make absolutely sure nothing would bleed. With an air of satisfaction, he placed the books back on the shelf. "Thank you very much, Mr. Youssef. I'll treasure them even more now."

"Call me Rasul, please." He winced inwardly at how flirty that came out. What in the world was wrong with him?

A strange expression passed over Jacob's face before he replied. "Thank you, but I couldn't." Rising, he smoothed the front of his trousers and adjusted his sweater. He looked about to say something, but then a knock came at the back door. "Ah, that will be Simon, here to take you home."

A bright, cheerful man in scrubs stood on the other side of the door. Rasul shook his hand for the introduction, then stood patiently as Jacob gave a summary of the situation, distilling it to the essential elements. Visiting professor, needs to get back to his apartment, but some girls in the store behaved badly and may be looking to cause more trouble, so please get him home discreetly.

Simon's polite expression morphed into cold outrage. "Are you kidding me? Why? Do you know who they are? Their parents?"

Jacob held up a hand. "I do, and I've contacted them. I don't think any harm was meant. Mr. Youssef is… a bit infamous online."

The careful way the bookseller phrased that, as if dancing around a highly sensitive topic, made Rasul more abashed than anything Elizabeth could have hurled at him.

Simon, however, brightened, understanding dawning. "Oh—*oh*. You're *that* guy. The author! My husband bought your books because you were coming. He keeps nagging me to read them. Welcome to Copper Point."

There were a few more pleasantries, and then Jacob gently ushered them out the door and onto the stairs leading to a small parking lot behind the building. With his hand on the rail, Rasul turned to Jacob, trying to work out how to thank him.

He was cuter than Rasul had initially given him credit for, but the sweater still bothered him. It was like he was hiding behind it, dressing like a grandfather *so* no one noticed him. Rasul wanted to know that story. He wanted to sit in that charming kitchen and listen to the careful man talk while they drank good tea and soaked in excellent atmosphere. Hell, he wanted to *write* in that kitchen.

Right now, though, all he could do was thank the man for all his help once again.

"It was my pleasure," Jacob replied politely in that bookseller voice Rasul was starting to resent a little. "Please come by the shop anytime you like."

With that, he shut the door, and there was nothing for Rasul to do but to follow Simon down the stairs and go back to his terrible apartment with no company except for his ancient phone.

Chapter Two

As soon as Jacob Moore heard the doors to Simon's car close, he shut his eyes, slid down the back of the door, and curled into a ball on the floor of his apartment. After a few minutes he withdrew his phone and texted his friend Gus with trembling fingers.

anybody in shop still

The reply came back swiftly. *No, and I was about to ask if you wanted me to close up. Everything ok up there?*

lock door, make sure nobody in shop, then come up please

After sending the text, he put the phone facedown on the floor and resumed his fetal position, where he remained, deliberately not allowing his brain to function for more than the bare minimum of survival, until Gus crouched in front of him.

"Oh my God, hon! Are you okay?" Gus put a hand on Jacob's shoulder. "What happened—"

With the touch, Jacob's dam broke.

"*Rasul Youssef*, Gus. *Rasul. Youssef.* Was here. In my apartment. Tea! He had tea! His cup is still there! I can't ever wash it!" He tipped his head against the door and stared at the ceiling, too lost to function. "He signed my books. *My books.* Called me his hero. But first I helped him pick out almost one hundred and fifty dollars' worth of books and gave them away."

"Why in the world did you give them—"

"*Because he's my favorite author ever and he stood there in my shop and I was trying to be all smooth and casual but eventually I couldn't take it anymore.* It's honestly a miracle I didn't hand over the deed to the building."

Gus stroked Jacob's arm now, a quiet smile on his face. "It's rare for you to break your composure like this."

Jacob pressed his hands to his eyes. "I'm trying to pull myself back together."

Gus sat back and folded his legs in front of him. "Why was your favorite author here, anyway?"

Jacob gave him a long-suffering look. "It's only been in every edition of the local paper for the last month. Rasul Youssef, international award-winning author, is one of the visiting professors at Bayview University this year."

"I know, hon. I'm saying why was he *here*?"

"I suspect because he wanted a book." Jacob sighed. "I hate that the girls made a scene, but sadly that's more what he's known for lately, his notoriety instead of his incredible fiction. His latest release has been bumped indefinitely, and he's been in the news partying with a string of partners all year. The latest is a model known only for escorting celebrities to ruin, who he's been consistently on and off with. Half her brand right now is making people wonder when she'll destroy him as she did so many others."

Gus raised an eyebrow. "Seriously?"

"The tabloids are calling it the Clash of the Sirens, because *he* is also known for leading people astray."

"It's difficult to grasp how someone like this can be your favorite author. Also, how in the world did Bayview get him?"

"I *detest* the playboy narrative hung around Youssef's neck, but I'll admit his behavior hasn't helped his case. I've been privately hoping his arrival in Copper Point would be good for him, since we're so far removed from the gossip mines, but the herd of teenagers in my bookshop makes that seem impossible." He pushed off the door and rested his elbows on his knees. "I don't know how Bayview convinced him to come. I've honestly thought it was a hoax, like the time the drama department said Russell Crowe was coming to teach a seminar and it turned out to be someone's uncle from Michigan. But no, today Youssef waltzed into my bookstore and asked for recommendations."

Gus grinned at him. "So. Is he as handsome in person as he is in his pictures?"

Despite his best efforts, Jacob blushed. "Of course he is. But he was also so calm and centered while he shopped, just a regular guy, and endearingly polite. Except where I had to chase off his stalkers, it was my dream encounter with him. I honestly hope he never comes back so I can keep it crystal clear in my mind."

"You *don't* want to meet him again?"

Jacob drew his knees to his chest and hugged them. "Youssef's debut novel helped me through my parents' death, and his second led me out of depression and inspired me to open this bookstore. The last thing in the world I want is for that sacrosanct individual to fall in any way. The tabloid reports are bad enough. I can't afford to let anything else intrude."

"Huh. Well, now I want to read his books."

"You should. They're incredible."

"So it seems."

Jacob straightened a bit. "Thank you again for coming over on such short notice. I'm sure it put you out."

Gus waved this away. "You did me a favor. Ben Vargas was doing his regular afternoon decoration of my coffee counter."

Jacob raised his eyebrows. "He's still here? I thought he graduated."

"He shifted to part time since his mom's diagnosis. His parents moved to town for their retirement and the new oncologist, and he's at home with them helping out. So he's going to be a fixture around here for some time, it seems." After pushing himself to his feet, Gus held out a hand to Jacob. "You still need to deal with the cash register, but I did everything else associated with closing. But hey, we never did settle things at the last Mini Main Street. Are you going to the university gala?"

Jacob shook his head. "I had planned to, but I don't think I have it in me."

"Damn. Okay, Matt and I will rock, paper, scissors it to see who goes. Though I think Matt's dad was on him to attend. We can let him take the hit this time."

Now Jacob felt bad. "Maybe I can go. Especially since I was the one who pointed out we couldn't let Clark get a talking point that 'the youth' on the Copper Point Chamber of Commerce don't know how to represent at community functions."

Gus shrugged. "It's fine. We'll deal. I'd prefer you go, as you're our best bet at getting into leadership, but it sounds like you have had a day."

"Thank you. I appreciate it."

"Are you sure I can't convince you to come to dinner with the guys, though? I mean, a significant chunk of them will be at the gala, but I know the quieter atmosphere is a plus for you."

"I need to be alone, without *any* people. But maybe I'll stop by if you end up at your shop like usual after."

"I'll hold you to that. Matt or I, whoever loses the draw, will give everyone at GAG your love."

Jacob's lips thinned into a line. "I seriously wish they'd change the name of that group."

Gus grinned. "No chance. I know Owen started it as a joke, but you're the only one who hates it."

"It isn't even properly descriptive. Gay Area Guys? Seriously?"

"Well, you can't say Gay Copper Point Guys. One, because a lot of the members come from out of town, and two, GCPG sounds like some kind of Soviet acronym."

Jacob tipped his head back again.

Gus regarded Jacob carefully. "Will you be all right on your own? I've never seen you this rattled."

"Yes, yes. I'll be fine." Running his hands over the front of his cardigan, Jacob took several fortifying breaths. "Thank you for allowing me a moment to melt down. I needed that more than I knew."

"Let me know if you need another round." Smiling, Gus rubbed his shoulder affectionately. "I'll give your regards to GAG."

Jacob waved Gus down the stairs, then locked the door. After a few deep breaths, he sat in the rocking chair near his shelf of literary treasures, withdrew the books Youssef had signed, and ran his hand over the inscription to *The Sword Dancer's Daughter.*

To Jacob, who has the loveliest bookstore I've ever seen. Rasul Youssef.

This was his original copy of the book, the first-edition hardcover he'd picked up in the hospital bookshop. It had a coffee stain on page 34 from when the nurse had startled him as she dragged him to the ICU so he could be with his father in his last moments. Jacob hadn't picked up the book again for a week, not until his mother had followed his father, not until the funerals were well over. He'd tripped over the book in a deep depressive funk as he wandered alone and despondent through his parents' house, then stayed up all night reading, stopping to cry every few chapters even when there was nothing remotely sad in the text, finally able to do the mourning he'd been too stunned to do. He'd purchased the audiobook and listened to it on constant repeat as he went through his parents' belongings and did enough repairs to sell the house.

Now here was the author of that book's signature, scrawled across the title page, along with a compliment for the bookstore that had given Jacob back his life.

Jacob's heart beat a desperate flutter against his throat as he opened the cover of *Carnivale*, this inscription calling him a hero, the word *love* etched above Youssef's scrawl. This was a bit dangerous. While reading *The Sword Dancer's Daughter*, Jacob had worshipped Youssef in his mind's eye. During that breathless, initial read of *Carnivale*, he'd fallen a bit in love. He was hardly unique in this aspect. *Carnivale* was insightful and critical, but also sensual and immersive in a way that tended to make the reader feel they'd stumbled into a forbidden garden. He'd read reports of people going to Youssef's promotional junket for *Carnivale* in full cosplay, and the movie adaptation was reportedly still in the works, which would only revive everything again.

For Jacob, reading *Carnivale* had felt like meeting a kindred spirit. He picked up on references so buried you had to have a book lover's encyclopedic database to catch and felt as if they were sharing a secret handshake. He loved the way Rasul embraced his half-Brazilian, half-Syrian heritage while harkening both to Middle Eastern and fully modern Western story and character conventions. *Carnivale* was the book Jacob chose to read when he wanted to feel wicked.

Now his copy had *Love, Rasul* on the title page.

It was as close Jacob would come to a confession from his secret, silly crush, and he honestly couldn't decide which was better, the memory of having him in his two most sacred places, his store and his apartment, or possessing these inscriptions. He couldn't possibly go to GAG after this. Today called for a glass of wine, pizza delivery, and a bubble bath as he let everything marinate.

He didn't even have the cork out of the bottle, however, before his phone rang. It was a local area code and prefix, but Jacob didn't know the number, so he assumed it was spam. At the last second, though, instead of letting it go to voicemail, he answered anyway.

It wasn't spam.

"—lo! This—President Larson—view. How—you?"

The president of Bayview University's age-roughened voice was difficult on a good day, but with this bad connection, it was nearly intolerable. But why was Larson was calling him? "I'm fine, Mr. Larson, but I'm afraid we have a bad connection. I can barely hear you."

"Evan—you to come—gala tonight—escort—" This time the break was of significant length. "—big favor."

Jacob frowned at the cupboard, wine bottle still in hand while he tried to figure it out. "Dean Clare wants me to escort him to the gala tonight? Why?"

"No, no—" Another long break in the connection. "—visiting professor—handholding. All about appearances because—" The air filled with crackles. "—good opportunity—"

Jacob set the bottle down and sighed. "I'm very sorry, Mr. Larson, but I have absolutely no idea what you're saying or what you need from me."

"—coming out of a valley. Can you hear me now?"

Jacob straightened. "Yes, perfectly."

"Can you come to the gala at eight tonight?"

"I can, but I don't understand—"

"Going into another valley. Evan will call you later and give more details. Can we count on you?"

Count on him *for what*? Jacob absolutely didn't want to go to the university gala. He'd been issued an invite both as a member of the chamber of commerce and someone on the hospital board, but he wasn't part of the university, he hated parties, and he truly did want to soak away the day in hot soapy bubbles. But he was a sucker for someone in crisis, which Larson probably well knew. "I suppose I can come, but I really want to know more about—"

"—about to—reception—counting on you—appreciate it—"

The call went silent, then disconnected. When Jacob tried to call Larson back, he got an automated message that the caller was unavailable.

Jacob set his phone on the table with his lips tightly sealed. The gala was a welcome party for new professors and staff as well as a chance for people who enjoyed doing so to rub elbows with what passed for celebrity in northern Wisconsin. Rebecca Lambert-Diaz, the hospital board president, had suggested it would be advantageous for as many members of Mini Main Street to attend as possible and network with the community, and of course it would be good for him to make more networking connections in case he decided to run for chamber of commerce president. But he so wanted to stay home. It seemed like all he did was go to parties like this lately. And now the Gay Area Guys met every Friday night. *Every* Friday!

Why did everyone in this town live for an excuse to get together? Why were they determined to fill every hour of his life with activity?

Jacob ran a lint roller over his good suit, the one Matt had selected for him before all the doctors at the hospital had started getting married. Well, correction. Matt had selected several different ones first, all of them too flashy and showy, and Jacob had made him go back and find him something conservative and nondescript. He regretted this now. It wasn't that he wanted to impress anyone! But if his favorite author gave him an approving glance, that would be a nice flutter to keep him warm in the winter.

He thought of the YouTube interview Youssef had given after *Carnivale* when he'd been asked if he liked parties. "I hate them," he'd replied immediately, which had made the interviewer laugh and assume he was being facetious, because even then he was known as a party animal. "No, I'm completely serious," he went on. "Parties are like cotton candy. Dazzling and sweet but ephemeral, evaporating in your mouth so all you want is more and more and more. And once you've gorged yourself, you're sick, but you're still dreaming about that sugary floss."

Jacob didn't like cotton candy or anything excessively sweet, but he'd still loved the metaphor, as well as the knowledge his favorite author felt the same way about them as he did. Did that mean, though, he should give Youssef a wide berth? He at least had to exchange pleasantries, but beyond that felt like a mystery.

Who was he kidding, he'd never have the courage to say anything meaningful.

What *was* he doing at this party, though? He remembered Larson said Evan Clare would call and give him further details, but Clare hadn't reached out by 7:40, at which point Jacob couldn't put off leaving any longer without showing up late.

With a frustrated sigh, he put out food for the cats, gathered his wallet and keys, and set off for the community center.

Since it was on the same block as the bookstore, he walked, waving to people he knew along the way. It was a busy section of town at this time of day, with parents picking up and dropping off kids from library events, church youth group, and tae kwon do practice. With the parking lot of the community center cordoned off for the gala, cars vied for precious real estate in the street, honking and edging toward parking spots about to open up. Meanwhile, Jacob enjoyed the cool breeze from the bay and wished he could spend the evening at the park, or in his apartment reading. He was going to resent not getting that bubble bath all night long.

There was a line at the entrance, which Jacob kicked himself for not anticipating. It wasn't until he was through the door that he was able to search for the dean, and an immediate scan of the room didn't help. All he saw were men in variations of gray and black suits and tuxedoes, and women in gowns in a dazzling array of colors and styles.

"Jacob."

He turned at the sound of his name, but it wasn't Evan calling to him. It was Matthew Engleton, the manager and heir to the Copper Point institution known as Engleton's Fine Clothing. He was also one of Jacob's closest friends. Smiling, Jacob waved to him, relaxing a little. "Hey."

Cradling his glass to his chest, Matt lifted an eyebrow at Jacob. "I thought you weren't coming."

Jacob couldn't help noticing how Matt's lips flattened slightly at the sight of his boring suit.

"I wanted to skip it, believe me, but I got a mysterious call from Larson a little while ago asking me to come. The call had terrible reception, so I don't really understand what's going on. I was hoping to get more answers when I arrived. Evan Clare was supposed to call me, but he never did. Have you seen him?"

"Hmm. I think I did a few minutes ago, but he was on the move. Come on, let's go hunt him down."

Jacob was grateful for Matt's assistance, which Matt probably knew. Though both their jobs required interacting with people, Matt was significantly better at it. Jacob was perfectly at home with anyone who wanted help locating a book or doing essentially anything in his store, and though it was exhausting, he did enjoy his work on the hospital board. He didn't even mind being pointed and argumentative in a meeting. However, any situation where he was expected to *mingle* was pure torture. If he wasn't careful, everyone he met asked him what was wrong. He couldn't very well answer that all he could think about was going home.

God, but he wanted to go home.

They couldn't find the dean, but they did run into several people from the chamber of commerce, including, of course, Les Clark.

Clark was the eighty-year-old, semiretired president of Copper Point Bank and Trust, an institution that had dodged corporate takeover only by Clark's iron will and determination that nothing *ever* would change. He was the current president of the Copper Point Chamber of Commerce, and he'd held that title off and on regularly over the years. He was either the rock of city business or the boulder holding back progressive innovation, depending on who you talked to.

Clark didn't like Jacob, Gus, or Matt. He thought they had too many wild ideas, and of course the fact that they were all three gay and out was also a scandal. He never missed a chance to needle any of them.

That included right now.

"Moore." Clark grimaced at him. "I'm surprised you made it. I thought you'd still be busy with the chaos at your store."

Jacob gave Clark his most patient smile. "Just a bit of high spirits. Everyone is excited to meet our new celebrity, it seems."

Clark huffed at the very idea of celebrity. "I expect there will be something nasty written about it in the paper. You'll be the downfall of this town one day, boy, with all your *ways*."

Jacob had no idea what those ways could possibly be, since all his friends gave him grief for being so analog, but he suspected this was his orientation again and so simply continued to smile.

Matt also smiled as he took Jacob's elbow. "So sorry, Mr. Clark. We're on a mission to find Evan Clare. Enjoy the party."

But as soon as they were out of earshot, Matt muttered, "Old coot."

Jacob had to agree.

They found Clare talking to several professors from the college, all men, so they were a sea of monotone suits and tuxedos. When the dean saw Jacob, however, he broke away and rushed over. "Oh good, you came." He nodded to Matt. "Good to see you too. Having a good time?"

"Of course." Matt inclined his head to Jacob and stepped away. "I'll catch you later."

Jacob didn't want him to go, but he supposed his friend had his own mingling to do. Events like this were critical for a clothing store with the entire internet competing with it.

Suppressing a sigh, Jacob turned back to Evan, but the dean was already dragging him away.

"Larson said he gave you the details over the phone?"

Jacob had to walk double-time to keep up. "Not really. The connection was bad."

"Oh. Well, honestly, I don't understand much of it myself. All I know is we got a call from the agent asking if we could provide an escort for the evening, someone highly respectable and no-nonsense. We all thought of you right away."

There wasn't any insult in anything Evan said, and yet Jacob felt an annoying prick along the top of his head. "I see." Except, wait a minute, he didn't see at all. "What do you mean, escort? What agent?"

Evan cast a questioning look over his shoulder. "He really didn't explain anything?"

Jacob flushed. "It was an exceptionally bad connection."

"Well, thank you for coming anyway. Though I shouldn't be surprised. You're so dependable."

This time the prick of annoyance manifested in Jacob's cheeks as he sucked them against his teeth. "Would it be too much to ask what it is you want me to do?"

"Oh, sure. One of our visiting professors needs to be kept out of trouble, is what it boils down to. Larson was supposed to ask you to be his date for the evening. He says we'd owe you a big favor."

At the word *trouble*, a low buzzing began in Jacob's ears. It intensified as Evan led him around another group of suits and past a clutch of women in an eerily coordinated set of pastel gowns.

No, the part of him that still craved the bubble bath whispered. *No.*

But of course, as the crowd parted, there was Rasul Youssef in a stunning, vibrant floral jacquard tuxedo, standing in the center of a clutch of people, dark curls a riot around his bearded face and cast in a pleasant glow from the light positioned as an accidental spotlight above him.

MR. ROGERS looked a hell of a lot better out of his cardigan.

He was still pretty straitlaced in a somber gray suit and powder blue tie with soft geometrics, but the just-pressed look about him was a nice departure from the cardigan. He didn't look happy, however, and Rasul was surprised at how intense his urge was to fix that. Of course, he wasn't sure how much help he could be once his minder showed up. He still chafed at Elizabeth's intervention and the tense phone call they'd exchanged over the teenage girls. Being assigned a date was his penance, though he'd done nothing wrong.

Not this time, anyway. But if Elizabeth was going to retroactively punish him for everything he'd ever done, things were going to get grim fast.

Gently extracting himself from the woman who'd attached herself to his left arm, Rasul came forward to meet Jacob with a grin. "Hello again. You're a pleasant surprise."

It made him pause when, instead of melting into a demure expression, Jacob shuttered further and put up a thin *I don't want to be here* smile.

Dean Clare raised an eyebrow and glanced between Rasul and Jacob. "You two already know each other?"

"You bet." Rasul winked at Jacob, thrilled that this time he was rewarded with a blush, though he'd had enough champagne to make him want even more of a reaction. "He rescued me earlier today in more ways than one."

"Well." Clare looked confused but also relieved. "That certainly makes this easier. Mr. Youssef, this is Jacob Moore, your escort for the evening. Jacob, this is Rasul Youssef, who apparently I have no need to make an introduction for."

Rasul straightened, his gaze darting from Jacob to the dean and back again. "Wait—you're serious? Mr. Rogers is my babysitter?"

"No, Mr. Moore," Clare corrected, looking concerned. "I just said."

Jacob had flinched and seemed slightly hurt.

Rasul rushed to fix it. "Sorry, complete slip of the tongue. Until I got your name when I signed your books, your sweater and sneakers reminded me of Mr. Rogers, and I guess the nickname stuck in my mind."

This explanation, however, only further irked Jacob. Clare, on the other hand, was apparently satisfied. The dean patted them both on the shoulder. "Well, you two boys have fun. Let me know if you need anything."

He left, and Rasul and Jacob were alone, or as alone as they could be in a room full of people watching their every move.

A chill Hozier song played through the sound system, an offering from the bored DJ on the stage. Rasul was keenly aware of Jacob's bad mood and his part in it, but he wasn't entirely sure how to fix it. His brain was still adjusting to the fact that the *steadying influence* Elizabeth requested turned out to be his charming bookseller who, equally surprising, looked hot in a mediocre suit. Well, hot was probably the wrong word. Fussy and delectable, that was closer to the mark.

It helped that Rasul's brain kept playing over and over that one moment where Jacob had shown a hot flare of passion, projecting it onto the shuttered individual striving not to meet his gaze.

Time to fix whatever I broke here. Rasul made a grand bow. "I'm sorry, I seem to have upset you. Is it something I said, or are you this unhappy to be my minder?"

"I'm not—" God, Rasul kind of dug how Jacob kept trying to button himself down and failing. "It's a bit of a surprise, is all. I honestly wasn't sure why they asked me to come."

Heavy subtext there made it clear Jacob would have preferred not to perform this role, and surprisingly, it seemed finding out his mission was Rasul hadn't moved him much. Interesting. What was up with this guy? Suddenly Rasul had to know.

"Well, thank you for making the time. You're keeping me out of serious hot water with my agent for the second time today." Rasul gestured to the bar. "Can I buy you a drink?"

Jacob followed his gaze, his lips thinning into a line. "There are so many people looking at us."

"Not a problem. I'll deflect them." He grabbed Jacob's hand.

To his surprise, Jacob flinched and pulled away. Then he put on another plastic smile and looked near but not at Rasul. "Could I trouble you to get me a rum and Coke?"

"Sure thing."

Rasul charmed his way through the line, though he kept glancing back at his date. Something had upset Jacob pretty intensely, and he had a bad feeling it was him. He wasn't sure why. It felt bigger than the Mr. Rogers comment, but he was at a loss as to what else he'd done that was offensive.

Had something else damning shown up online? He reached for his phone to check, felt the dull lump of the flip phone, and muttered under his breath.

Armed with a pair of drinks, he wove his way back to Jacob, smiling and accepting compliments and well-wishes. A few women flirted openly with him, and though he instinctively reflected it back to them, he didn't linger, too interested in his date. Just as he returned to him, however, the college president took the microphone at the front of the stage, welcoming everyone to the gala and cutting off Rasul's charm offensive. So he studied Jacob, noting the way the man's lips touched the glass Rasul had passed him, the manner in which his suit—remarkably well-fitted—shifted and glided with his movements. He was about to compliment Jacob on his tie when a rough and shaky voice shouting his name his name into a mic pulled his focus again.

"—Youssef, internationally acclaimed author of *The Sword Dancer's Daughter* and *Carnivale*, will be heading up an evening seminar at Bayview in the Creative Writing department for the duration of the school year." Larson beamed, not noticing the winces from the crowd at the feedback coming from the mic. "Mr. Youssef will use the rest of the time here to finish his upcoming novel, *Veil of Stars*."

The crowd clapped enthusiastically, and Rasul smiled and waved back at them. When Larson moved on to the next new instructor, however, Rasul glanced at Jacob and saw he looked even more wooden than before.

Seriously, what in the world had he done to the guy?

Rasul wanted to interrogate him as soon as the president's speech finished, but of course that was when the hordes descended, everyone and their pet rock coming up to welcome him to Copper Point and ask him a million questions. Normally he didn't mind this, or at least understood it as part of his job, but he particularly resented it when all he wanted was to sit and talk with his date.

Some of the people greeting him acknowledged Jacob, though, offering him a polite smile and greeting. "Good to see you, Jacob. How's business?" He would always give the small smile and nod, telling them business was good, thank you. A few of them mentioned something about a hospital board, and another seemed to be nudging Jacob about some leadership position on the chamber of commerce. An older gentleman with an expression like he was some kind of 1880s schoolmarm pulled Jacob aside and said something to him that made Jacob return to Rasul's side with a flat and thinly veiled annoyed expression.

"Didn't realize my escort was a celebrity," Rasul murmured to Jacob. He'd meant the remark to be a bit of playful levity, but again, it seemed to upset Jacob more than anything else.

Eventually he couldn't take it, and with an apology to their admirers and a promise to be right back, he took Jacob's hand and led him down a hallway marked with an Exit sign. When the darkened area revealed itself to be full of people waiting for the bathroom, he sighed and tugged

Jacob out of a fire door and into the purple-orange light of the sunset. With the gray-blue of the bay behind him, he faced his date.

Jacob hadn't relaxed at all coming outside, and if anything he looked more apprehensive than ever. "Is something wrong?"

"Funny, that's what I was going to ask you." Rasul rubbed at his beard, not sure how to phrase this. "Did... did I offend you in some way? If so, I'm sorry, but I've been racking my brain trying to figure out what I did, and I can't come up with anything."

Alarm flashed across Jacob's face before being buttoned back down. "I'm not offended by anything, no."

You are. Rasul studied him carefully, looking for a clue. "Did something get posted online?"

Now Jacob seemed confused. "I'm sorry?"

"A rumor about me. Did you hear something? Anything?"

Why did everything Rasul say only fluster the man more? "I'm not on social media."

Rasul blinked. "*No* social media? Not even Facebook?"

Jacob's lips thinned as he shook his head. "I'd never used it much, but after Cambridge Analytica I closed my account."

Was this person real? "No Twitter? Tumblr? Snapchat? Pinterest?"

"I don't even know what most of those are. Twitter I know, but I've never had an account."

"Surely you at least have an Instagram."

He opened his mouth, then stopped, considering something. "I suppose *technically* the bookstore has an Instagram account, though it's run by an employee. I don't like it because it's connected to Facebook, but I had to have it for some local event."

Rasul threw up his hands. "What in the world do you use your phone for?"

Jacob appeared to be confused again. "Texting and phone calls?"

Unable to take it anymore, Rasul sat on a short railing with his back to the bay. "Wow."

Folding his arms over his chest, Jacob seemed annoyed. "Did you bring me out here to quiz me on my social media usage?"

"No, I—" Rasul paused a moment to appreciate how much he'd messed this up. "I wanted to know why you were acting so weird around me so I could fix it."

"I'm not...." As he trailed off, Jacob's shoulders rounded forward and his hands fell back to his side. "Very well. I'm probably a little awkward. But it's not because you did anything to upset me."

"You're *sure* it's not something lousy about me online? Not even one of the news articles?"

"No—I mean, yes, I've seen some articles, but they don't upset me."

Liar. The gossip did upset him, Rasul could tell, but he could also tell that wasn't the source of his date's irritation. "Then why—?"

Blushing, Jacob half turned away. "I don't really want to talk about it, please."

"Why not?"

"I just said I didn't want to talk about it."

"But what's the *reason* you don't want to talk about it?"

Jacob pressed fingers to the side of his head as if he were warding off a headache.

Part of Rasul was able to see he should leave the poor man alone. He owed him a lot, so at the very least he could pay the man back with silence. Except another part of him—the part that was still mad about the loss of his phone and really, really wanted to call Adina—that bit of him was desperate for something to soothe his ragged edges, wouldn't let it go.

As it had for the last few months, that part of him won. "I'm happy to apologize," he said. "Generally or specifically."

Sighing, Jacob lowered his hand. He stood at the rail beside Rasul, put his hands in his pockets, and stared across the greenbelt at the bay beyond. "You have nothing to apologize for, and I'm not angry."

"But you *are* upset."

Jacob tipped his head back and stared up at the sky. Rasul shifted so he could study him. The guy really was cute, in a buttoned-up way. Not at all Rasul's style. Not usually. But still cute.

"Do you read Neil Gaiman?" Jacob asked at last.

"Obviously. What does he have to do with this?"

"He's said on numerous occasions it's best not to meet heroes, that even if they become good friends, they can't be heroes any longer." He extended an arm and picked at invisible lint in a meticulous way. "I think he's a wise man, and he's also a hero of mine, which is why I've gone out of my way never to meet him."

The puzzle pieces began to click into place. "Wait. Are you trying to tell me…." He stopped, uncharacteristically too shy to finish the thought.

"Your novels and your early interviews have been a very important part of my life. Yes, you're a bit of a hero to me." Jacob folded his arms again, his cheeks staining red. "Fine, you're *quite* a bit of a hero to me. I had fully intended to spend tonight processing the fact that you came into my bookshop, asked me for book recommendations, had a cup of my tea, then signed my original copies before escaping out my back door. Now I'm expected to behave normally while being your date at a city function. It's a lot."

Many, many people had worked hard to flatter Rasul over the years, but nothing had ever affected him quite like this. For a moment he couldn't reply, could only watch Jacob as his hair and the tails of his suit ruffled in the evening breeze.

Eventually he said, "You sure played it cool at the bookshop, if that's the case."

"Well, I didn't want to look ridiculous."

He said it like it was a cardinal sin. "For the record, I think you'd look good ridiculous."

Jacob cast him a cool glance. "I thought I looked like Mr. Rogers."

Yep, that one had gotten under his skin. "Look, I'm sorry. It's the navy blue sneakers. Well, and the cardigan. Plus you're a little prim. You wear it well, though." He winced as Jacob turned annoyed again. "Sorry. Probably your hero never said that."

"It's fine." Jacob sat beside Rasul and stared at the concrete patio in front of them. "I don't have some delusion this is a real date or that someone like you would be interested in someone like me. I don't *want* you to be interested. I just…."

God, but it was weird how drawn Rasul was to this guy. Not sexually, not like he wanted to tear his clothes off, but… drawn all the same. He wanted to know what he'd said or done that had made him this guy's hero, but in such a controlled, calm manner he could hold him at arm's length. He wanted to know what about his work had drawn him in.

He wanted to see another flare of visceral passion in this guy's eyes.

That he was Jacob's hero, though…. He'd been told that before, but never like this. Never by somebody who seemed to know exactly what it meant.

Probably he should settle down and try to respect this man a little more.

"Do you want me to leave you alone?" he asked at last. When Jacob shook his head, he pressed the issue. "I won't be upset. I'm flattered as hell and sure I don't deserve it, but I'm ready to honor your wishes."

"No." Something about Jacob's heavy sigh broke Rasul's heart. "It's fine."

"It sure doesn't sound fine. I mean, I know I've already been a disappointment, but maybe we can put putty in the dam leak or something."

Jacob regarded him quizzically. "How in the world have you been a disappointment?"

Rasul snorted and kicked at the pavement. "God, where do I start? How about with the fact that you were asked to babysit me?"

"I was asked to *escort* you."

He should shut up and change the subject. "Yeah, because I'm in serious hot water with my agent."

So much for changing the subject.

Jacob frowned. "Why?"

Rasul laughed. "Uh, let's see. Missing my deadline three times, partying too much, missing my first flight here because I let my ex talk me into something stupid, trending on Twitter and Instagram with my name linked to high school girls—"

"That last one wasn't your fault at all. I'm happy to speak up for you."

He waved a hand at Jacob. "Won't do any good. I've blown it too many times." He pulled his horrible phone out of his pocket and waved it in the air between them. "See this? It's my new phone."

Jacob tilted his head to the side. "It looks like a very *old* phone."

"Bought it at that cellular place on University. Or rather, my agent did, and she made me mail her my actual phone. No internet, no photos, no nothing except her number, Dean Clare's, and both my parents'. My punishment, my last chance." He hunched forward. "Except honestly I don't know that it's going to work. I think I've lost my edge. I'm not the writer you made into a hero. I'm a mess."

A heavy silence settled between them, one Rasul sank into like a bog. When Jacob held out his hand, he frowned at it, unsure what he was supposed to do.

"May I see your phone?"

Jacob's quiet, prim tone was soothing, and Rasul obeyed, curious to find out why. He watched as Jacob flipped it open, fussed with the buttons a bit, then passed it back.

"There," Jacob said. "The next time you're convinced you've lost your edge, if you forget what kind of a writer you are, call me up and I'll tell you."

The phone felt heavy and significant in Rasul's hand. "What kind of writer am I, to you?"

Jacob rose, brushing off his suit. "We should go back inside. I'm sure someone's looking for you."

Rasul stood as well, but he didn't move to go inside. "Tell me what kind of writer I am."

Jacob faced the bay. He stared out at it for some time, but Rasul only waited. Eventually Jacob spoke.

"You weave worlds like no one I've ever read before, and I've read a lot. You write with a rich tapestry of diversity, not only of race and nationality but orientation, occupation, and personality. You put real people in your stories, or people who feel real, and you let them be messy but urge them to arc toward redemption. That's a good word for your work: redemptive. I've lain awake trying to decide if you're writing to redeem yourself or humanity, and the only conclusion I can make is that it's both. There are worlds inside your stories, and I'm happy to descend into them every time."

The sun burned orange-red, casting Jacob in a fiery glow. The wind picked up too, ruffling his tie, his suit, his hair. It pulled Rasul's hair across his face as well, and it stirred him the same way Jacob's words had.

Unfortunately, the shadows inside him insisted on tearing those precious castles down. "I can't write like that anymore."

"You can. You will."

"I'm just a playboy spinning out. Everybody's eating popcorn while they watch me go down."

"Not me."

Rasul shut his eyes and ran a hand through his hair.

Screw it.

Grabbing Jacob's hand, he tugged him toward the door leading inside. "Come on."

Jacob stumbled after him. "Where are we going now?"

"To party."

Chapter Three

As Rasul dragged him by the hand back into the gala, Jacob's heart threatened to beat out of his chest. Why in the world was this the man's reaction to him baring his soul like that? He'd never told anyone that was how he saw Rasul Youssef's work, not even in an online review. It was the truth he kept in a turret inside him, but Rasul had seemed so low, he'd been compelled to tell him.

So why in the world did that inspire him to pull Jacob along like they were a pair of toddlers going out to play?

Gaiman was so right. When Jacob had heard Rasul was coming to Copper Point, he should have sold the store and moved to Yellowknife, Canada, and let his image of his hero keep him warm at night.

He was plenty warm now, though. He was hot from embarrassment and nerves, his hand fully captive in Rasul's palm. Also he kept getting whiffs of Rasul's woodsy, spicy aftershave, and it made his knees weak.

"What are we doing?" he asked again once he gathered his wits enough.

Rasul paused at the edge of the room, not letting go of Jacob. After looking around a moment, he grinned. "We're going dancing."

Jacob tried to pull away. "Oh, no. I can't dance."

"Liar." Rasul winked at him as he tugged him forward. "You dance alone in your apartment, I know you do."

He did, but the hell he was going to admit that. Jacob tried for another angle. "I don't even know what this music is."

Rasul wrinkled his nose. "You're right. Come on, let's go fix that."

"Wait—" But it was too late. Jacob was once again tugged across the room.

He tried to keep his composure and nod politely to people he knew as they passed, but it was a struggle, just as everything had been a Herculean effort ever since he'd found out his date was Rasul. *I'm being dragged across the Copper Point Community Center by Rasul Youssef.* Jacob couldn't decide if he wanted to fly to the stars or curl up and die.

Rasul took them to the stage where the DJ was set up and gestured the man to come out from behind the table. "Hey, you take requests? What system are you using to play music?"

The DJ, a bored-looking man in his early twenties, shrugged. "A Spotify playlist some committee made up. I'm mostly here in case of a technical difficulty."

Rasul dug in his wallet, then passed over a twenty. "Play 'I'll Never Fall in Love Again' by Dionne Warwick." Then he pulled out another bill and passed it over too. "Follow it up with some Air Supply."

"You got it, boss," the DJ said, suddenly a lot more animated.

"Hold on," Jacob said, but then they were off again, this time headed for the dance floor.

They'd caught the DJ at the end of another song, so the muted horn opening of Warwick's song drifted through the community center speakers as Rasul pulled Jacob into dance position, making Jacob the follower. "Think you can do a simplified swing?"

Jacob's knees threatened to turn to jelly. "No."

Rasul, already swaying to the beat, winked at him. "Sure you can. Rock step, triple step."

He led Jacob through the steps patiently, constantly repeating the litany that it was easy, Jacob could do it—*look, you're doing it!* Jacob wasn't convinced he was doing anything but stumbling to the beat, but he'd only stepped on Rasul's toes twice, so perhaps that was some kind of progress.

Then, without warning, Rasul spun him out. Jacob barely had time for a yelp before he was drawn back into Rasul's orbit.

Laughing, Rasul resumed the pattern they'd fallen into before. "See? You're a natural."

"I absolutely am not." But it was getting easier. Unfortunately it meant Jacob had more brain cells available to notice everyone looking at them and worry that he was making a spectacle of himself. The bank president glared.

How in the world am I dancing with Rasul Youssef? How?

The second time Rasul spun him out, he handled himself better, but his heart still raced.

"You look terrified," Rasul said as they slid back into the main dance. "Am I terrifying you?"

"A bit," Jacob admitted. "I'm not used to this kind of thing."

"What, dancing?"

"Attention." He decided to ask the question rattling around in his brain. "Why *are* you giving me this much attention?"

Rasul didn't answer right away, some of the light going out of his face. Before Jacob could apologize for being rude, the music switched to Air Supply's "All Out of Love."

"Hmm, let's go with seventh-grade sway for this one." Rasul shifted his grip on Jacob and slowed them into a more traditional dance floor shuffle. The corner of his mouth tipped into a quirky smile. "Man, you gotta love Air Supply."

So they were switching the topic. Not a problem, Jacob could do that. "Do you prefer music from the seventies and eighties?"

"I've got a soft spot for it. My parents were busy a lot when I was young, my grandparents too old, and one of my most regular babysitters was a big ballad fan. I can sing every word of this song and most of Air Supply, honestly. I associate the music with summers in the backyard, floating in the pool while Carla belted out old-school love songs with a heavy accent."

Jacob smiled, his own memories overtaking him. "My mom liked Whitney Houston."

"Another good choice."

They swayed in comfortable silence for a while, Russell Hitchcock's vocals swirling around them, but as they cleared the bridge, Rasul moved in closer and spoke almost in Jacob's ear.

"I wrote my first novel because I was in the biggest depressive funk of my life. I didn't know what I was supposed to do, I felt like everything I did turned to ash, and I hated myself. The only time I felt good was when I wrote, so I wrote so much I had to be reminded to eat. I wrote my second novel because I was angry—with my parents, with the media who kept telling me who I was, with myself because I still didn't understand who I was or what I was supposed to be doing. I really liked that novel, and when it was received with even higher praise than my debut, I thought, well, that's it, then. This is what I'm good at, what I'm doing. I'll write books, and that'll be that. Except it's as if as soon as I let the idea float through my head, everything broke."

He sighed, and for a second Jacob thought he would lean against Jacob's shoulder, but he didn't, only continued talking. "Now I'm just lost. Everybody has an opinion on what I'm supposed to be doing, who

I am, what mistakes I'm making, how I should correct them. Everyone takes one look at my career and puts me in a box." His grip on Jacob shifted slightly, then tightened. "You didn't do that, though. You treated me like you would any other customer, you helped me like I was simply a human who needed aid, and you accepted the job of escorting me with grace. Except when I signed your book, you flared to life, and I can't get it out of my head."

Jacob tripped.

Rasul righted him, kept talking. "It's like you're the kind of calm, rational being I wish I could be. I'm emotional and messy and dysfunctional. I ricochet around like a Ping-Pong ball. You, though, see something in me, you know my work maybe better than I do, and yet I can't help feeling as if you'd love to bolt away from me if you had the chance. Yeah. I'm interested in you."

Jacob was dizzy. He didn't know what to say, how to respond. He had a million questions, though. What did Rasul mean, he was interested? Interested how? Curious? Bemused?

Attracted?

The song ended, and in a somewhat awkward transition, Billie Eilish's "Bad Guy" belted through the room. Rasul broke into a grin, his hold on Jacob shifting again. "Damn, I've gotta go tip the DJ again. But first…."

He spun Jacob into another dance.

This time there was no swaying, no swing steps, only grinding. Jacob felt more self-conscious with these moves than he had with the others, especially with all of Copper Point looking on, but Rasul wouldn't let him retreat into himself.

"Let go. Relax and move." Meanwhile, he had turned into some sort of boneless creature who apparently felt the beat inside his soul.

"I can't," Jacob protested, which was the wrong thing to say because then Rasul pulled him against his chest.

"Feel how I'm moving and match it."

God, he was so close. Jacob had been smelling him all night, but now he could taste him. He tried to mimic Rasul's movements, but they were so erotic and smooth, he felt foolish.

"Relax. Relax." Rasul's hands slid to Jacob's hip and spine, further guiding him. "Stop thinking you look ridiculous and move with the beat."

The seventeen-year-old singer's sultry whispers that she was the bad guy kept creeping into his brain. There certainly was a bad guy, and he was luring Jacob into a wicked dance. This wasn't the Rasul Youssef that Jacob imagined as he lay in bed with *Carnivale* clutched to his chest. This wasn't the Rasul who had just whispered all those stunning things to him, sad confessions about how he'd arrived at this moment.

This was the Rasul from the tabloids. The party boy. The dangerous bachelor. The seducer. The sinner.

The temptation.

Rasul pressed in so close to Jacob his lips brushed Jacob's ear. "Let me see that flare again, baby."

Jacob's eyes fluttered closed as he felt some clasp break free deep inside him. Drawing a breath, he opened his eyes. Rasul was right in front of him, staring back like every kind of erotic dream Jacob had ever had.

Jacob let go.

He wasn't sure if he danced any better now than he had before, but he released the part of him that was afraid he looked ridiculous, that he shouldn't do this. He shifted his hips, rolled his shoulders, felt the fast pulse deep in his belly.

He never looked away from Rasul, and Rasul never looked away from him. It was the most intense moment of his life, which felt strange to acknowledge because his life, contrary to what most people thought, hadn't been all quiet days at the bookstore wearing cardigans. There on the community center dance floor, grinding to the goth whispers of a child, Jacob set free the part of him that would have recoiled to learn his thirty-four-year-old self was this buttoned-up.

Rasul liked it.

Jacob could see it in his gaze, the way his eyes widened, then narrowed, focused even harder on him. He *wanted* Jacob, that was absolutely clear. With one stroke of his thumb along the man's throat, Jacob could seal his invitation into his hero's bed. Which was funny, because Jacob had always disliked the playboy side of Rasul. He'd told himself it was because he could never play that way.

Well, he was playing now.

As the song came to an end, shifting into a slower, heavier bass beat, Jacob and Rasul matched the music with their moves, still staring at one another. As Eilish whispered, it was as if Jacob and Rasul were whispering with her, each of them confessing to the other.

The song stopped, the spell broke, and Jacob regretted everything. Packing that part of him back into the box it had come from, he drew away, smoothed his suit, and put on the politest face he could manage.

"I'm sorry, but I need to get going. Please give my apologies to President Larson and Dean Clare."

He turned and bolted before Rasul could reach for him, not running exactly but moving as fast as he could go through the crowd. He saw Clark glaring at him, but he ignored him, just as he ignored the clutch of excited women in the foyer. He didn't have time for anyone right now. He *had* to get home.

Jacob triple-timed it out the door, down the street, and back to the bookshop. For a moment he thought he heard people calling after him, but when he glanced over his shoulder at the corner, he was alone on the street.

Halfway up the back stairs, he started to tremble, and he had to stop twice and grip the rail to steady himself, whispering that he was all right, that he was fine, that he'd never do anything like that again.

When he opened the door to his apartment, all three of his cats stood in the foyer waiting, regarding him with part curiosity, part annoyance.

Locking the door behind him, he greeted them with a warm, if not slightly watery, smile. "Who would like a wet food treat?"

With three felines weaving gently around his legs, Jacob stumbled to the kitchen and turned on NPR, willing the replay of *Marketplace* to erase the evening from his memory.

ONE SECOND Rasul's blood coursed through him, lighting him up and insisting he'd just found north again, his libido firing on all cylinders and whooping because he *knew* he was going to get laid—and then Jacob ran away into the night.

He was so startled it took him a second to get organized enough to follow, and by then not only was Jacob halfway to the door but the vultures who had been waiting to pounce on him realized they finally had their chance. People who wanted Rasul to look at them the way he'd been eye-fucking Jacob, who wanted their turn at the dance, who liked the idea of a celebrity in their midst and wanted to punch their ticket. Also in the foyer to the event there was, somehow, a group of overexcited twenty-year-olds who kept trying to take selfies with him.

Rasul dodged them all, but they slowed him enough that by the time he made it outside, Jacob was blocks away. Rasul made one halfhearted call to him, then stopped.

He'd already pushed the man more than he should. It would be borderline cruel to pursue him now.

God, but why did that thought make his chest pinch?

As he headed back into the venue, he dredged out a winsome smile for the cluster of people at the door, but he noticed that mixed in with the bright, interested gazes, the usual sort of glances were already appearing. Suspicious, annoyed, dismissive. Well, that was always going to happen, because it was what always happened. He was a biracial, pansexual man with a huge personality and wild reputation. Some people were intrigued, some wanted in on the game, and some resented him for perceived slights. Hogging the spotlight was a favorite callout. Being narcissistic was right behind it. Plenty of people were simply jealous, usually of something Rasul didn't even have.

The gazes, though, especially right after whatever that had been with Jacob, made him crave a drink. Several drinks. Also, something about that gaggle of women in the foyer had a foreboding feel to it. He aimed himself for the bar.

The dean of faculty intercepted him with a polite, professional smile. "Everything all right, Mr. Youssef?"

Nope, not on a bet. He beamed and winked. "Absolutely. Having a great time. Do you guys do this every year for new faculty?"

"Yes, but the crowd is decidedly bigger this year." Clare's tone indicated this was entirely due to Rasul.

Yeah, he needed that drink right now.

Rasul had never been at an event quite like this. He'd been to exclusive gatherings full of people who bought and sold the equivalents of nation states every day, and celebrity gatherings populated almost entirely by the A-list of entertainment. He'd been to house parties thrown by the known and the unknown, by the movers and shakers and the hipster chic. Never this, though, never some sad backwater trying to echo what some movie in 1990 had told them was high society. Never somewhere *he* was the A-list celebrity. He didn't know the moves to this dance. He couldn't find the cache of edgy and slightly disinterested people he liked to adopt at an event where he didn't arrive with his own squad. Well, he kind of knew where they were, but they didn't feel right. He floated from group to group, sipping a seriously terrible martini, trying to make polite conversation but mostly wondering how far away the bookstore was from here. It had to be close. Jacob had walked.

He should have followed him.

He couldn't stop thinking about him.

Eventually he excused himself from the group of doctors and hospital administrators he'd been pretending to chat with and sought out Clare to tell him he was heading back to his apartment.

"Everything all right?" Clare asked.

"Just a little tired from traveling. I'll be at the orientation for new professors tomorrow, don't worry."

"Would you like me to get someone to drive you?"

Drive him? His apartment was three blocks away, and even he with his terrible sense of direction and no GPS could find it. He could very nearly *see* it. "I'm fine, thanks."

He regretted this dismissal, though, as soon as he was back in the foyer. The selfie crew was still there, and this time they surrounded him so he couldn't get away.

"Rasul, Rasul!"

"We're going to take selfies with you for Adina! She misses you *soooo* much."

Rasul blinked and shook his head. "What?"

The delay cost him. Three of the girls surrounded him, and as the camera on one of the phones clicked, two girls kissed him, one on each cheek.

"*Hey.*" It took him several second to fight them off, after which many more pictures and probably some video had been taken.

"Ladies. That's enough."

Rasul turned as a tall, imposing Black man in a *very* nice suit loomed over them. Beside him, a white man with a menacing snarl took point. "You ladies don't look like you're from around here, and I don't see tickets in your hands."

An Asian man appeared on the other side of Rasul. He said nothing, only folded his arms and glared. The girls looked like they wanted to protest, but when two more men appeared with equally inhospitable expressions, the ladies took off.

Rasul rubbed at the back of his head and tried to quell the queasy feeling making him want to go hide under a blanket. "Thanks, I—" He stopped as he got a better look at the men surrounding him and something clicked. "Oh, hey, you're the doctors I was talking to earlier."

"Three of us are doctors, the other two just sign our checks." The surly white guy who had appeared initially reached out to take Rasul's hand. "Owen Gagnon. Anesthesiologist at St. Ann's Medical Center." He gestured to the blond man. "This is Jared Kumpel, pediatrician, Jack Wu, super-surgeon. This guy"—he gently elbowed the shorter, slighter white man with curly hair—"is my husband, Erin Andreas, VP of the hospital. And of course we can't forget our CEO, Nick Beckert."

The man who'd initially come to Rasul's rescue shook his hand. "Pleasure. Sorry they swarmed you like that."

Kumpel frowning in the direction the girls had left. "Honestly, I think they were from out of town. It's not like I know everyone in town and all the students on the campus, but someone said they saw a group of girls with Minnesota license plates casing out the college earlier and carrying on at the McDonald's on the edge of town. My instinct tells me this was them."

"What in the world are twentysomethings from Minnesota doing here?" Andreas asked.

Rasul didn't know, but he had a bad, bad feeling.

This time when he was offered a ride, he accepted. He'd wanted to meander past the bookstore, but clearly that wasn't a good idea right now.

Thankfully Wu let him lapse into silence for the most part on the short drive, and after thanking the man for the ride, Rasul let himself into his depressing accommodations. He paced around for a few seconds, then got out his phone. At least he could call Elizabeth first this time.

She answered immediately, which he knew was a bad sign even before she spoke. "You can't go five hours without a scandal? Is that it?"

He sat down on the couch, sending up another cloud of dust. "I swear on my next advance I had nothing to do with that. Or any of this. I went to the gala like you told me, met the escort."

Chased him away. His shoulders rounded slightly.

Elizabeth sighed. "I know. I know the look on your face in those selfies. Plus, I've been haunting your ex's Instagram and YouTube. She got dropped by her agent. She's desperate, and she's sending her fans to you. Everybody who tags her with pictures of her precious Rasul who she misses so much gets a shout-out."

"What?" Rasul remembered the doctor's remarks about Minnesota license plates, and the pit in his stomach grew. "She sent people here? Why?"

"We've had this meeting. While you were dating her, she saw a four-thousand-percent rise in social media hits. You broke up with her and she went way down and couldn't get it back. Then you answered her booty call and got her on the lips of everyone again. You're the meal ticket. She's not letting go."

"I'm *in Wisconsin*."

"Who cares? She operates online. She's billing this as a sad separation and she's the dutiful wife at home holding up the fort. Her agent, damn him, spilled the beans about you not having social media access, and so she's filling the void. Apparently you called her before the gala. You miss her so much."

Now Rasul felt *sick*. "I didn't call her. I swear. I *swear*. Call the mobile carrier and ask for my phone log."

"You act as if I don't have access to that already. I did set up the account. But no, I was pretty sure you didn't do that. All the same, this is a problem that needs to be nipped in the bud."

"You want me to call her and tell her to back off?"

"Absolutely not. You'll just give her clear voice samples."

He wanted to object that this was too much, Adina wouldn't do that, but he did know how desperate she was to get a toehold on real fame. He hated to think she'd fallen this far, but Elizabeth was right, he couldn't get involved. "So what do I do?"

"Avoid selfies. Exercise restraint. Honestly, I wish you had a legitimate, stable relationship with someone else to end this before it gets started, but I also don't want you distracted from your work."

Jacob's fussy face appeared in his mind's eye. "You want me to document a different relationship online?"

"No, she'll just see that as a war. But hmm, I wonder if her *fans* assumed someone was a significant other, that might help. Maybe, but maybe not. Look, like I said, I don't want you to be distracted. I certainly don't want you to upset people there. At some point this should die off on its own, but I want you focused on your work, not your unstable ex."

Rasul couldn't get Jacob out of his head. "But if I did legitimately have someone, that would be good?"

"If you had a stable relationship with someone who truly appreciated you, didn't use you, and actually supported you? Yes. That would be amazing. But I'm not holding my breath. You certainly don't know how to pick a winner."

"*Hey.*"

"Show me the evidence to the contrary."

Jacob. He could show her Jacob. He didn't say anything, though.

Elizabeth sighed. "I'll keep monitoring your social media and keep you apprised if there's anything you need to know. They just started posting things." There was a pause. When she came back, her voice was sharp. "Who is this guy you're dancing with?"

They had pictures of him and Jacob? Damn, Rasul wanted to see. He cursed his lack of internet. *Need to fix that.* "That's my escort for the evening. The guy who owns the bookstore from earlier, actually."

"You look like you're about to eat him for dinner. And he looks like he wants to be on the menu."

Rasul went warm. Jacob looked like he was into him too? Really?

There was another pause on Elizabeth's end, and then she grumbled. "These comments are going to send Adina into orbit."

The bad idea formed in Rasul's mind. He tried to push it down. But all he could think about was the way Jacob had felt in his arms, the way he'd smelled like the bookstore. "I... might have asked Jacob out."

"Wait—you asked who out?"

"The escort. The bookstore owner. Guy in the photos. His name is Jacob Moore."

"If you get distracted by dates instead of work—"

"Hey, I thought you just said a significant other would be good to deflect Adina."

"Yes, *potentially.* But I want you working."

"I understand."

Her tone was softer now, though. "It is true that this would be fortuitous. I don't know that you dating someone would truly put her off, but I worry about what this chick is going to pull. I'll take what I can get. And if this is the guy the president of the college insisted was a quiet, dependable, upstanding citizen, that could be good for you in general, not simply deflection." She sighed. "All right. Date your bookstore guy. Just remember. The book is your priority."

When Rasul hung up, he stared at the ceiling a moment, digesting the gravity of what he'd done. Then he opened the contacts and read the new contact name nestled between the others.

Mr. Rogers.

Smiling sadly, he shut the phone.

Probably he should call Elizabeth back and tell her he'd lied, that he only *wanted* to date Jacob.

A real hero would leave him alone and go work on his manuscript, not force him into a relationship.

With a sigh, Rasul put his phone in his pocket and shuffled through his boring apartment to his boring bedroom.

When he couldn't sleep, he turned on the bedside light and started to read *I Capture the Castle*. Except just as he thought, it depressed him. When he was young, he'd seen himself as Cassandra. Now? Now he couldn't deny that he was anything but the self-absorbed, fragile patriarch who couldn't get organized to publish another book or work in any fashion. He could only hide in his gatehouse refuge, reading.

This isn't a gatehouse, and it's no refuge.

Jacob's bookstore was, especially his apartment.

Rasul forced himself to keep reading, not allowing himself to plot how he could maneuver his way back there.

Chapter Four

JACOB DIDN'T sleep at all after the dance, only lay there tossing and turning until four in the morning, when he finally gave up and started his day. The cats glared at him because he'd dislodged them from the bed all night and then didn't feed them immediately upon rising as they were accustomed to.

"You'll get fed at six as always," he told Susan as she glared at him from the end table beside the chair where he was trying to read his usual round of digital news and failing.

Susan, unimpressed by this answer, tucked her striped tail around her body and continued to stare daggers at him. Occasionally Mr. Nancy would yowl in an attempt to get his attention, and the whole time this went on, Moriarty batted a felt mouse across the kitchen floor with a carefully calculated degree of aggression.

Doing his best to ignore them, Jacob switched to another news site and continued his attempt to ground himself in normalcy, but nothing could pull his focus from the continuously echoing truth that he had spent the evening talking, dancing, and flirting with Rasul Youssef, and then had bolted into the night. Even when he surrendered the tablet, gave the cats their morning kibble, and descended into the bookstore to distract himself with inventory, the events of the previous evening continued to play through his mind. The things Rasul had said, the way he kept studying Jacob with an intensity that made him want to purr.

What would have happened if he'd let the date continue? What if he'd brought the man home, had sex with him? Would he be cuddled against him right now instead of doing mundane shop owner tasks?

He knew that was exactly what would have happened, and that was the trouble. It was important he do his best not to think about it until his efforts stuck. He had a good life, he honestly loved what he did for a living, and he wasn't disrupting that for anything.

Except half an hour before the store was set to open, he learned how impossible a task that was going to be.

Gina Wilkerson had been with Jacob since he'd first opened the shop, using her connections to get him started. Her husband was an accountant, her sister was a real estate agent, and she'd been one of his mother's closest friends. Now she was one of his, in addition to being his only other full-time employee. His part-time workers came and went on the regular, but Gina was a constant. She used her salary to boost her retirement and had taken several handsome vacations on the bonus income.

He knew it was her when he heard the key in the lock and the door's bell jingled, and he was about to call out a hello, but she'd hustled through the stacks at double time, and when he turned to see what was going on, she had a seriously strange look on her face. "Is it true? Is what I read online true?"

Jacob put down the books he'd been shuffling on the shelves. "What are you talking about? What did you read online?"

Eyes alight, she whipped out her smartphone and showed him a photo from Instagram. "Look. They all tagged the bookstore, probably because you don't have an account of your own."

Taking the phone from her, Jacob frowned and tried to make sense of what she was saying. He was looking at the bookstore's profile, that much he knew, but instead of the usual photo of that month's staff picks or charming photos of the cats nestled on shelves, he saw a page full of stills of him dancing with Rasul.

Photos of Rasul looking like he wanted to devour Jacob, and a few of Jacob making it clear he felt the same way.

His stomach was already twisting into knots when he accidentally opened one of them and saw the captions and comments on the image.

This dude shows up out of nowhere and swoops up Rasul Youssef like a boss.

OMG Rasul's new boyfriend is a snack. What was Adina on about? Rasul is TAKEN.

IKR? Keep those pics coming.

How dare Rasul cheat on Adina!

We have to stop this, guys.

Eyes wide, Jacob swiped to another photo. Hypnotized, horrified, he read that caption and comments too.

They danced three dances in a row. I am LIVING.

Cheating bastard!

God but Rasul's fuck-me face is hot AF. Give me a man who looks at me like that.

Jacob's face flamed as he moved on to the next one.

They are so fucking. Somebody figure out where this guy lives and get us some live video!

Pretty sure that's the owner of @moorebooks. AUTHOR AND BOOKSTORE OWNER. I ship it.

Guys WHY are we ignoring Rasul's traitorous infidelity?!

BRB gotta go shopping. In Wisconsin.

With a gasp, Jacob dropped the phone and covered his mouth with his hand.

Gina picked it up. "I'd heard the two of you danced quite a bit, but I hadn't thought much of it until I saw the pictures. Is it true? Are you dating him? Because I know he's your favorite author, and I rushed over to get all the details. How did this happen?"

That was the question, all right. How had *any* of this happened? Jacob couldn't dwell on that, though, too preoccupied with what he'd seen in those photos. "Who are these people who took pictures?"

"Kids from the college, I think, and a few locals. Usually hardly any of the Bayview kids go to the gala, but it sounds like several of them came exclusively for Youssef."

Jacob sank back against the bookshelf behind him, then glanced toward the front of the shop. "Oh God, are they going to come *here*?"

Gina's eyes sparkled. "I think so. I'll make sure they buy things. We'll turn this to our financial advantage." She leaned forward. "But is it true? Are the two of you dating?"

Jacob ran a hand through his hair. "No. Evan asked me to escort him at the gala, that's all."

"It's just that there's also these photos." Gina swiped at her phone before handing it over again. Now the screen showed a video of Jacob tugging Rasul through the store until they disappeared up the stairs. "I can't believe he was in the shop and I missed it!"

Taking the phone back again, Jacob swiped to see more photos and more video from inside the shop. "*Why* are they taking so many photos of us?"

Gina's eyes widened. "So there's an us? It's true?"

Why was this so out of hand? *Why were there so many photos?* "There's no us. I told you. I was his escort. And I helped him get out of the store because Jodie apparently called all her friends to come mob Rasul. That's all that happened."

"You've never been able to lie to me, Jacob. There's more to the story, and I see it on your face. Spill it."

"It's not what you're thinking. *At all.*" He ducked his head in case she tried to read more into his obfuscation of the truth. "He signed my books as a thank-you. I gave him some books because it was impossible for him to check out with the chaos."

"And what about the dirty dancing?"

"It wasn't *dirty dancing*, for heaven's sake."

"There's video. It absolutely was." Gina's expression went soft. "I haven't seen you light up like that since the accident. He's good for you, honey."

Jacob tipped his head back and stared at the ceiling. He didn't need someone to tell him that. He'd spent all night alternately trying to deny and obsess over that fact. "He's a celebrity. I'm a nobody bookstore owner. Plus he's so important to me as an author. I absolutely can't afford to destroy that."

"What's to say it'll get destroyed?"

"Logic and reason." Jacob sat up and looked Gina levelly in the eye. "Yes, I think he wanted to take me to bed last night, and that alone has rattled the foundations of all my fortresses. But that doesn't mean he wanted to date me, and even if he did, I'd be a lark while he taught here, at best. Meanwhile, it would be a struggle for me to maintain a *friendship* with him without dragging in all the stars I have in my eyes over him. I'm sure I'll run into him in town from time to time while he's here, and that'll be thrilling enough. Anything more wouldn't be fair to either of us."

Gina huffed. "If you ask me, you're far too logical and reasonable for your own good. You should take a chance with him."

"I don't take chances, which you know very well."

"You *used* to."

That was true, he acknowledged as he finished up his inventory and made himself a cup of coffee in the small office behind the cash register. People who had known him since he was young, especially adults who had been contemporaries of his parents, liked to tease him about how nobody would have ever expected the wild child who had been Jacob Moore to not only come home to Copper Point but become such an upstanding citizen. If he'd told his teenage or even college self he'd be sitting on the hospital board and would be considering taking up leadership in the Copper Point Chamber of Commerce, he'd have laughed in his own face. Back then he'd been determined to go anywhere but here. He'd gotten out too, and had put his foot firmly on the business ladder in Chicago.

And then everything had changed.

He was still in the office when his phone rang. It was Gus. Jacob grimaced, hoping this wasn't about the Instagram posts.

It wasn't. It was about the Facebook videos.

"I didn't know you had moves like that," Gus said after describing an absolutely sensationalized account of what had happened. "And you told me you were going to take a bath and read a book!"

"I *was* going to do that, yes. But Evan called, and I couldn't say no."

"Who would want to if that guy was going to be your date? Man, but he's hot. Now I wish I'd gone to the gala. Everybody at GAG is saying the same thing. Jared is bragging it up on Copper Point People too. He was one of the people who posted video. Clark is fuming, apparently, but you look like you were having so much fun, I think it was worth it."

Jacob set his teeth. *Et tu, Jared?* "Why is our pediatrician the worst gossip in town?"

"Is it true, though? Are you dating him?"

"I already told you, I escorted him as a favor to Evan."

"You didn't say, actually. So Evan set you up? Bold, and awesome of him, to fix the guy up with a male date."

Jacob was about to protest it had *not* been a date when Gina stuck her head into the office, looking even bouncier than she'd been when she came in. "Sweetheart, you should probably come out here."

Why? They weren't open yet. But something in Gina's face brooked no argument. "I gotta go. I'll call you later," he told Gus.

Gina gestured wildly as he stood and pocketed his phone. "Come on, hurry. I think there's going to be a riot if you don't let him in."

"What's going on?" he asked as he followed Gina out of the office. "Let who—"

He stopped as he saw the front of the store, the huge crowd of people filling the sidewalk in front of the door. Every last one of them had their phone out, and all the devices were aimed at the individual standing at the top of the ramp, on the other side of the antique door, peering at Jacob through the glass.

Obviously it was Rasul.

He looked incredibly nervous and delectably disheveled.

Butterflies leaping around his insides, Jacob unlocked the door and pulled it open enough to regard Rasul without obstruction. He wanted to ask what was going on, but the cameras made him uneasy, so he simply raised his eyebrows.

"Can I please come in and talk to you?" Rasul spoke low enough there was no way anything he said would end up on the many videos being taken.

At least, Jacob hoped so.

Rasul smelled just the way he had the night before, except now he was slightly rumpled and had the tiniest hint of sweat. Jacob's entire body reacted on a visceral level.

Clearing his throat, he opened the door wider and let Rasul in.

As Jacob locked the door and tugged down all the shades, Rasul noticed the man was back in Mr. Rogers gear again. It was probably some strange side effect of a night of insomnia in the terrible apartment followed by another call from Elizabeth, but this morning Rasul found it hot.

The tinkling of the bell as the door closed soothed him, and the book smell of the store settled the ragged edges of his soul. Honestly, he might have slept if he'd been able to make a nest between the stacks. He wondered if there was any chance that could happen.

Probably not, given what he was about to ask. Jacob didn't seem happy even before Rasul brought it up, and something told him it wasn't entirely because his business was besieged by Rasul's fans, though likely that didn't help much.

A brightly smiling plump woman with light auburn hair that was probably dyed beamed near the checkout desk. "Want me to duck out so you two can talk, or are you going upstairs?"

Jacob glanced at the clock on the wall, then at the door. "We're supposed to open soon."

The woman waved a hand. "I'll take care of that. You boys go chat." She crossed to Rasul with her hand extended. "Gina Wilkerson. Pleasure to meet you."

He accepted her handshake with a smile that was soft and warm. "Rasul Youssef. Likewise."

"I know who you are. I love your work." She said it calmly, as if complimenting him on his shirt. Not false praise, just not… the young ladies in front of the shop. To Jacob, she suggested with a smile, "Why don't you two head upstairs and have a cup of tea?"

The idea of sitting in that delightful kitchen again, combined with another cup of Earl Grey, sounded like heaven to Rasul. "Sounds good to me, if it's all right with you."

Jacob looked unsure, but he nodded and led Rasul through the shop to the door he'd unlocked the day before.

No cat sat on the stairs this time, though all three of the ones he'd seen previously sat in or near a window in the kitchen where morning sunlight streamed through. The tabby occupied what seemed to be the prime spot, glaring at the longhair who ignored her from the other end of the long window, nestled between several plants. Moriarty sat on the far end of the table, looking as if he were plotting how to vie for his own space but wasn't quite ready to hatch the plan.

Jacob went straight to the counter, where he filled the electric kettle. "What type of tea would you like? The Earl Grey again?"

He'd noticed what type of tea Rasul drank. Why that pleased him so much, he didn't know. "That would be perfect, thank you." Moving cautiously toward Moriarty, he extended a hand for inspection, smiling as the cat sniffed him cautiously. The tabby stopped glaring at the longhair and turned its ire on Rasul, making it clear there was absolutely no room in the window for *him*. As Rasul stroked the black cat's cheek, he offered his other hand to the tabby, waiting as she decided what to do with it. He grinned as she allowed him to stroke her too, then laughed as the longhair shifted position to sniff him. "I love your cats. What are names of the other two? I already was introduced to Moriarty."

Glancing over his shoulder, Jacob softened slightly. "The longhair is Mr. Nancy. The tabby is Susan Sto Helit."

"Excellent cat names."

Mr. Nancy meowed softly and pawed at Rasul's face.

"He wants you to hold him," Jacob said as he fussed with a pot and tea leaves. "Don't feel obligated, but if you do, be aware he'll nip your chin as a sign of affection. He does that to everyone, but he especially loves beards."

"He likes to be picked up? Really?"

"Really. He has a lot of fans in the children's department."

Rasul let go of the other two cats and held out his hands to Mr. Nancy, who meowed again and then all but leapt into Rasul's arms. He laughed as he cradled the cat to his chest and, yes, received a series of nibbles on his beard. "I've never seen a cat who *wants* to be picked up."

"All three of them are originals, but I suppose most cats are, in their own ways."

Moriarty leapt immediately into the place Mr. Nancy had vacated. Cradling the cat closer to his chest, Rasul crossed to the counter beside Jacob and leaned against it. "So, first of all, I'm sorry about the scene outside."

Jacob cast a confused glance at him. "Why? Are you saying you invited them?"

"God, no. But if I weren't... me, they wouldn't be there."

Jacob shrugged. "Gina will get them all to buy books, so it's fine."

Okay, not the reaction he expected. He scritched the back of the cat's head. "Do you have many of mine in stock? I could do an impromptu signing."

"I have about thirty of each. People have been interested in picking them up ever since they heard you were coming, but I assumed more would be curious once you arrived."

"Well, like I said, I'm happy to sign them, and that's a standing offer." He shifted the cat slightly. "That wasn't why I came here, however. I have something I need to ask you."

Jacob kept fussing with the pot and cups in a way that made it clear he was distracting himself. "I'm listening."

Where to start? The beginning, he supposed. "I told you a little of this last night, how I'm behind on turning this book in. I mean, I think the whole world knows that. But it's causing a lot of trouble for my agent and my publisher. My agent is ready to chuck me out the door, and I live in fear that my publisher will ask for the advance back because of my failure to deliver."

Jacob turned to him, suddenly focused. "Do you still have the money?"

Rasul snorted. "No." Sighing, he shut his eyes and submitted to another round of Mr. Nancy's nips of love. "I've compounded everything by being visible to the public while I'm not writing. For a while I could get away with saying I was trying to find inspiration, but it's gone on too long. And I just can't sit in a room and force myself to work. I've tried, believe me. So Elizabeth—my agent—came up with the idea that I should come teach somewhere remote where I couldn't get into trouble. She was hoping the experience might be focusing for me. I had my doubts, but I was willing to try anything at this point. So I came here. But I panicked at the last minute and got back together with an ex, and not only did I miss my initial flight north, I was also plastered all over the gossip sites. This infuriated Elizabeth so much she confiscated my phone. Then, as you know, there was the incident here yesterday. There was another last night after you left. And now this stuff outside this morning."

He put the cat down and paced a bit, the nerves starting to get to him. "Adina is playing some kind of game, which isn't surprising but is a big problem." How did he explain Adina? "I actually like her, even though she does some questionable things. If she would apply the hustle she has for cultivating a social media presence into getting gigs as a model, she'd have an incredible career. But she dreams of being an influencer, and I guess I was good for that route when we were dating. Then I got back together with her and it spiked again. So now she's telling everyone we're still dating, it's in secret. We're not dating, and I don't think she actually cares about me. Just her fame."

Jacob frowned at the tea. "That's a bit rude."

"Yeah, well. She might have been able to make it work, but she shot herself in the foot by sending people to keep tabs on me last night. They saw the two of us dancing instead."

"And now they're outside the bookstore?"

"Yes. I guess Adina has posted again, insisting this is a farce, you and I. Which...." He ran a hand through his hair. "Anyway, the bottom line is that Adina is messing up an already tense situation for me."

Jacob finished pouring the hot water and turned around to face Rasul. "Can you talk to her about it?"

"Wouldn't do any good. It's attention she wants, and she's decided I'm a good way to get it."

"So in addition to rude, she's callous and inconsiderate."

Rasul shrugged. "Yeah, but I can't cast too many stones. She's my go-to bad choice path. We've gotten together and broken up six times now, and every time it's like I'm willingly leaping into the snake pit, thinking somehow this time it'll be full of sinful goodness that will set me free. We're the worst match for each other, but neither of us is good at quitting." He sighed. "But none of that matters. Well, it does, because it's the problem, but I just made a bigger one." He fidgeted, hating himself worse than when the original sin had fallen out of his mouth. "My agent saw the social media blowup—" He stopped, realizing, and glanced at Jacob. "Oh, wow. You're not online much, you said, so maybe you don't—"

"Gina showed me." Jacob didn't look at all happy about it. "Apparently several people at the gala uploaded photos and video. Some of them are my friends, which I apologize for. Believe me, I'll be having a word with them later."

Rasul resumed pacing, a slow, agitated meander back and forth across the kitchen tile. It was cream-colored with faint red and blue flowers and scrolling greenery. He loved it. He also loved that this morning he saw a few errant cat hairs that hadn't yet been whisked away. It felt like he'd been let a bit behind the curtain. "Well... anyway, my agent called me last night because of the photos and video." His stomach knotted and he leaned against the doorway between the kitchen and the living room. "And I did a stupid thing."

After the pause went on too long, Jacob asked, "And the stupid thing is?"

Rasul didn't want to say it, but he had to. He didn't even know how to spin it. *Say it, apologize, and see what happens.* "I... told her you and I were going out."

Jacob didn't say anything, didn't even gasp in shock, which Rasul took as a very bad sign.

He hurried to fill the dead air. "It slipped out. It's horrible of me. Presumptuous, awful, rude, inconsiderate—" *everything you said Adina was.* He winced. "I'm sorry to say, that's me when I get in a bad place. I think it was the apartment that did it."

"Apartment?" Jacob blinked in confusion.

"Yes. The apartment. My awful one, your amazing one." Rasul gestured accusingly at the space around him. "Look at this. Why do you have such an amazing space? I can't even determine what it smells like, but I want to bottle it and wear a sachet of it around my neck so I smell it all the time. Meanwhile my place is horrible and sterile and stinks like grease, and I can't sleep there. All I can do is think about your space and how much I want to write a novel in it."

"You… told your agent you're dating me because of my apartment?" Jacob spoke slowly, as if trying to make something nonsensical logical.

Out with it. All of it. "I told her that because I keep thinking about you. Your apartment, your bookstore, your Mr. Rogers sweaters, your way of talking about my work, your way of being all buttoned-up except sometimes you're not, and I want… more of that. Which I'd been thinking about how to make happen anyway, and then Elizabeth called getting angry at me again, and I couldn't even check what she was looking at because I don't have Wi-Fi set up yet, and… I blurted out that we were dating."

Rasul slid down the doorway to the floor, drawing his knees to his chest. Mr. Nancy immediately jumped on top of them and tried to bite his beard again. Rasul let him.

Meanwhile, Jacob fussed with pouring the tea. "So is that why you've come here? To ask me out? Or try to muscle me out of my apartment?"

Rasul tipped his head back, letting his gaze sweep the space around him. "I mean, both? Not muscle you out, though, more worm my way in with you remaining."

"I'm not looking for a roommate." Jacob set the teapot back down on its trivet. "And I'm not going to date you."

That hurt more than he'd expected. "Because of the crappy way I asked and how I told my agent first?"

"Because I don't want to."

Double ouch. "Ah." He didn't know what else to say.

Jacob came over with the two cups and, to Rasul's surprise, folded himself gracefully to the floor beside Rasul. He handed him tea with the same calmness he'd exhibited since he'd opened the door of the bookshop. "I think there's more to your story. How did your agent react when you said we were dating?"

Rasul clutched his cup in his palms, willing the warmth to seep into him. "She wanted an explanation, and details. So I told her the truth. She already knew about the part where people tried to shanghai me at the store, or whatever it was Adina had inspired them to do, but I told her how you ended up also being my arranged escort and... well. She liked that you'd been hand-picked by the dean." He clutched harder at the tea. "I almost came to legitimately ask you out last night, but I got the feeling you wanted to be alone, so I didn't."

"I did want to be alone, and thank you for noticing." He nudged Rasul's knee. "Drink your tea before it's cold."

Rasul did. It was as good as the day before. "But now you're angry with me?"

Jacob also sipped his tea. "I'm not. Perhaps a bit annoyed, but there's a distinct difference."

"But you don't want to date me?"

"I don't. Though that has nothing to do with your agent, your lie, or the girls outside."

Rasul set his cup aside. "Seriously? Because I really thought we had something going last night. Was I completely off?"

"You weren't wrong. But for many reasons, all of which are my own business, I don't want to date you. Which is part of why I left when I did." Jacob sipped again. "That said, I appreciate your current dilemma and am open to helping you solve it, with some ground rules."

Rasul had been all set to push for Jacob's damn reasons when he realized what else Jacob had said, and now he was just confused, though also slightly hopeful. "Do you... mean you *will* date me?"

"I will *pretend* to date you."

"You're going to fake date me? To keep my agent happy and my stalkers off my tail?"

"Something like that, yes. But with several important conditions."

Rasul shifted so he was cross-legged and facing Jacob. "Okay. Hit me."

Jacob stared into his cup as he spoke. "First, I need to understand why hearing you're dating me soothed your agent."

"Because she thinks you sound like a good influence. She called me again this morning after researching you further. She highly approved of the fact that you weren't on social media and had such great Google results. Apparently you're some kind of upstanding citizen. She said, in fact, that she could see this relationship being the impetus that finally gets me to work again." He rubbed his cheek. "I don't know about that, but I mean, I'll take anything."

"So she expects me to… keep you in line? Out of trouble?"

"I don't know that she expects that precisely, but she's hoping for it, and at the very least wants to take me out of this weird limelight Adina put me in. Which is not what *I'm* hoping for. I seriously wanted to ask you out. Properly. Legitimately."

"But it would help you if I filled that role?"

God, this was *not* how Rasul had wanted this conversation to go. He was hoping for angry passion. He could work with angry passion. He would've used it to launch Jacob straight into bed, or maybe onto this fine kitchen tile. He hunched his shoulders. "Yes. It would help. With the image problem. I don't know about productivity."

"You said, though, that you wanted to write at my kitchen table."

Rasul glanced at it longingly. "I do. I really do."

"Then it's fine. We'll pretend to date, you'll use my kitchen to work, and everyone is happy."

Rasul sure wasn't happy. "How in the world are we supposed to pretend to date?"

"We say we are, to start. We meet for coffee, to go to dinner, and I drop by the college to say hello while you're there. We take walks along the bay, and when people ask me if I'm dating you, I say that we are. You do the same. That's how."

Everything about that sounded exactly like what Rasul wanted, excepting one important thing. "But you won't have sex with me."

"I will decidedly not have sex with you, no."

"And you won't tell me why."

"And I won't tell you why."

Dammit. Rasul picked up his tea and took a large sip. "I take it I'm not to try to change your mind?"

"You can try, but you won't succeed."

The cool, indifferent way Jacob told him he had no chance really turned Rasul's crank. He settled against the doorframe again and studied the man. "Can I stay overnight?"

Jacob opened his mouth, paused, then frowned. "I don't want you to, no. Not right now. But I understand that interrupts the fiction in a significant way."

"I can stay late and work sometimes and then go home. That'll give tongues enough room to wag."

"That sounds feasible." After draining his tea, Jacob set it aside.

He was maddeningly calm. Rasul wanted to rattle him, make him react. Yet at the same time, he wouldn't dare. Not someone who so graciously offered to help him.

Not someone so obviously not interested in him.

Rasul gave in. "So, what's next?"

"Next we go downstairs and let the fiction begin. If you still want to, I'll get out the books for you to sign, but it's not essential."

Just like that. Goddamn. "Should… we set up another time to meet?"

"I'll text you." He paused. "Well, texting is probably difficult on your phone. I'll call you."

"Great."

It was surreal as hell to climb to his feet and follow Jacob back down the stairs into the shop. Noise bled through the door, making it clear they were about to descend into chaos.

"Hey," Rasul said before Jacob could open the door. "I've never fake dated before. Are there rules I should know?"

Jacob glanced over his shoulder at him. "What do you mean?"

"Like, touching. Can I do that casually, or no? Usually I do, but…."

He'd meant it to come off as flirtatious, but mostly he sounded pathetic.

Jacob turned back around. "We'll play it by ear."

The room was brightly lit and crowded with people, mostly women, who turned on the pair of them like locusts. They were huddled farther back in the stacks, except for one white girl with blond hair pulled back in a tight ponytail right beside the door. She looked familiar for some reason.

Rasul spied the store apron and realized she was the employee he'd startled that first day. He tried to give her a winsome smile, but he must have still been rattled from Jacob's cool refusal, because she gave him an inscrutable expression and ran off.

The crowd pressed in, and for the first time in his life, Rasul wanted nothing to do with the people pleading for his attention. He'd resented the attention before, but right now he absolutely hated it. He wanted the safe cocoon of Jacob's kitchen again.

He wanted Jacob.

Before he had a chance to wallow in the depressing truth, Jacob captured his hand and held it loosely as he addressed the room. "Rasul has agreed to a small signing of his works I have in stock. Anyone interested should see Gina at the checkout desk." Then he turned to Rasul, giving him a smile that made his heart stop. "I'll go get the stock. You go get settled with Gina, all right?"

"Sure," Rasul agreed, too dazzled to argue with anything the man said.

Then Jacob lifted his hand and kissed it, and Rasul knew then that no matter what else happened, this man was going to ruin him completely.

He absolutely couldn't wait.

Chapter Five

JACOB WAS fully aware he'd signed on to a disaster, that he shouldn't have agreed to a relationship of any kind with Rasul. This said, he knew if he could go back in time and do everything again, he wouldn't change a thing.

By the time he'd returned to the sales floor with Rasul, his phone had started buzzing constantly with notifications, so he put it in a drawer. He busied himself with talking to people, patiently enduring their quizzing about his new relationship, not giving them many answers but a lot of professional smiles, and always redirecting them to a selection of books they might enjoy. More than young women were in the store now, as Copper Point loved nothing more than a spectacle. Included in that number was a reporter from the *Copper Point Gazette* who took several photos of Jacob, the crowd, and of course of Rasul.

"Is it true that you're dating Mr. Youssef?" the reporter asked.

Imagining Clark's lemon-sucking face, Jacob kept his demeanor cool. "He asked me out, yes, but I didn't realize my private life was headline news in Copper Point."

The reporter glanced over her shoulder at the crush of people hanging on Jacob's every word.

Rasul stepped in then, putting on the bright, easy countenance Jacob recognized from his other interviews. "Don't mess this up for me, guys. I haven't had the date with him yet. I don't want to scare him away."

"That wasn't a date last night?" someone called from the crowd.

"No, that was just flirting," Rasul fired back. Everyone laughed.

After a few more back-and-forths, Jacob got people calmed down and organized for the impromptu book signing. Moore Books had hosted signings before, but they'd always been local authors who, even if they had some significant following and respectable sales, mostly sat alone in a corner, trying not to look dejected. Jacob did what he could to support them, but the truth was most people weren't attracted to signings unless they were at a large event designed for that purpose. He'd known the situation wouldn't be the same with Rasul, but he was taken a bit aback by *how* different it was, and how good Rasul was at his job. Gina had instituted a number policy for claiming books, and when his supply had been quickly depleted, she took down their contact information so they could order a copy and get their book signed on a different day. They still stood in line to see him, though, and even when his fans came up to him to do nothing more than giggle and gush and ask him to sign blank pieces of paper or various parts of their body, Rasul took it in stride and gave them as much attention as the people who'd been able to buy his book.

He was good at making people feel as if they were the only person on the planet, which was probably a lot of why he had such an intense fan base, whether or not they'd read his work. They approached him, desperate for a slice of him, and in a way, he delivered. Jacob noted, though, that Professional Rasul wasn't the same as the Rasul who had sat on his kitchen floor, drinking tea and despairing, nor was he the man who had confessed his fears by the bay and then drawn Jacob into a dance so intimate he'd forgotten himself. Well, there was a little of that Rasul here today, but there was a shutter over him, welcoming people in, but only up to the fire door.

Perhaps it was hubris, but Jacob had the feeling he'd been admitted significantly further.

Rasul signed for three hours, and with the crowd showing no signs of stopping and Rasul exhibiting no indication he would turn a single soul away, Jacob called Gus.

"Can you send three lunches over here and three huge coffees?" He paused, realizing he didn't know how Rasul took coffee or even if he drank it at all. Or if he was vegetarian or had any dietary restrictions. "I'll text over more details, but do you have the staff to step out?"

Gus snorted. "Um, yeah, and I'll bring it down myself. It's pretty slow here, since everyone is down at your end of the street."

Jacob winced. "Sorry. Though, hey—why don't you bring some signage and coupons? I have the ones I usually pass out with purchases, but we could use more. We'll send some of this traffic your way. They have to be hungry and ready for caffeine."

"Will do." A brief pause. "You gonna have some stories for me later?"

Jacob had already decided Gus and Matt were the two people he'd tell the truth to. "Can we have a Mini Main Street meeting for dinner?"

"*Ooh.* Absolutely. Text me what you need and I'll be right down, but I'll contact Matt in the meantime."

Pocketing his phone—which still buzzed with notifications—Jacob wove his way through the crowd to Rasul.

Rasul gave him a bright smile as he approached. Astonishingly, he didn't seem tired. "Everything okay?"

Jacob crouched to talk to him, aware of the many pairs of eyes watching him. "I have a friend bringing over lunch and some coffee. Do you have any requests? He runs Café Sól on University. They have soup and sandwiches and protein bowls."

Rasul touched his stomach as if just remembering he had one. "I'm in the mood for a lot of meat with some fresh veg, especially tomatoes. Coffee sounds excellent."

"You probably want the steak protein bowl, then. How do you take your coffee?"

"Strong, hot, and black."

Jacob leaned in closer so his next question wouldn't be overheard. "Do you want me to find a way to wrap this up?"

Rasul waved a hand. "Nah. Food and coffee and a little more water will get me through." He grinned. "I get a contact high off of signings."

Jacob put in the order and went back to managing the crowd. Before he knew it, Gus walked down an aisle toward him bearing a large bag, a tray of drinks, and a flask under his arm.

"Matt's in for a seven o'clock meeting in the back room of my shop, and he's bringing pizza." Gus peered around the room, taking it in. "Wow, I've never seen it like this in here. You doing any sales, or are they all gawking?"

"Gina and I have nudged several of them into buying, and we sold out of Rasul's books in the first hour, with over one hundred special orders of each title. He's doing signings on paper now and posing for selfies. But they're buying plenty of books."

Gus whistled. "Nice. All right, let's drop Gina's order off, and then take me to the man."

Jacob insisted on Rasul taking a twenty-minute break to eat, which caused a minor ruckus, but he whisked Rasul and Gus up the stairs to his apartment before anyone could complain too loudly.

"I'm August Taylor, nice to meet you," Gus said to Rasul as they went up the stairs. "You can call me Gus. I own Café Sól up the street."

"Oh yeah, I saw that shop on my way by yesterday. Looks like a nice place."

"Thank you. Feel free to stop in anytime."

They sat at the kitchen table, which had three chairs because a lot of the Mini Main Street Meetings were held here. For now it was Gus, Rasul, and Jacob, and Gus and Rasul immediately bonded when Rasul fell in love with his food and exclaimed loudly over the coffee.

"*My God*, this magical brew...." He took another sip and rolled his eyes back in his head. "Are you kidding? Is this vacuum coffee?"

Gus beamed, chin in hand. "It is. I'm impressed you can tell by the taste."

"A friend took me into a shop in San Francisco that made it, and I wanted to live there." He shook his head. "First a great bookstore, then culinary-level coffee. This town is full of surprises."

Gus and Rasul chatted amicably all through the break, further bonding over coffee brewing techniques and international travel, since both of them had been a few places in their time. Jacob mostly listened, using the time to craft an exit strategy for Rasul and plotting what he wanted to say to Matt and Gus alone later. Thankfully Rasul gave Jacob the space he needed, and once they returned to the main floor, he went along with Jacob's announcement that the impromptu signing would be over at three.

"I assure you, we'll have Mr. Youssef back here again," he told the disappointed hangers-on.

"And I intend to be here a lot, so feel free to say hello if we bump into one another," Rasul added. This went over very well with the crowd.

Jacob arranged for Gina to give Rasul a ride back to his apartment so he wasn't mobbed, since she got off at the same time, but he did speak to his fake boyfriend alone in the office briefly before he departed. "We can talk on the phone later to strategize some public dates."

Rasul nodded. "I'll leave you alone through the rest of the weekend. I should go get settled in my campus office anyway." He ran a hand nervously through his hair. "I would love it, though, if I could try to work in your apartment during the day sometimes. I promise not to get in your way."

"That's fine. I assume you have a laptop? I can get you the Wi-Fi password, but I warn you, my connection isn't the fastest."

"Not an issue. I'll work better if social media doesn't load very well. Mostly I need to be able to look up research things on the fly."

Jacob couldn't hide an amused smile. "You do understand you could walk out of the apartment and into more research notes than you could possibly need? The library is also across the street."

Rasul grinned back. "I did think of that, yes. I can order books through you too. Who needs Amazon Prime?"

Jacob sobered completely. "While we're fake dating, I forbid you to utilize that site unless absolutely necessary, for anything."

He held up his hands. "Understood."

It was wonderful to watch the shop empty after Rasul left with Gina, though Jacob didn't mind the influx of cash at all. He often operated at a razor's edge, buoyed by the money his parents left him and some shrewd investments, and days like this translated into much-needed breathing room. He spent the remainder of the store's open hours straightening the first-floor shelves and making notes on what needed reordering. Once he closed shop at five, he did the same thing to the upstairs. He had a shower and a change of clothes, then a cup of tea as he indexed his online newspapers again once that was finished.

At a quarter to seven, he stuck a bit of cash in his wallet and started up the street to Café Sól.

Several people waved hello to him on his short journey, perhaps a few more than usual and with a bit more interest, but that was it. Inside the coffee shop itself, the patrons were a mix of students and local residents, and all of them tracked his progress through the main area to the small door that read STAFF ONLY beside the order pickup area.

The barista waved him through, used to seeing him there. Mini Main Street met a *lot*.

Gus and Matt were already established in the small staff room adjacent to Gus's office at the back of the shop, cups of coffee and a pizza between them. Gus rose and waved at Jacob as he entered. "Excellent. I'll go ask Lisa to start your order."

Jacob acknowledged this with a nod and murmur of thanks, then sank into his usual chair.

Threading his fingers together and resting his elbows on the table, Matt leaned forward. "I don't want to get ahead of things before Gus comes back, but *holy cow*, Jake."

Matt and Gus were absolutely the *only* people allowed to refer to Jacob as Jake, and only in private. He slumped forward, then gave up and all but collapsed onto the table, his hand brushing the edge of the pizza box. "I feel like I've been run over by a fleet of tanks but had to pretend nothing was happening."

Gus was already back and waving his hand impatiently. "How *dare* you start without me. Rewind and do it all again."

"He's exhausted," Matt said to Gus, pulling out his chair for him without getting up. "Let the poor boy be."

Gus wasn't much for empathy, though. "Is it true? Are you actually dating the guy you've been fantasizing about for ten years?"

Jacob rolled his body to the side on the table and poked at the cardboard box. It was takeout from the Italian restaurant, not the chain store out in the strip mall. Mini Main Street had a code. "I'm not dating him, but you two are the only ones who get to know that. If anyone else asks, the answer is yes."

"You're *fake dating*?" Gus pursed his lips before sipping his double espresso. "I don't like this."

"You mean he's just using you?" Matt looked displeased. "I don't like it either."

Jacob held up a hand. "No, this was my idea. He wanted to actually date, but I can't handle that."

Gus settled into his chair and propped his feet on one across the table from him. "So he legitimately asked you out, and you said no?"

"Well… it's a little more complicated than that." Jacob told them the story of the gala and the horde on his doorstep the next morning, plus Rasul's confession of his lie to his agent.

Matt shook his head. "I don't like this. It sounds like a bad deal for you."

"He did sell a lot of books today," Gus pointed out.

"It's not a bad deal for me. A little dangerous, maybe, but not awful. And I'm not doing it to sell books."

Gus waved this away. "Obviously not, but perks is perks."

"Clark is going to have a fit," Matt pointed out. "He's already going to be upset about the article in the paper."

Yes, Jacob was sure he would be. "Do you think I shouldn't have agreed to the fake dating because it'll upset our plans for getting on the leadership of the chamber?"

Gus shook his head. "Naw, he's going to resent you no matter what. Besides, he doesn't get a vote on your personal life."

The smell of the pizza was getting to Jacob. He withdrew some money from his pocket and passed some to Matt for the pizza, some to Gus for the coffee. Then he opened a pizza box and took several slices.

A knock at the door signaled Jacob's beverage had arrived, and while Gus went to collect it, Matt also took a slice. They busied themselves with their food until the door had closed again.

"Is this going to be a problem, you being in love with him?" Matt asked eventually.

Jacob wiped grease from his lips. "I'm not *actually* in love with him. Not the real him. Do I idolize my mental image of Rasul? Of course. Will that fade away as I get to know him? Yes, but that's going to be impossible to avoid. We're going to be friends. I'm going to help him with a problem, and I'll get to watch him write his novel."

"But you're both attracted to each other," Gus pointed out.

Jacob busied himself with his pizza.

"I still don't like it," Matt said at last. "There's not a lot in this for you. Plus I know you. You're *going* to fall in love with him."

Jacob sighed. "I know. But there's not much I can do."

"Just be smart and safe," Gus advised. "Including with these lies you're going to tell everyone. Especially the ones you're telling yourself."

Jacob drew his mocha latte closer to him and cradled the warmth in his hands. "I know. Believe me, I know."

RASUL DIDN'T mind Bayview University as much as he'd thought he would, but he still hated his apartment, which was unfortunate because he spent far too much time in it.

Sunday and Monday he kept himself busy arranging his few belongings in his university office. He begged a ride from the dean and went shopping at the discount stores in the strip mall, trying desperately to find things to cheer up his living space. The junk store on the street behind the Wiccan shop was a true score, full of funky knickknacks and small practical items he hoped would make his apartment more palatable. A few hundred desperate dollars made it tolerable, but all he could think about was how great Jacob's place was and how much he wanted to be in it.

He had his first seminar Tuesday night—he only met with students in class Tuesdays and Thursdays at six, and had to keep four office hours a week. The understanding was that he'd spend the rest of the time writing, and probably not at the university. Elizabeth would expect him to be in his apartment, but he truly couldn't stand it. He'd scrubbed every wall and set up an essential oil diffuser, but he still smelled grease every time he opened the door.

Moore Books didn't smell like his place. Moore Books smelled like literature and Jacob. It drew Rasul like a siren's call.

On Sunday he'd had a long conversation with Jacob laying out ground rules for their fake relationship. Rasul could come over any time during store hours, which were eight to five Monday, Tuesday, Wednesday, Friday, and Saturday, and from eight to nine Thursdays. Traditionally Mondays were Jacob's day off to run errands, leaving Gina in charge of the place, though he said he often popped into the office to catch up on paperwork during that time as well. This meant Monday wasn't the best time for Rasul to occupy his kitchen table, but Jacob had said they could work something out if he needed to be there.

Rasul had already decided he'd only appear on Mondays if he had no alternative.

They still hadn't worked out how they were going to perpetuate their fake dating, something Rasul thought a lot about. Every fiber in his being wanted to use this as a lure to woo the man, but he knew that was a slimy thing to do and he should in no circumstance act on that impulse. He still didn't understand *why* they couldn't date, and he desperately wanted to know. Was it because he was such a disaster? Did Jacob have some kind of hang-up? Was it the shitty way he'd trapped him into this? The latter seemed the most likely, despite Jacob's protestations otherwise, which meant pushing the man was the worst thing he could do.

The problem was this whole thing was the best setup ever to get Rasul to pine like mad for the man. He had a bad feeling about where this was headed.

As he walked to the university for his first seminar, he got plenty of looks and a few photos taken. Elizabeth had given him a brief social media update Monday afternoon, reporting that there were still plenty of tags of him popping up, but Adina had gone quiet, with the excuse that she had a sudden call for work and would be taking a brief hiatus. Given what Elizabeth had said about her agent, that was a lie. Rasul was a bit sorry for Adina and wished her well, but he was glad everything was over.

He felt a bit guilty that technically he didn't need to fake date Jacob anymore, but it was probably safer to let it go on for a bit.

He wasn't excited for his class, he had to admit. He'd done a bit of teaching here and there at conferences, but never anything as sustained and organized as this. Usually his "classes" were people asking him questions and him pulling strategies out of his ass. Though he did have an MFA, he wasn't sure how qualified he was for this.

His class waited for him as he came into the room, every seat full, about twenty people in total. To his surprise, only a handful of the students were in their early twenties. There was a wide expanse of age, gender, and race in the room.

Putting on his convention smile, Rasul put his bag on the desk and withdrew his lecture materials. "Wow, a full house. Good to see you guys. I'm Rasul Youssef, author of two speculative fiction novels and your instructor for this term. Pleased to meet you. Why don't we take a moment to go around the room and have everyone introduce themselves as well?"

They all did, some sticking to the facts, some taking the time to talk about the novels they intended to write. One woman, though, Meg Yardley, was already published with six novels under her belt.

Rasul was intrigued. "That's excellent. Where are you published?"

Meg's chin went up a little, but her expression remained cool. "I'm indie. I write lesbian romance."

There was defiance in her tone, waiting for him to challenge her credentials, but Rasul wasn't going there. He'd already picked up some heavy butch vibes from Meg, and now he saw hints of Elizabeth overtones. Besides, he loved lesbian fiction. "That's great. I'm sure you'll have a lot to teach everyone as well." He glanced around the room. "Not trying to get ahead of the introductions, but is anyone else published?" His eyebrows rose as several hands went up. "Wow. Well, mention that when you introduce yourself. I love this level of expertise we have going on here."

It turned out there were several poets, two novelists, and two nature writers in the class. Every last one of them was self-published. Well, Rasul supposed that was the new thing, though given the grim looks on their faces as they talked about their publication experiences, it sounded like the self-pub game was as rough, if not rougher, than the New York game.

This could be an interesting undertaking.

He rubbed his hands together when they all finished with introductions. "Right. Okay. I'll do my best to remember your names, but feel free to correct me when I invariably misremember some of you. Let's dive right into it: so I can continue to get to know you better, I wanted to start today with a writing sample exercise. I'll do some instruction after, but I don't want to color your efforts. My goal is for you to be able to look back at what you started with and see your improvement. Your assignment: pick your favorite novel, or one of your favorite novels, and write a scene based on it. You can give us a scene you wish would have happened, put the characters in a different setting, whatever you like. Just make sure it's your voice and your style shining through. I'll give you half an hour for the exercise, and then I'll have you turn it in. No worries if you don't finish it, and there's no minimum or maximum word count. This is diagnostic only."

A college-aged girl in the front raised her hand tentatively. Rasul tried to remember her name, then decided not to risk it. "Yes?"

She lowered her hand. "So you want us to write fan fiction?"

Rasul paused. "Huh. I guess I do."

Another hand went up, this time from the older gentleman named Ron who had taken great pains to talk about his unpublished novel's hero, who liked to go fishing. "Are you going to do the exercise too?"

Rasul shrugged. "Sure. I'll do one, then share it. I'm going to type on my laptop, and if you have one you can do the same, but no worries if it's handwritten. Ready?" He reached for his phone to set a timer, then stopped. "Ah. Anyone have a smartphone with a timer?"

They all did, of course, but Meg took charge and kept the time. Rasul sat down at the desk, pulled out his laptop, and stared at the blinking cursor. The novel that flew into his mind, of course, was the one he'd recently reread, *I Capture the Castle*.

Well, why not?

He wrote a small scene between Cassandra and Simon, though very quickly it turned into Rasul and Jacob, respectively. Cassandra was trying to be glib and catch Simon's attention, but Simon kept her politely at arm's length, despite their obvious attraction. He was getting into a good attempt by Cassandra to lure him out on a walk through the castle when Meg's phone went off.

The room filled with groans and protests. Most people had barely gotten started, and everyone hated what they'd written. A few of the college-age girls and one of the older women, though, looked quite confident and almost smug.

Rasul let them vent for a minute, nodding. "Sure. It's tough to write on the spot, and tougher to write with someone else's characters." He plugged his laptop into the overhead projector and turned it on. "This is what I did. I worked from *I Capture the Castle*, though my Cassandra and Simon aren't terribly accurate. There are elements of them there, but they quickly turned into my own creations."

"But what is this going to teach us? How are you grading this?" a woman asked. Rasul was fairly sure her name was Tina.

"What it tells me isn't very important. What it tells *you* is far more interesting. So that's your next assignment. Twenty minutes, a quick paragraph about what you learned from this. No wrong answers. 'I hate fan fiction' is a valid response, the same as realizing you love it. Just take a moment to examine your work, your reaction to the exercise."

This time Rasul watched them while they worked. He would have played on his phone, but that was impossible, so he studied his charges instead. He hadn't been sure how to go about this class exactly. The dean had said it was supposed to be very introductory level and free-form, so he was doing as requested so far. There were so many different ability and experience levels here. He hoped he could do a good job.

Once they finished their exercises, he had them share them, which was fun. They gave a variety of answers and had some lively discussion, and all of a sudden it was time to end the class.

Rasul pointed to the corner of the board. "For Thursday, read the short story I uploaded to Google Classroom. Come ready to discuss it. You have my office hours on my syllabus too, so if you have any questions, let me know."

They filed out, and several of them came up to tell him how excited they were about the class. The dean stopped by too, and he was smiling.

"You're off to a great start. Looking forward to seeing what else you do here." Evan handed Rasul a flyer. "Also, I wanted to officially invite you to the Founder's Day celebration next weekend."

Rasul threw away the flyer as soon as the dean was out of sight. He thought about the class all the way back to his apartment, though. It hadn't been bad. He'd worried somehow his complete lack of ability to do his own work would translate into being a crap teacher, but it seemed like he'd done all right.

He opened his laptop to see if he could work on his novel, but the same heavy, twisted feelings of anger, regret, and terror swamped him immediately.

He shut it and lay back on the bed, staring up at the ceiling.

JACOB ABSOLUTELY hated chamber of commerce meetings.

He didn't at all resent the idea of them—he *wanted* to connect with his community and share new ideas, to find ways to promote other local businesses. Problem was, the meetings were never about that. They were just another chance for Clark and his crew to complain about the internet and be suspicious of anyone under fifty.

Every Copper Point small business could become a member, in theory, but traditionally only businesses of a certain type were welcomed. There had been a small scandal when the Wiccan shop, for example, had joined, and a certain set of members ensured the owner's membership only lasted a brief time. Jacob had tried to help her, but Clark and company did too good of a job making her feel unwelcome. It was shortly after that Jacob organized Mini Main Street so they could coordinate their plans and counter whatever Clark and company were up to.

Lately the controversy in the chamber had been that the Chinese restaurant owner had joined. The same clutch of members who had turned up their nose at the Wiccan shop owner were now working on Yi Fu Zhang. He was more difficult for the naysayers to take down, though, because in addition to MMS, Zhang had Rebecca Lambert-Diaz and her partner at the law firm, Julian Steele, on his side. It was difficult to say which one of the lawyers was more terrifying.

They were so terrifying, in fact, MMS hadn't worked up the courage yet to ask them to join even though they desperately wanted them to. But they knew Rebecca better now because they were all on the hospital board together, and Julian had joined GAG, so he wasn't as scary. Maybe they'd ask them both soon.

Being part of the St. Ann's Medical Center board and watching that group take on long-established local institutions had given MMS the courage to take on the Main Street cabal. They didn't have any coordinated attacks planned yet, but they did their best to keep in touch with each other and work behind the scenes and sometimes in front of them to manipulate things to get what they wanted. Jacob always thought of it as "Emma-ing," but he was the only one in the group who'd read Austen. The other two called it scheming.

Originally Mini Main Street had planned for this chamber meeting expecting they would need to shore up support for Zhang, but it didn't take a genius to know that given recent events, the focus would be on something different. Or rather, someone.

"I should like to know," Clark began with a sharp glance at Jacob, "how it's becoming of a community leader to cavort around a public function and then be written up in gossip columns."

"He actually just said *cavort*," Gus murmured under his breath.

Jacob kicked him gently under the table as he folded his hands together and gave Clark his best *and screw you too* smile. "I assume you're talking about me, Les? Yes, I danced at the university gala and did an interview for the *Gazette* the next day. What of it?"

It pleased him to see how much his use of Clark's first name bothered him. "It was highly unseemly."

Rebecca beamed a smile that matched Jacob's. "I thought it looked like Jacob was having a great time. And I heard the Sunday edition of the *Gazette* sold out completely, something that hasn't happened in a while." She glanced around the table. "Am I misinformed?"

Beside her, Julian didn't look up from the legal pad he was perusing and replied in a bored voice, "You're not. The paper's owner asked me to personally thank Jacob, since he couldn't be here tonight, and said to be sure to let him know of any more exciting events in his shop."

"I saw quite an uptick in sales that day as well," Gus ventured.

"*We* didn't." This was Matt's father, the owner of Engleton's Fine Clothing. "If anything, our sales were down."

Matt studied the table.

Rebecca laughed. "Well, I doubt a bunch of eager young women and curious residents would naturally run from a bookstore and coffee shop to start suit shopping."

Zhang, who had been consulting his translator, popped into the conversation here. "We have good business Saturday."

Clark, annoyed this wasn't going his way, launched into a fifteen-minute diatribe about respectability, morals, and community image. As he wound down, he fixed his gaze on Jacob. "I hope we're not about to see some kind of repeated spectacle. Our businesses are struggling enough as it is."

Jacob offered a serene smile. "I don't see how my love life could affect other businesses, but I'll certainly keep your remarks in mind."

He enjoyed watching Clark's mouth pucker at the idea of Jacob's very gay love life.

"If you think about it," Gus ventured with a thread of maliciousness in his tone, "Jacob and Rasul will be *contributing* to the local economy. Dates mean restaurants. And wherever they go, others are sure to follow."

Every restaurant owner immediately perked up.

"Do you think it's too late to ask our new celebrity to be featured at Founder's Day?" someone asked, sending Clark into another round of bluster.

The meeting droned on until well past ten, at which point Jacob only wanted to bolt home and soak in the tub. Instead, he lingered afterward, making small talk with the restaurant owners who suddenly had great deals for him, especially if he booked in advance, and with Rebecca, who drew him aside.

"Thank you," he said to her before she could say anything.

She waved a hand at him. "Nothing to worry about. I've got your back. But speaking of that. Are you still open for running for office?"

Jacob startled. "You knew I was considering that?"

She winked at him. "I had a feeling, but thanks for confirming. Wanted to let you know I was behind you."

"I'm not sure I have a real chance, though."

"You have more of a shot than you think. Everyone knows you're absolutely dependable and respectable."

Why did people keep saying that, and why did it bother him so much?

She kept going. "This town needs new blood in all its leadership. I can't do it—they hate me too much, plus I'm still busy with the hospital board for a bit. I pity you in advance, because I know Nick is going to turn to you to be president next after my term is up."

Good Lord. Jacob wasn't looking forward to that.

It's probably because you're so dependable.

Rebecca continued. "That won't be for a while, yet, though. Besides, right now I want you to serve office here. There's no one better suited. You're not as young as Gus and Matt, but you're not so old you're... well, them. You embrace new ideas, but you're still conservative in some ways, like how you resist social media. I just wanted you to know I have your back completely, and so do several others."

He thanked her, hugged her goodbye, and went to join Matt and Gus.

"Does everyone really see me as dependable and boring?"

"Not boring," Gus said. "But yes, very dependable. Loyal, dependable, solid. That's Jacob Moore."

Not the adjectives he wanted to be used to describe him.

He thought of Rasul telling him he liked his brain and wanted to see more sparks of passion.

Sighing, Jacob ran a hand through his hair. "I need to get home, feed my cats, and finish the books."

Matt grinned. "See? Dependable as the day is long."

Jacob frowned all the way back to his apartment.

Chapter Six

ON WEDNESDAY Rasul packed up his laptop and headphones and headed down Main Street toward Moore Books. He was a little apprehensive about going, despite having explicit permission.

It was ten in the morning, and the place was decently busy. It seemed there was some sort of book club going on in the circle of chairs near the front window, and the collection of mostly older women waved to Rasul as he came through. The blond ponytailed employee was also there, watching him intently as she loaded books from a cart onto shelves.

Ah, he finally saw her name tag. Jodie. He waved at her.

She ducked her head and turned away.

He frowned, then shrugged. Weird to have a teenage girl hate him for no reason, but at least he could be in the store without having his photo taken.

Jacob was at the checkout desk, working at the computer. He glanced up at Rasul and gave him a polite smile as their gazes met. "Good morning."

Rasul had to fight the urge to straighten his clothes and run a hand through his hair to smooth any errant strands. "Hey. How are you?"

"I'm well, thank you."

Rasul was highly cognizant of the other patrons in the store getting quieter to listen to them. He wasn't sure how to behave with Jacob. Normally if he were dating someone, he'd come up to them and give them a kiss, touch their face, their hair, their shoulders, their hands. He was a highly tactile person on a lot of levels, but especially in regard to romance. He knew being overly touchy wouldn't be a good way to approach Jacob for actual courting, but at the same time, Rasul worried their fake relationship would be found out if they weren't engaged enough with one another.

If Jacob had these same fears, he hid them well. After closing his computer, he glanced at the women in the front of the store. "Maryann,

I'm taking Rasul upstairs so he can start writing. Will you keep an eye on things for me for a few minutes?"

A spry elderly woman with a cane leaning against her chair turned so she could grin lasciviously at them. "You two lovebirds take your time. I'll keep people in line."

"Isn't there an employee here somewhere?" Rasul asked Jacob as they went to the back of the store. "That Jodie person?"

"Yes, and she'll do the official store minding, but Maryann likes to feel important, so I always tease her about taking charge. Besides, she'll actually greet customers, whereas Jodie won't. She can be painfully shy. I let her work here against her grandfather's wishes because I think it's good for her."

"Why in the world does her grandfather have a say in what she does?"

Jacob sighed. "One, because he's a rather significant person in Copper Point, and two, because it's Copper Point."

As they headed to the door leading to the apartment, Rasul glanced around to see if he could spy the cats, but the space was currently unpopulated by humans or felines. Moriarty was on the stairs again, however, waiting to bolt until Jacob shooed him, at which time he darted away with a hurt glance.

"I do appreciate that you're letting me use your space," Rasul said as they cleared the landing. "I promise not to get into anything but the tea."

"Well, I'll be a little disappointed if you don't poke around my bookshelves." They were in the kitchen now, and Jacob gestured to it expansively. "Feel free to rearrange things on the table if you need to, and of course make whatever tea or coffee you need. It's all in this cupboard here, the pour over and the tea strainers, and the pots and mugs are in this cupboard."

Rasul put his hands in his pockets to keep himself from fidgeting. "Sounds good, thank you. I'll restock anything I use too much of."

"I buy everything from Gus."

"I'll take any excuse to go get some more of that vacuum coffee."

Jacob narrowed his eyes at the two cats in the window, who were having a subtle battle for space. "If Mr. Nancy or Susan bother you, kick them out into the main part of the bookstore. Also, fair warning, if you leave your laptop open, especially on the table, they'll sit on the keyboard. They're a little better if you leave it on the ottoman, but they've been known to hop on it there too. You're free to write from the armchair or couch in the living room—I have a small lap desk tucked behind the end table. In essence, make yourself at home." He glanced at a living room wall and added, "Also, go ahead and stop the clock if the tick bothers you. Would you like me to do it now?"

Rasul followed Jacob into the living room and saw the impressive wooden clock complete with pendulum swinging back and forth as a rather pronounced *thunk, click, thunk, click* radiated into the room. The clock had gold edges around the clock face, and the numbers were written in Roman numerals. It looked old but not ancient. "Go ahead and leave it. It's a great clock. Seems like it would be good company."

"It doesn't toll the hour, at least, which is a small mercy. I have to reset it once a week, as it doesn't keep time as well as it did when I grew up." Jacob's gaze didn't leave the clock, but his thoughts seemed to be very far away. "I didn't keep many things from my parents' house, but this was one of the most important."

This was the second time Jacob had spoken of his parents as if they were no longer in the picture. Rasul struggled for a moment to find the most delicate way to ask about them. "You keep referring to your parents in the past tense."

Jacob kept his gaze on the clock. "When I was twenty-four, my parents were in what would eventually become a fatal car accident. They were hit by a drunk driver coming home from a charity event."

Rasul's heart fell. "I'm so sorry."

"I was in Chicago at the time, but I made it back to say goodbye. Well, they were both in comas at that point, but I was there when each of them passed." He hesitated, then touched the back of his hair before speaking again. "I started *The Sword Dancer's Daughter* while I was in the hospital. I finished it in the days after the funeral. It was a huge comfort to me at a very rough time."

Many, many people had showered Rasul with praise for his work, had told him how much his stories meant to them, but not a one of them shook him like this confession. "I'm… honored to have written something that was able to help you," he said at last.

Jacob's sad smile made Rasul want to draw him into his arms. He resisted the urge.

With a no-nonsense sigh, Jacob straightened and gestured to the clock again. "If you'd like to stop it, all you have to do is open the glass doors at the bottom and still the pendulum. I don't have any kind of superstition about it and have turned it off for guests before. It's another one of those things that annoyed me when I was young, but after my parents' death, I changed my attitude about it. The clock feels like soothing company now. A steady grounding beat I barely hear consciously but would miss if it were ever gone." His smile was the polite, distant one he used on the sales floor. "Anyway, I should get back to work. Let me know if you need anything. I'll probably pop in for lunch once my afternoon worker shows up, but I'll eat downstairs in the office."

With that, Jacob was gone.

The ticking of the clock was louder when Rasul was alone, but he already knew he'd die before he stopped the pendulum for his own sake. Jacob had been so matter-of-fact when he talked about his parents dying, but it was clear nothing about their absence in his life was simple or tucked neatly behind him.

Sitting down in the rocking chair, Rasul stared at the clock and rocked unconsciously in time to the clock's beat. It was quite loud with no other sound in the apartment save the occasional growls from Susan and Mr. Nancy. But it was soothing and hypnotic too.

He started my book while his parents were dying, finished it when they were gone.

Rasul had never been in such close, repeated proximity to someone who responded so much to his work, not anyone who didn't work for his publisher or literary agency. *He'd* never responded to a book or author like this. While he had books that were important to him for deeply personal reasons, he didn't have anything like what Jacob described.

Jacob had said all that, but he didn't hang on Rasul or try to kiss his ass, or gaze at him with a kind of adoration that made his stomach queasy. He'd basically just said, "Your work is incredibly important to me and got me through a very bad time, thank you," and then continued with his day. While letting Rasul exist in his space and use his name to deflect bad PR.

Thunk. Click. Thunk. Click.

Would *Veil of Stars* move anyone in that way? God, but Rasul wanted it to. He was aware his debut novel had received a huge boost from the serendipity of the Syrian conflict and stories about refugees drifting into public consciousness at the same time. Critics had loved that he was half-Syrian and could speak with some authority about the culture—not as much as people thought he could, not always, but he wasn't ignorant about that side of his family's homeland, no. There was also something about putting a literary polish on complicated matters, and of course delivering everything in an engaging way. *Carnivale* had been for his mother, a nod to her homeland of Brazil, but he'd also made her angry because he'd touched on political things her family hadn't liked.

Veil of Stars was for himself, though he'd only recently realized it. In so many ways it was his story. Sometimes he worried it was *too* autobiographical, that people would call him on it. Of course the only real biographical part was the main character's orientation. Bisexual instead of pan, but it was close enough he'd own it. Well, and the part about him being part Arab. Maybe it was pretty autobiographical. Yet all the surreal bits where he could manipulate the universe with his thoughts were not even remotely how his own life had played out.

Thunk. Click. Thunk. Click.

He was scared to write. This wasn't the first time he'd acknowledged that. He was scared he'd suddenly suck at it. Scared of what he might poke inside his own head. Scared it would be great to him but nobody would buy it and people would curl up their noses at him. Several times his agent had suggested he write something, anything, else.

But to turn away from *Veil of Stars* felt like turning away from himself. He was in a sticky trap, flailing and making himself more stuck, all while dangers closed in around him.

Thunk. Click. Thunk. Click.

What if he let the main character borrow even more of himself? Would that help, or make things worse?

What if he let some of Jacob bleed into the love interest?

What if he made this more of a love story than he'd initially planned?

Was that wrong, to base the character a bit on Jacob? Should he ask permission? How would he do that without making things more awkward? Wasn't that even more of an aggression than what he'd done already?

Could he write anything *other* than a version of Jacob right now, though? That had been the element he'd been missing this whole time, a better characterization for the love interest.

Could he write such a simple story? Boy meets boy, boy falls in love with boy, boy accidentally rearranges the universe, learns to manage himself, and everyone lives happy ever after? Was that *allowed*?

Thunk. Click. Thunk. Click.

The clock was seriously soothing. Sometimes Rasul became aware of it, but mostly it marked off the seconds of his life one at a time. Every time the clock *thunk*ed or *click*ed, another measure of Rasul's life was spent. Another second he was past his manuscript's due date. Another moment closer to his death. Another breath drawn in, pushed out.

What did Jacob think about as he sat in this chair in the evenings, his life marked into increments by the clock on the wall? Did he think about anything at all?

Did he think about his parents, whose lifetimes had already been measured out?

Did he think about Rasul?

Thunk. Click. Thunk. Click.

He became so engrossed in the rhythm of rocking and listening to the clock, allowing his mind to unravel, that when the door to the apartment opened and footsteps sounded on the stairs, Rasul startled and leapt to his feet. He stood awkwardly in the center of the room, probably looking guilty, as Jacob passed through the kitchen.

"Sorry," he blurted, averting his gaze. "I… got caught up thinking about things and listening to the clock."

Surprisingly, this pleased Jacob. "I do the same thing. Sometimes when I'm too overwhelmed from dealing with people, I turn on the electric fireplace—just the light and faux flames in the summer—and rock, listening to the clock, letting my mind unravel. Gus and Matt hate the tick, though. They say they feel like someone is hacking off pieces of their life."

Well, yeah, but Rasul kind of dug it. "I met Gus, but who's Matt?"

"Matt's family owns the clothing store next door. Engleton's Fine Clothing."

"Oh, I think I saw him at the gala."

"Yes. He was there. He's the store manager. We sort of have our own unofficial gay chamber of commerce club. It meets here frequently."

"That sounds lovely."

"It is." Jacob was back in the kitchen now, putting together a very healthy and delicious-looking sandwich from the fridge. He glanced over his shoulder at Rasul. "Can I make you something?"

"Oh, no. I don't want to impose more than I already am, but thank you."

"It's not an imposition, just a sandwich. Do you want turkey, ham, or vegetarian?"

"Uh, can I have turkey *and* ham? And all the veggies?"

"Of course. Pickles? They're dill, not sweet."

"Yes, please."

Despite what he'd said he would do earlier, Jacob sat at the table with his sandwich, and Rasul followed suit. All three cats appeared from wormholes and placed themselves as close to the table without being on it as possible. Mr. Nancy chose the post beside Rasul's leg and meowed while scratching his trousers.

When the same technique was applied to Jacob, he deftly nudged the cat aside. "I advise against giving them scraps. Once they take you as an easy mark, your life is over."

"I am kind of an easy mark, though." Rasul gave Mr. Nancy an apologetic glance and telepathically told him he'd square up with him once the boss was gone.

"I was wondering," Jacob said around a bite of sandwich, "when would be a good time to go on a date together?"

Rasul's heartbeat, which had synched with the ticking of the clock, briefly stuttered ahead. "Oh? I mean, anytime really, except for my class and office hours. My class is Tuesday and Thursday, six to eight, and my office hours are Monday and Friday ten to noon. Other than that I'm supposed to be trying to write. But I do need to eat. And take breaks. And come listen to your clock tick."

God, he hadn't babbled like that to a crush since he'd been fifteen. In love with the shy boy in the library, unable to sort himself out enough to get a date.

I should start the book right there. In the library. The two of them alone, listening to the clock tick, and when he can't bring himself to say anything, the rush of his power stops the moving hands, drops the veil of the universe, and abruptly the two of them are inside their personal nest of stars, unsure of how to get out again.

With a cry, Rasul rose to his feet, heart galloping now, every sense wired to ninety.

Jacob regarded him with concern, rising more slowly. "Rasul? Are you all right?"

He must've had wild, terrifying eyes as he turned to his pretend boyfriend. "I just figured out the opening of the book. Maybe. But I really think it will work."

A smile, the real smile that made Rasul's heart skip, spread across Jacob's face. "I'll leave you to it, then."

Rasul didn't wait for him to leave, only plunked down in his chair, sandwich forgotten as he opened the word processing document with trembling hands and started typing.

When he looked up an hour later, dazed and quietly euphoric with victory, there was a metal water bottle and a note beside Susan, who sat, legs tucked, on the other side of the laptop, eyes shut as she dreamed.

The note said,

The remainder of your sandwich is on a plate in the fridge. I'll make us a reservation for seven Friday night. If Indian isn't okay, let me know and I'll change it.—Jacob

Rasul rubbed the edge of the paper between his thumb and forefinger, reading it through a second time. Then he tucked it into his pocket, saved his file, took a drink of water, and started in on the next scene.

JACOB WAS nervous about his date with Rasul all day Friday.

It didn't matter how much he told himself it didn't matter because it wasn't a real date. It was Rasul Youssef, the author he'd been calling his favorite for ten years. It was the intense but charming man who kept barging his way into Jacob's life.

It was the man Jacob had been attracted to for a long, long time, first in the abstract and now in the very specific.

He left for India Palace at twenty to seven, far earlier than necessary, but he didn't want to be late. It was on the University Avenue side of what the locals thought of as Front Street, the name it had borne until sometime in the middle of the twentieth century when Bayview had been founded and some city planner felt having a campus town sounded nice. It was the same small-town phenomenon that made Copper Point Pharmacy's unofficial name Peeley's, which came from it being known as Peeley's Drug in the 1960s and early seventies.

It was another nice day, though a bit windy as a front edged over the bay. Soon Jacob would need a jacket when he took this walk, which usually ended at Gus's shop. He glanced through the window of the café as he passed, but the windows didn't let him peek too far in, still reflecting the street in front of them.

India Palace was in essence a slightly upscale diner, boasting a buffet at lunchtime for the students and professors, and a fancier dinner service complete with candles on the table for the locals in the evenings. The owners were a lovely Indian couple who tended to come out to the guests' tables and ensure they were having a quality dining experience. Jacob also knew them from chamber of commerce meetings, the same way he knew most of the Main Street and campus-town proprietors.

Avni met him with a smile as he came through the door, drawing him in for a quick embrace. "Jacob, so good to see you. Your boyfriend is already here, so I seated him."

A thrill of delight and terror ran through Jacob at *your boyfriend.* "Thank you."

She beamed like a proud mother as she escorted him to the booth near the window where, indeed, Rasul sat gazing out the window, a cup of chai in front of him, as well as a spread of naan and samosas. As Jacob expected, the restaurant was full to bursting, and everyone had their eye trained on Jacob and Rasul.

He didn't blame Avni or her husband. He'd chosen them because he liked them and wanted them to do well. Also he knew from online interviews that Rasul loved Indian cuisine.

Rasul rose, smiling as Jacob approached. Then he put his hand on Jacob's shoulder. "I ordered already because I accidentally skipped breakfast and lunch and I thought I was going to faint. Avni's been taking care of me."

Jacob went still as Rasul leaned in and bussed his cheek with a dry kiss. It was a perfectly acceptable part of the ruse, he acknowledged. All the same, it short-circuited all his nerve endings and made him long to curl into a ball on the floor and expire quietly.

Instead, he returned the kiss with what he hoped was a cool gesture, and sat down. To Avni, who hovered like she was watching the best television episode ever, he said, "Another chai, please, and a glass of water."

"Of course." She drifted away, casting several glances back at him.

"She's wonderful," Rasul said, dragging a samosa through the mint sauce. "And so is this food. Holy cow. You're welcome to have some of this, of course, but I'll warn you I asked her to make the samosas extra spicy."

"How spicy is spicy?"

Jacob's heart sped up again as Rasul dredged the samosa through the sauce and held it out for Jacob. It was intimate and sensual and made Jacob want to melt. He wanted to lock his gaze with Rasul's and drag his tongue across those long, dangerous fingers.

Instead, he politely took the food from Rasul with his hands and steadied it before taking a bite. His eyes widened as the spice hit him. "That's *hot*." He caught some crumbs falling from his lips as he gave the samosa back. "But very good."

Rasul's eyes sparkled as he passed Jacob some naan and his cup of chai. "We can order some more."

"I want room in my stomach for the main course."

"Look, I have absolutely no argument with leftovers. Also I'm in the mood to pack away everything they have in the kitchen."

They ended up ordering more samosas and naan and three main dishes to serve family-style in a variety of spice levels.

"I love samosas." Rasul dipped the last of the one in the mint sauce again and paused to chew it with obvious pleasure. "They remind me of my grandmother's kubbeh. Not the same at all really, but they're similar enough to make me nostalgic."

Jacob sipped his chai as he watched Rasul enthusiastically consume his food. "Your grandmother emigrated from Syria, yes?"

"Grandfather and father too, back in the 1960s. Dad was only seventeen when they came over, but he leapt headfirst into assimilating as an American. Got himself a high-powered job in New York City and flirted with a Brazilian model, who became my mother." He wiped his fingers on a napkin, his lips thinning briefly into a line. "Mom thought Dad was richer than he was, but in the end she decided a green card marriage would do well enough as compensation, so she got pregnant to force his hand. Then got divorced and took off as soon as she was in the clear."

What? "I never heard that in your bio, only that your parents got divorced when you were young."

"Yeah, well." Rasul shrugged and sopped up more of the sauce with his naan this time. "Doesn't sound as nice, plus she's mostly rehabilitated herself now. She—" He stopped short, his entire face lighting up as he froze. "Jacob, listen. They're playing our song."

Jacob glanced around, then realized Rasul meant the atmospheric music. During the day they played Indian music, but at night they put on various Spotify soundtracks full of soft rock. Right now Air Supply sang with heartfelt intensity.

Jacob couldn't help smiling. "I don't think we danced to 'Every Woman in the World,' though."

"Every Air Supply song is our song, babe." Rasul put a hand on his chest and lip-synched along with the singers as if he were on stage with them.

Blushing, Jacob tried to bat him away. "Stop, you're making a scene."

"I love scenes." Rasul calmed down, though, resting his chin in his hands. "I sat up a lot trying to figure out what that song meant when I was little. Why is she every woman in the world to him? The only thing I could come up with was that when he was with her, all the women on the planet sucked into her and became a single entity. It was terrifying and wonderful."

"Your speculative fiction roots being formed."

Jacob had meant it as a gentle ribbing, but Rasul deflated and curled around his cup. "Do you know, sometimes I hate that I got boxed into that genre? I feel like I always do the same thing and people are going to call me on it. They already do. If they're not bitching at me for taking so long to finish my book, they lambaste me for doing the same thing over and over."

"What do you mean? You've only written two novels and a handful of short fiction. Your editor says this, or reviewers? That's impressive, though, if it's the latter, still giving you ink after all this time."

"No, no. Readers. People online."

Jacob leaned back in the booth, even more confused now. "They email you this?"

"No, though I think my publisher gets letters. They don't know my email, thank Christ. This is on social media. Go read the comments on my Instagram sometime. They're a nightmare. And on Twitter and on my Facebook page I get a lot of random posts about how I should be writing. And input on how I could improve in general. I should be more diverse. I should include more marginalized groups. I should stop doing diversity theater. I shouldn't hate white people so much. I shouldn't use Oxford commas. There was an error on page forty-five and when am I going to fix it, could I notify them so they can redownload their ebook. Would I like to hire them as a proofreader and here are their rates. Though some are only there to see me party, so there's a clash." Rasul laughed sadly and ran his finger through the mint sauce. "The look on your face."

Jacob hoped the look on his face was that he was horrified, because that's exactly what he was. "So people come up to you constantly and… what, give you advice? Yell at you?"

"Some comments are amazing. Sometimes someone tells you how much your book meant to them, and it hits at just the right time. Sometimes someone tags you in an awesome personal review and it makes your day. Other times it's the other way. When I'm in a healthy mental place, I thrive on it. All that feedback. But Elizabeth says even when I think I'm okay with all that input, it affects me in complicated and detrimental ways. I hate to admit it, but I think she's right. I have so many voices in my head all the time. Sometimes the most random remarks will stick to me, and instead of writing for days I'll mentally masticate, worrying all the bits and corners for truth and things I should improve on. The problem is often the volume of feedback. For each online poster, it's simply them saying something. When I log on to see how people like the photo of the sunset I posted, though, and somebody feels the need to complain about how I'm not writing fast enough or offer commentary on how I treated the shopkeeper on page forty of *Carnivale*, it can be a bit derailing."

"I should think so." Jacob frowned as he sipped more chai. "You should stay away from social media, or at least not read the comments."

"But reading the comments is why I go, and I go the most while I'm writing. Sometimes the solitude gets to me, and I need some contact, any contact. Except I'm doing okay in your apartment. That clock is a gift. Well, and of course the cats."

Their food arrived then, and after they loaded their plates, Jacob indulged in a moment of watching Rasul enthusiastically enjoy his food. "Can I ask how your writing is going there, or is that a bad question?"

Rasul wiped his lips with a napkin. "It's a delicate one, for sure, and I think every author has a different attitude regarding someone asking how their work is going. For me right now, it makes me tense when my agent or editor ask, or random people online. What you just did is okay. Because you framed it like you wanted to know if *your space* was working for me, and in general I felt more like you were making sure there wasn't something additional I needed, or giving me an invitation to talk about it." He arranged another bite of food. "And to answer your question, yes, your space is excellent. I decided to restart the draft completely—this is the tenth time I've done that, but I stopped feeling horrible about that seven versions ago. In this new draft, I only have one scene. I like it. At your place that first day I barfed out the bones, and today I shaped it up a bit. It's in the beginning of the book but not the opening, so I'm curious about what ends up coming before it."

"Wow, you don't write from beginning to end?"

"Eh, kind of? For my first book I did, but my second one was all messy in my head, so I jumped around. Doing that with this one hasn't worked, so I'm trying a modified version. I work on the opening, with all of it loosely plotted, but I leap around and alter things as I go. I have an outline for the whole novel, but I'm already sure the ending is completely wrong."

Jacob had stopped with his fork halfway to his mouth, and now he set the utensil down. "I had no idea this was how writing worked. It sounds so intense."

"Writing a novel is like finger-painting in your own blood while blindfolded alone in a room without light, and without windows or doors. Except sometimes you find a magical paintbrush bleeding light and wonder, and you feel like you can whip up whole universes with a fell swoop. You basically screw around and try not to cry while waiting for those eureka moments to come."

"That doesn't sound very pleasant, I have to tell you."

Rasul winked at Jacob as he lifted his water glass to his lips. "Writers are masochists at heart."

It sounded like it. Jacob resumed eating, but his thoughts didn't stop. "So I know not to ask you how your writing is going, or at least to ask in a careful way, but how about *what* you're writing? Can I ask about that?"

Rasul's whole demeanor brightened. "Oh, absolutely. Authors *love* talking about their stories. Be careful, because it's like opening Pandora's Box."

"Mmm, I'm okay with that. Tell me about your story."

"*Veil of Stars*? Well, my editor and the publicist argue a lot over whether it's young adult or not, because the hero is in high school. That's where my first hang-up started, I think, because they wanted it to be a certain way to fit into that market, and then I turned in my initial drafts and they changed their mind and said I should write normally and they'd tweak it later. That weirded me out, though, because when I asked what they wanted to tweak, they said it would depend. After that, I didn't write for six months."

"What got you started again?"

"Elizabeth cracked some heads, and she said ignore everything, just get a story out and she'd go to bat for me if they wanted to do something weird."

"Good. I like Elizabeth already." Jacob took some more naan. "I knew this new book had a younger protagonist, but that's all the detail I had."

"They kept it under wraps pretty tight. That was the other thing that held me up the first year. I wanted to write a bisexual protagonist trying to find a way to confess to his crush. His gay crush. Except his suppressed intensity activates latent powers and he starts spawning alternate universes instead."

Jacob's whole body reacted like an antenna picking up a heavy signal. "Oh, *wow*."

Rasul grinned. "See? That's what I told them would be the reaction. But they worried it wouldn't sell and asked me to make the crush a girl and to not talk about the protagonist being bisexual. The girl could be a tomboy, they pointed out."

Jacob recoiled. "Tell me you're kidding."

"Absolutely not. That was another eighteen months of me circling the drain, alternately arguing with everyone and attempting to make the wrong character work. When I turned in a forty-thousand-word partial where the love interest turned into a monster and started ripping people in half, they had a meeting and decided the book should be shelved and

I could maybe write something else. I think that's when I started going out and partying."

"My God, I had no idea about any of this. I can't believe they told you to change the orientation and gender of your characters. Did they not read *The Amazing Adventures of Kavalier & Clay*?"

"I think they got hung up on the part where I made the character bisexual. In their mind, that meant he could go either way, so why not the way that made them feel safer? The only reason they changed their tune was that there were a few minor hits with gay characters in young adult." Rasul pushed his food around his plate. "Wait until they find out I want to make it even more of a romance and give it a happy ending."

"Can you tell me more about the story you *want* to tell? Forget what other people have said."

Rasul became animated as he talked in granular detail about a Los Angeles high school and a sixteen-year-old boy serial dating girls but pining for what Rasul described as "a high-class gay." In the library the protagonist manages to get his love interest alone, but instead of a confession, an electric wall of emotion sends a wave over everyone and tugs them into the first alternate dimension.

"I want to keep escalating them," Rasul said. "At first I splatter-shot a lot of fun dimensions, but now I want them to build. Fun, but with a secret ladder underneath so you look back and realize they were all his subliminal attempts to communicate. At first Adam thinks he's the only one aware they keep jumping dimensions, but my plan right now is for him to find out at the midpoint that the love interest has also been cognizant all along. I want it to be that Milo is also manipulating things, but I feel like that's too obvious."

"Oh, I like that." Jacob gave up on eating and rested his chin in his hand, letting the story spin out in his mind. "I don't think it's too obvious. If it's a story about connection and emotion, that makes perfect sense, don't you think? The thrill won't be in how clever your twists are but how deeply and originally you allow them to connect."

Rasul stared at Jacob, eyes shining. "Okay, if we were actually dating, you'd get so laid tonight."

Ears burning hot, Jacob fussed with the napkin in his lap. "Stop."

"God, now I want to go write more. I just know there's no way I'll get anything done in my apartment. I hate it so much."

"You've said that several times now. It still feels sterile? I thought you went shopping."

"I did, but it's still bad. I don't know why I have such a strong reaction to it, but I do. The only time I feel okay about it is when I curl up in bed reading the books you gave me. Which, I hate to tell you, I've blown through."

"Come get some new ones, then. Feel free to raid my personal shelves."

"Can I come tonight?"

If it had sounded even a little like a come-on, he would have refused. Mostly, though, Rasul sounded desperate. "You can come over long enough to get some books." He paused, considering. "Well, if you wanted to write in the bookstore, you could do that too."

It was as if Jacob had told a child they could get anything they wanted from a candy store. "Seriously? What time do I have to be done by?"

"When I go to bed, which is usually around eleven."

"Deal." He looked pleased. "Now all I need is a magic wand to fix my own place so I don't have to bug you."

"Actually, I might be able to help you there as well. Or rather, I know some people who can. What are you doing next Friday night?"

"Hating my apartment and wishing I could take a walk without being bothered every few feet. Why?"

"There's a group I go to sometimes for area gay men. I think you could make some connections there of people eager to help you fix your space. Plus you could make some more friends."

"Just gay, or gay and bisexual and pan men?"

"Yes, sorry. I didn't mean to exclude. Though I don't think we have many bi men."

"Probably the advertising strategy. Do you usually talk about it only being for gay men?"

"I think so. Sorry."

Rasul shrugged, but he didn't have the same breeziness he usually did.

Jacob felt awkward, aware he'd stepped in something but unsure of how to fix it. He'd been hating on the group's name since its creation, but only because it sounded ridiculous. He was mortified with himself he hadn't considered how exclusionary it was. Should he say something to them? Well, obviously.

What happened if they brushed it off, though? Should he keep pushing? What if Gus or Matt were ones who thought it wasn't a big deal?

Wrong question. How about wondering how many other bisexual and pansexual men feel shut out? What about trans men?

Rasul interrupted Jacob's musings by loudly patting his belly. "Well, I'd planned on getting some dessert, but I don't think I have it in me. What leftovers do you want?"

"You take them all." Jacob knew his whole face flamed with the still-blooming embarrassment of his faux pas, but he made himself push through it. "I meant to ask you. How are your classes going?"

"Good, actually."

"You sound surprised."

"I am, I guess. It's my first time teaching in this kind of setting, but the students are eager. All over the map, but that makes it great. I'm into the lesbian romance author."

"Oh, Meg? I've had signings for her. She does well. I'm not surprised she's trying to hone her craft." He hesitated, then pushed on. "Are you interested in coming to the meetup next week?"

"Sure, sounds interesting."

"Okay. I'll tell them we're coming." Why did he feel so self-conscious? "Um, did you want to have another date before then?"

Rasul's smile made him dizzy. "I want as many as you'll give me."

"Ah. Okay. I'll... look at my schedule and call you." Unable to handle it any longer, he pushed out of the booth. "I'm going to run to the restroom quick. But here's my debit card so they can split the check."

Inside the bathroom, Jacob locked the door and slid down the wall, pressing his hands to his temples.

When he came out to rejoin Rasul and walk back to his apartment, Avni winked at him. "Come again soon."

Chapter Seven

RASUL WONDERED why he'd broken form and let Jacob know the local gay group's bi/pan erasure bothered him.

It wasn't the first time something like that had pissed him off, far from it. He had a lot of banked anger going all the way back to high school, where he'd kept a tight lid on his orientation and only dated girls because coming out as bi or pan felt far too dangerous. There were several peaks of fury from college, when he'd finally started opening up about it, and gay and straight friends and lovers would wrinkle their nose at him like he'd admitted he only washed his hair once a month. "Are you sure?" was a common refrain. "But you're dating a guy," someone would point out, insisting that meant he was gay. "But you're dating a girl" would come another time, and now his pansexuality—they'd called it gayness—had been a phase. His whole life, people had lined up to explain his orientation to him as if he weren't personally living it. But as he did with almost everything, usually he pasted on a smile and laughed it off.

Never had he let the awkwardness go on so long he sent his date, or even his fake date, running for cover.

Once Jacob had come back to the table, they'd fallen into something more amicable once again, chatting about how Rasul's classes were going on the way to the bookstore. This dovetailed, somehow, into a loving discussion about *I Capture the Castle*, now fresh once again in Rasul's mind.

"Their poverty astounds me. Every time I read it, I try to imagine what the equivalent would be today. Because back then goods were sold and managed differently. Also, can you imagine everything being made locally? Or rather, trade wasn't remotely on the level then that it is now. Which always makes me think of how many goods flow across the oceans daily from China to basically everywhere. From everywhere to everywhere. I can't fly to London without spending an arm and a leg, but I buy cheap clothing made on the other side of the world."

He'd ended up not writing at Jacob's place, only talking endlessly about books until he'd seen the time and realized he needed to let Jacob sleep.

"Oh, but I meant to give you this earlier." Jacob fished in a small drawer in the kitchen and came back with a key. "It'll only get you in through the back door at the top of the stairs, but I thought this way you could come and go without having to be let in."

The key felt heavy in Rasul's hand, weighty with the gravity of the gesture. "Wow, thank you. Do you move this fast with all your fake boyfriends, or am I special?"

Jacob rolled his eyes, but he smiled. "I'm assuming eventually you'll want to come work while I'm out. For example, Tuesday I have back-to-back meetings first at the hospital and then at the chamber of commerce. If you're here that day and write past closing, you can let yourself out the back."

"Thank you. I appreciate it, sincerely."

Jacob nodded and averted his gaze again. "So… the meeting next Friday night is at six. It happens to be a potluck in City Park this time, but we can pick something up on the way."

"If you let me use your kitchen, I can whip something up."

"Of course."

Rasul stayed up late that night reading new books he'd borrowed from Jacob, sleeping until midmorning without meaning to. The urge to write had left him, but he went over to Jacob's anyway and put in the time, managing to drag a thousand words of dreck out of himself. He stayed away on Sunday, half hoping Jacob would call him for a date, telling himself not to be disappointed when his phone remained silent. On Monday, though, Jacob invited him to lunch at the Italian restaurant. It was busy, and he felt lucky they got a table.

People still watched him everywhere he went, but he was getting used to it.

He also hit the library on Monday, losing himself in the stacks for hours and coming out with a pile of books he could barely carry home. He ate leftovers from lunch for dinner.

Tuesday he worked at the bookstore until class, enjoying a lunch break with Jacob. He did the same thing on Wednesday and Thursday, except when he was at his office hours. Class continued to go well too.

He'd assigned more reading to his students and asked them to have a short story ready to group critique in two weeks.

His writing was… going. He'd managed to get a whole scene done, and when he sent it to Elizabeth, she didn't hate it, just told him to keep going.

She hadn't mentioned Adina, and he didn't ask.

On Friday he cooked.

He'd spied a food processor on top of Jacob's fridge the other day, and when Jacob mentioned the picnic was a potluck, he knew right away he was going to make his grandmother's hummus and pita bread. He soaked fresh chickpeas overnight, then hauled them in a container he'd also purchased so he could boil them at Jacob's while he worked. He also started making the bread, and toward the end of the afternoon when it was baking, he had difficulty focusing on his work because of the olfactory explosion.

He was cutting up vegetables for a tray when Jacob came up the stairs. "Wow, what smells so good?"

"Hummus and pita bread." He ripped off a piece of a mostly cooled round, dipped it in the hummus, and fed it to Jacob. "My grandmother's recipe. What do you think?"

Jacob's groan was answer enough. "Oh my God. It's amazing."

"I haven't made it in a while, but it used to be my go-to stress-relieving activity, making pita and hummus."

Jacob stole more bread and helped himself to a generous amount of hummus. "I like how you say it. *Homm-ous.*"

"My grandmother would rise out of her grave and smack the back of my head if I didn't."

They finished up the last of the prep together, then packed everything in a box and took it to Jacob's car. "They're going to be surprised," Jacob said, "because normally I'm the one who shows up with a two-liter and bag of chips, or store-bought cookies."

"Do all of them know we're dating? Or rather, do all of them think we're dating?"

Jacob snorted. "In this town, everyone knew in twenty minutes, and most of them thought we were even before it was official. A word of warning: don't tell anyone anything you don't want put on blast. Especially Jared Kumpel. He's the worst gossip ever."

"Noted."

"Has our pretend dating helped you the way you wanted?"

Rasul nodded. "I think so. My agent seems happy, but she still won't give me my phone back."

"Well, I'm glad our arrangement is helping. I haven't had many people bother me about it, though I have sold more books this week than I normally would due to people dropping by hoping to see you."

"Why, do they know I write in your kitchen every day?"

"They know you come over every day, and apparently this is an exciting development. I get a lot of people wanting more information, but I don't tell them anything."

"My students ask me about our relationship a lot, and people at the college. Also my next-door neighbor. And people at the grocery store, including the checker. I had to go pick up something from Elizabeth at the post office because it wouldn't fit in my box, and the counter clerk, the same one who sold me the mailer for my phone, grabbed my hands and told me she was rooting for us. Honestly, for a second I thought she was going to cry, she was so emotional about it. Does this happen a lot when people date here?"

"Even with virtual entertainment studios in their back pocket, the people of Copper Point can't resist a drama unfolding right in front of their eyes."

Rasul considered this statement as they drove the rest of the way to the park and had almost grasped a corner of how this might relate to his story when Jacob stopped the car and a large cluster of men came over to introduce themselves. He saw several of the doctors and the hospital CEO he'd spoken to at the gala. Rasul remembered Jacob's warning about the pediatrician and gave vague answers during his grilling.

There were too many people to remember, but Rasul did his best. Gus he'd already met, and Matt. There were also several professors from the university. Ram Rao was in the music department, and Christopher Miller was a math professor. Rasul was pretty sure he'd seen them at a staff meeting, but he hadn't had a chance to talk to them until now. There was also a lawyer, Julian Steele, who looked as if he were super aggressive and calculating in everything he did, and boy would Rasul have tapped that in any other circumstance.

Several students from the college were there as well, a few he recognized from class. One of those was Ben Vargas, who turned out to have grown up in the same town as Gus. He made, Rasul noticed, a lot of puppy eyes at Gus, ones Gus worked hard to ignore.

"I don't think I've ever seen this many people at a GAG event," Jacob mused as they set out their pita and hummus.

"They all came to meet your boyfriend," Owen said with a wink at Jacob.

Rasul, meanwhile, was stuck on something Jacob had said. "Hold on. This group is called GAG? As in, the reflex?"

"Gay Area Guys," Owen said, looking pleased. "Funny, right?"

Jacob decidedly did not look amused. "I've never liked the name, but honestly, Owen, it should be more inclusive. Unless you don't want to be welcoming to *all* queer men?"

Owen frowned at Jacob, looking seriously confused. His husband Erin, however, regarded Jacob thoughtfully. "You're right. That's why it's been bothering me. Well, that and GAG is ridiculous." He tapped his cheek. "It could be QUAG."

"No double entendre, but it would get the job done." Owen scratched his chin. "Dang. Feel like an ass I didn't think of it. That's what I get for getting all focused on making puns and jokes."

"What's this?" Julian asked this as he came in closer, gaze sliding to the hummus Jacob had just unwrapped.

"We're changing the name of GAG," Owen told him. "To QUAG."

Julian arched an eyebrow at him. "Well, at least it doesn't make me think we're all coming here for some sort of oral sex fest." He smiled at Rasul with a look he suspected was saved for jury members who needed to be swayed. "Would you mind terribly if I tried some of your pita and hummus? It looks amazing."

Rasul lifted the plate for him, though he kept glancing to the side to look at his fake boyfriend. He was blotchy red all over, the way he got when he was embarrassed, but he looked relieved too. So he hadn't known how that conversation would go, but he'd brought it up anyway. In a way that wasn't a big deal, just addressing an issue, and people had simply rolled with it.

Honestly, it was a damn shame they weren't actually dating, because the man had a lot of gratitude sex backlogged at this point.

The picnic was fun, and the food was pretty great. Rasul enjoyed watching the men interact with each other as much as he did getting to know them. He got to hear Jared and Nick's announcement of how they'd finally settled on a surrogate and hoped to be expecting their first child by the end of the year. Jack, the hospital's surgeon, and Owen, the anesthesiologist, had some kind of good-natured rivalry going on that seemed to extend to everything they could possibly compete over but was brought to a head in the food they brought to the potluck. Owen presented a killer potato salad with whole baby potatoes and seven-minute eggs, and Jack had some sort of savory yogurt dish with cucumber, radish, and toasted sesame. They nominated Rasul to be their judge, and he struggled to choose.

"They're both amazing. I love the eggs and the mustard vinaigrette in Owen's dish, but I think I have to give ultimate props to savory yogurt. I have a huge sweet tooth, but my Syrian grandmother would kiss both your cheeks for this, Jack."

Owen grumbled about his loss, but he quickly recovered and started needling Jack over something else, which Jack clearly enjoyed. Jack's husband, Simon, who had taken Rasul home the day he'd met Jacob, chatted Rasul up to find out how he was enjoying Copper Point.

As they filled their plates, Jacob let the rest of them know Rasul was looking for help personalizing his apartment, and as predicted, everyone became interested in helping him problem solve. After complaining at the abysmal state of guest faculty housing, they shared design tips and volunteered things from their own homes to spruce things up. Ram said he'd nudge the dean about getting the place repainted, and Christopher promised to bring over some industrial-strength cleaner to get rid of the kitchen smells. Simon said he'd wheedle a new couch out of his uncle, who owned a furniture store. Rasul had several more numbers in his flip phone now, though every time he entered one, he had to endure their incredulity that he didn't have a more modern phone.

Fewer distractions, he kept telling them. It wasn't a lie.

To his surprise, several men pulled Rasul aside to passive-aggressively warn him that he needed to treat Jacob well, because apparently he never dated. Interestingly, Gus and Matt, Jacob's self-professed best friends, weren't among that number. They sure looked at him with menacing gazes, though.

At nine Rasul was trying to follow some story Jared was telling about a man everyone seemed to dislike but couldn't stop talking about, when Jacob tugged on his sleeve and announced it was time to go.

"I have to get up early. Unless you want to get a ride home with someone else?"

"No, I'm fine." Rasul followed him away from the group after waving goodbye.

Too soon they were back at Rasul's apartment. He thought about inviting Jacob up, then remembered why they'd left early. "Is it okay if I come over to write again tomorrow?"

"You can come over anytime. On Sunday I might set you up in the shop if you come, so I can clean."

Rasul lingered with his hand on the door, trying to figure out how to say the things he wanted to say. *I'd still like to date you for real* buzzed at the back of his mouth the way it had since they'd started this charade. *Thanks for speaking up about the group name* was another top contender. *I loved playing couple at a picnic with you. I've never done anything like that before, and I loved it.*

Instead, he sighed and gave Jacob what he hoped wasn't a sad smile. "I had a great time."

Jacob tried to give him his polite smile, but it frayed around the edges, like politeness was becoming difficult. "I'm glad."

"See you tomorrow."

"Yes, see you."

Rasul got out of the car, grabbed the bag of empty dishes, and headed reluctantly into his crappy apartment.

THE FIRST month of fake dating was fairly easy for Jacob. They slid quickly into a routine, and being with him was pleasant. He looked forward to their weekly dates, which started to feel like a tour of Copper Point restaurants. Despite Les Clark's continued dirty looks at chamber meetings, the restaurant owners were eager to have them, especially if Jacob called ahead to let them know they were coming. Apparently on Copper Point People, the infamous Facebook group, where Rasul and Jacob dined was a constant topic.

Rasul declined Jacob's invitation to walk around with him at the Founder's Day festival. Jacob was a bit relieved to simply go and enjoy it with his friends.

Jacob never heard anything further about Rasul's ex and whether she was still a danger. A few times he'd thought about asking, but he'd always invented reasons not to. He wouldn't let himself consider the possibility that perhaps he didn't *want* to end their fake relationship.

He had enough problems without worrying about that, he told himself. Rebecca still nudged Jacob on the regular to officially declare he was running for president of the chamber of commerce, something he'd have to decide one way or another soon, as he had to put his name in by November 1. The vote wouldn't be until May, but Clark had declared in 1980 that they should have a long period to get to know any potential candidates. In reality, it gave him and his friends more of a chance to beat them down.

One night when they were having dinner—at China Garden this time—he asked Rasul about it.

"Do I think you should run?" Rasul reached for the plate of beef and broccoli in front of him. "I mean, do you want to? That seems a more important question, or am I missing something?"

Jacob fiddled with his chopsticks. "It would be an advantage to a lot of us if I did, or if someone friendly to a broader set of businesses stood for election."

"Do you *want* to, though?"

"I mean... yes? And also no. I want it to happen, I want someone progressive in the position, but I would prefer, to be honest, that it wasn't me."

"So let someone else do it. You don't seem too excited about it."

"People keep telling me I'd be a good candidate. That I'm dependable."

Rasul snorted. "Well, you are dependable, but to me it sounds like they're looking for a patsy."

Jacob didn't like how that sounded at all. "I think it's more that they're looking for a leader."

"Well, fine if you want to be one. But I'm getting all the vibes like you're *not* wanting this."

"It's less that and more that I don't like how other people see me."

"What—hot, articulate, delicious?"

Jacob nudged Rasul with his foot, but he couldn't help a small smile. "No. Dependable, steady. Boring."

"I don't think you're boring at all."

No, Rasul really didn't. He flirted with Jacob all the time, and Jacob knew he could have a real relationship with the man just for asking. He told himself that wouldn't work, though. He told himself that every day.

It was becoming harder and harder to remember why he had to say no.

He tried to be content with their dates, with their conversations in his apartment when Rasul finished working for the day. Over tea in the evenings when Rasul didn't have a class, they talked and talked. About how much Rasul liked his class, how intriguing he found his students, about how his writing was going. They talked about books too, what they'd read recently and books they'd read long ago. Rasul was rapidly making his way through Jacob's personal inventory. He read voraciously, and quickly. Jacob had thought himself a pretty speedy reader, but Rasul put him to shame.

"It's kind of a curse," Rasul confessed one day as he picked up a new stack of titles from Jacob. These were from the bookstore itself, and he'd shelled out quite a bit of money for them. "I go through things so quickly."

"You don't have to purchase this many," Jacob said.

Rasul winked at him. "I know, but I feel like buying a bookseller's stock is a kind of flirting."

Rasul made casual remarks about dating every so often, not so much as to feel like pressure but enough that Jacob couldn't ever forget his fake boyfriend remained ready to be a real one at any time. Jacob still didn't want to touch that, but he couldn't help thinking about what it would be like. Essentially they *were* dating, though they weren't having sex. That and the veneer their ruse put between them felt like a fragile safety to Jacob. It kept him from getting too attached.

Gus and Matt, however, didn't buy it.

"You're even more in love with him than you were before," Gus said during a Mini Main Street meeting in Engleton's back room. They sat clustered on the far end away from the heap of alterations, and Jacob ended up facing the line of custom suits in various stages of construction. "Except this time he's not a fantasy. He's right in front of you."

"He's behaving," Jacob insisted, a little desperately.

"He undresses you with his eyes," Matt countered, and Jacob had to concede this was true.

Jacob wasn't sure what he wanted from Rasul any longer. Initially holding him at bay felt like keeping himself safe, but at this point Rasul was so entwined in his life his departure would leave a void. He told himself it was smart to limit how intimate they were because it would make things less painful later, but with every day that passed, he was less sure that was true.

Plus it was clear Rasul was holding back, that if allowed, he'd make their polite, nicely intimate friendship flame with passion well beyond the bedroom. There were more and more flares, Rasul's eyes lighting up as he seized on something he loved or bounced a plot point off of Jacob. All Jacob had to do was lower the gate and that intensity would come rushing at him.

The worst part was that Jacob wanted it. It made him remember aspects of himself he'd left behind in Chicago, when he'd transported himself back to Copper Point after his parents' deaths. But he *wasn't* that person any longer. And Rasul was never going to stay here. So why stir that part of him back up?

He did his best not to think about it, instead focusing on those custom suits in Engleton's back room as he walked home, and again as he lay in bed. They looked nice—still conservative, but something about them really drew the eye, even unfinished. They must feel amazing too.

Impractical for him, since he'd never have anywhere worthy of wearing them. Still. They were nice.

As September bled into October, when Jacob walked the distance from his store to Gus's for a Mini Main Street Meeting Matt had called, the leaves whipped around him in an increasingly bitter fall wind, mirroring the feelings of his insides.

I want him. I want to try this. I don't care that it's temporary. I want to ride the ride.

Gus and Matt were already in the back room discussing something, but they took one look at Jacob as he came in and called a time-out.

"You look… intense." Matt frowned at Jacob, then at Gus. "Did something happen?"

"I want to date him for real." Jacob sank into a chair and collapsed forward on the table.

"I'll get the whiskey," Gus said and disappeared into his office.

Matt patted Jacob's head. "You lasted longer than I thought. It's okay. We'll walk you through."

Jacob downed the shot Gus passed to him. "I *can't* date him. It'll be a disaster. Don't you get it?"

Gus sat beside Matt and threaded his fingers together. "No, hon, we don't. Why would it be a disaster? He's clearly into you, and you're into him—have been forever. What's the problem here?"

Matt had poured him a second shot of alcohol, and Jacob downed this too. "It's temporary. I'm going to get my heart broken as it is. I have to mitigate the damage."

"Why is it temporary?" Matt gave himself a little whiskey, but he drank it more slowly. "I mean, I know he's only here for a short time, but it's not like you couldn't—"

"He's going to go back to his exciting life of traveling the world and being with exciting people in exciting places. And I'm not exciting."

Gus folded his arms over his chest. "I take great issue with that self-assessment. I suspect Rasul would too."

Jacob snorted. "He called me Mr. Rogers when we first met."

Matt blinked a moment, then nodded. "Oh, the sweaters."

Jacob, always a lightweight, waved a drunken hand angrily. "He *doesn't know* why I wear the sweaters."

Gus remained patient and annoyingly sober. "You do know you could tell him?"

Snarling, Jacob poured himself more to drink.

"Careful," Matt warned. "Clark will have a field day if you drink yourself into the ER."

"I can't tell him." Jacob drank slightly slower this time. "I don't want to tell him. I don't want to open that door. I want to remain in my nice tidy life. I *like* my life. I love my shop, love my friends, my routine. I wasn't unhappy at all before he showed up."

Gus's expression softened. "But you are now?"

Jacob sagged. "I tried not to be. I couldn't help it."

"What do you think would happen if you told him some of this? Any of this?" Matt asked.

"We'd have sex. Wild, intense sex all over my apartment and maybe the shop."

"That doesn't sound bad," Gus pointed out.

"And then he'd leave when the school year was out, and all over my safe space that I love so much, I'd be surrounded by sadness. His new book would come out, and instead of being thrilled for its release,

I'd be too emotional to even put it on my shelves. I don't want this." He slammed his hand on the table. "I didn't want him to come to Copper Point at all. I just wanted things to continue as they were. But I don't think they can ever go back anymore. I think I'm going to be sad when he goes no matter what. And I don't like it."

He reached for the whiskey.

Gus pulled the bottle away and rose. "I'll go get him some coffee and a glass of water."

"I'm sorry." Jacob ran a hand through his hair. "This was supposed to be a meeting for you, Matt."

"Don't worry about it." He leaned forward on the table. "Can you explain something to me, Jake? If you know you're going to be sad no matter what, why not dive in and have a good time while he's here?"

"Because the very thought terrifies me." Jacob hugged his glass. "Heroes shouldn't come to life. He should have stayed up on his pedestal where he belongs." He reached for the bottle again, but of course it was gone. "I want to settle down with someone nice, maybe get a dog. I've assumed I'm a little too late for a relationship like that, but I have friends, so I always thought I was okay. Except now I'm not. I don't know that I'll ever feel okay again."

He wanted more alcohol, but they wouldn't give it to him, not until he had water and coffee. They listened patiently while he rehashed the same complaints over and over, doling out alcohol enough to get him drunk but not enough to kill him.

Then, like the friends they were, they poured him into Gus's car and took him home.

"Do you want me to stay with you?" Matt turned around in his seat. "Because I can. I'll just set an alarm with enough time to go back and change."

Jacob shook his head, carefully. "No. I'll be fine. I'll stumble through the shower, fall into bed, and have a headache in the morning."

Gus glanced at him in the mirror. "Call us, okay? If you need anything. Always."

"I know." And Jacob did. He was grateful.

He lingered in the small parking lot behind the store as they drove away, first waving them on, then letting the chill permeate through him as he stared across the greenbelt park behind the businesses on his side of Front Street. He could smell the bay in the distance, its cold waters feeding into the frigid Lake Superior.

It had been a night like this, the Lake Michigan version, when he'd received the call about his parents.

What would his life be like, he wondered, if his parents hadn't died? Would he have landed on this path anyway, only through a different route? Would he be happy with someone in a suburb, fighting over whose turn it was to mow the lawn or walk the dogs? Would he be disillusioned with life?

Would he have met Rasul? Would he have even cared who he was?

Am I happy with my life now? I always say that I am. I am lying, though, even to myself?

How could he possibly find the answers to those questions?

The wind picked up a bit too much, and Jacob decided it was time to go inside. He hurried up the stairs as best he could, almost falling down twice. That was the last thing he needed, to break his leg on his back stairs. He'd forgotten to bring his phone. He wouldn't be able to call for help.

I wish I had someone waiting here for me. I wish I weren't facing these questions alone.

He was fumbling with his key at the lock when the door opened. Startled, he looked up at Rasul, face framed by a pair of dark glasses.

You're not alone, he told himself, then thought, *no, I can't* just as quickly, and took a step backward.

He hit the railing and lost his footing, and for a terrible second he thought, *This is how I'm going to die, falling drunk off my staircase because the man I'm in love with surprised me by being in my apartment.*

Then strong arms surrounded him, righting him. The smell of Rasul enfolded him, undoing his defenses.

"I don't want to be alone," he said out loud, and sagged into Rasul's sturdy chest.

Chapter Eight

THE SOUND of someone on the stairs had shaken Rasul out of a deep trance, but a glance at the clock drew him back to reality. Ten thirty? It was *ten thirty*? He'd known Jacob was going out, so he allowed himself some leeway to stay later, but he hadn't realized it had gone this long. He'd been focused all afternoon ever since his phone call with Elizabeth, which for the first time in years wasn't full of tension and threats but problem-solving and plans. Even the Adina news had been good: she was back online and singing the praises of Korean skin care products, never mentioning Rasul at all. He was close to the midpoint of his story, trying to weave everything to the big reveal where Adam finds out Milo has been consciously jumping universes with him, so he kept pushing himself a little more and a little more, until the sounds on the stairs.

Then he opened the door, smelled the alcohol coming off Jacob, and nearly lost him over the edge of the railing.

"Easy, babe," he cooed, his tone belying the panic he knew at the thought of Jacob careening to his death before his eyes. "I got you. Come on inside."

"I'm not your babe." Jacob said this, but he clung to Rasul's shirt front and put his head on his shoulder. "Why are you here?"

"I'm sorry. I got caught up writing and lost track of time. I'll go, but let me make sure you're okay first."

"I'm fine. Just drunk." Jacob righted himself and glanced blearily around the room. "There aren't any dishes in the drainer. You didn't eat. Why didn't you eat?"

"I was really on a roll. I'll eat now, if it'll make you happy." He led Jacob to the table and sat him down. "Would you like to eat with me?"

Jacob made a noncommittal noise but sat obediently where Rasul planted him. Rasul hadn't even finished indexing the fridge, though, before Jacob spoke. "I can't believe Rasul Youssef's half-finished novel is sitting here on my kitchen table."

"Rasul Youssef's novel is half-finished *only* because of your kitchen table. And you." He grabbed a few vegetables from the crisper and a brick of fried tofu. "What about some stir fry over noodles?"

"Are they right? Are you actually interested in me? If I asked you to take me to bed, would you do it?"

Whoa. Rasul set the vegetables on the counter and came back to the table, sitting in the seat nearest Jacob. "This is a conversation I would like to have, but perhaps we should have it when you're not drunk."

Jacob blew a raspberry and tipped his head back to stare at the ceiling. "If I were sober, I wouldn't have it."

"True." Crossing his arms over his chest in a vain attempt to slow his galloping heartbeat, Rasul considered Jacob carefully. "I am interested in you. Very much. I'd go to bed with you if you crooked your finger at me."

Jacob looked Rasul dead in the eye, his gaze hot and intense. Lifting his hand, he crooked his finger at Rasul.

Rasul shivered and took hold of it. "Not while you're drunk. Not like this."

Jacob regarded Rasul with frustration. "I thought if I kept you at arm's length I'd be okay, but I'm not. I'm never going to be okay again."

"I'm sorry."

Jacob sagged toward the table, pushing Rasul's laptop away. "I want to tell you some things."

"I'm listening."

It was a long time, though, before Jacob spoke again, and he didn't look at Rasul. "I told you I discovered your first book in the hospital while my parents were dying. I don't know what would have happened to me if I hadn't gone to the gift shop when I did. You don't understand how much you were with me that day, or rather, your words were. They changed everything."

Rasul laced their fingers together. "Tell me. Because I want very much to understand."

Jacob stared off into the distance, lost in the past. "Chicago had been in the deep throes of fall, but a freak snowstorm had raged down from Canada into Copper Point, making the lake road hazardous. My father had been going half the speed limit, trying to keep track of the lanes, but the oncoming car came at full speed, right into them. The other driver died on impact. My parents were gravely injured, my mother lucid enough to call for help before slipping into a coma alongside my dad. They were transferred to Madison immediately, and in a bit of irony, I drove like a bat out of hell to get there before they died."

His face became incredibly sad. "They were excellent parents. Fully supportive of everything about me. When I moved into my first Chicago apartment, they came down to help me set it up. They never pressured me to come home, but when I needed to touch base, they welcomed me back, eager to hear about my adventures. Before they died, I was struggling a bit. Someone I'd thought I could have a relationship with turned out to be someone bad for me—nothing dramatic, only a disappointment. My work wasn't fulfilling me like I thought, and I was getting depressed. For the first time, my parents urged me to take a vacation and come home, saying they'd help me figure things out. I didn't go. I said maybe in a few months, but right now I couldn't afford it. I was about to admit I should go anyway, that only they could shake me out of my bad place, when the accident happened."

Rasul stroked the back of Jacob's hand. "I'm so sorry."

Though Jacob's eyes were wet, he didn't cry, and his voice was steady. "I never thought they'd leave me so soon, and not together. Not without a real goodbye. I took a leave of absence from my job, then outright quit, but it wasn't a smart move. I wandered around Copper Point, trying to figure out what I was supposed to do now. But that's when I started reading your book again."

He turned to Rasul now, his face twisted up in emotion. "It was like you saw right into me. The fight to find identity, dealing with loss but carrying on—that was what I needed. I read the book over and over, as if only these words could keep me alive. I understood at the time it was maybe a little unhealthy, but I didn't care. I didn't have my parents to be my anchor anymore, but I could anchor myself with your story."

Jacob might not be crying, but Rasul had to stop and wipe his eyes, and his throat was thick. "Jacob."

"I was living off my savings, and they were nearly depleted, but I had this huge inheritance from my parents. Life insurance, assets. I got tired of reading your book all the time, so I sprinkled others along with it. Fiction, nonfiction, everything. I feel like I devoured half the library, and the UPS driver brought me ten to twenty books at a time. I knew I was still escaping, but reading felt like a way out, so I kept at it, hoping for a lifeline. Then you wrote *Carnivale*."

Now a tear did roll down his cheek as he took his hand back and turned to Rasul, tugging at his cardigan. "You called me Mr. Rogers because of what I wear. Do you know why I dress like I do? Because after my parents died, I couldn't function unless I was wearing one of my father's old sweaters. Gus and Matt held me the first time I had to wash them because they were too filthy to continue, and I ached because I knew the smell of my parents would go. Also, at that point, several of them were all but ruined. Then the next day Matt came with a new set from his store. He said it was the brand my dad always bought, and he could get as many as I wanted."

Rasul wiped at his eyes. "I'm sorry. I'm so sorry."

"No. You see? Because in the middle of Cardigangate, that's when *Carnivale* arrived. I had it on preorder. I bought it in hardback, eBook, and audio. Wrapped in one of the manky old cardigans, the one I hid so it didn't get washed, I stayed up all night and read your second book. And for the first time since my parents died, I felt alive." He laughed, a soft and bitter sound. "Oh my God, but I fell in love with you so hard. I didn't even have the strength to mock myself. I simply thought, this is twice now that this man has dragged me out of the abyss. I'll have to love him forever. So I decided that I'd do just that, and I also started looking into what it would take to buy a bookstore. It was a lot easier than I thought." He shook a finger at Rasul. "It was supposed to be enough. It *would* have been enough. And then suddenly there you were. Here you are. Complicated and beautiful and sexy, flawed and messy and exactly what I never knew I needed. But if I let you in, all the way in, what comes next? You'll leave. I'll be alone. You won't be dead, but in a way it'll be worse. Because I don't want to leave here, I *do* love it here, but…." He shut his eyes and gave up.

Rasul drew several deep breaths, trying to gather himself after that emotional barrage. He couldn't do it. Running a hand through his hair, he glanced around the kitchen. "Do you have any alcohol?"

"If we're both smashed, this is going to be a disaster."

"I'm not going to get drunk. I just need to shave off a few edges. You're not the only one who has stuff to get off his chest tonight."

Jacob gestured at the far wall of cupboards without looking at them. "Top left, behind the paper cups. Should be some scotch."

"Excellent." Rising, he glanced back at Jacob. "Can I get you some water?"

"You can get me some scotch."

"Scotch *and* water. For both of us."

Pouring the drinks gave him something to do with himself, a chance to organize his thoughts. He didn't say anything until he'd sat down and gotten a heavy slug of the stuff in his system. How did he want to start this? Dive right in?

Might as well.

He drew a breath and let it out.

"I had a lot of abandonment issues as a kid. My parents were in and out, and so were my caregivers. My grandparents raised me officially, but there were nannies too. Essentially nobody hugely stable was in my life except for my grandmother, and she wasn't always reliable. Intellectually I can look back and see that I was set up, that this sense that people would abandon me no matter what I did wasn't my fault, but part of me can't let go of the idea that I might be the problem, that I'm unlovable." Smiling grimly into his glass, he took another drink. "Don't think the irony isn't lost on me that I draw all these people to me and I still feel that way. It doesn't matter how many ways I acknowledge I have a hole in me nobody can fill, it still eats at me. It drives me into relationships too fast, pushes me to ruin them." He dragged his thumb along his beard, his gaze unfocused on the table. "I think I sandbagged myself when I decided I'd write my way through the feelings. It worked for the first book and the second book, after all. What was the harm? Well, I think that was because somehow along the way part of me felt like even though the adoration couldn't completely satisfy me, it was enough. So long as I had that attention, so long as I was surrounded, I might be okay."

He shifted in his seat. "Of course, that became the trap. Because as soon as I disappointed people, I was lost at sea. I got really annoyed at myself over it. Here I was, thirtysome years old, and I was still trapped by the feelings I had when I was a kid. Worst of all, I'd decided to write *about* the feelings I had as a kid. About a real boy I had a crush on but couldn't tell. About how the world seemed to rearrange itself around me in order to keep me isolated. It was too much. I knew as soon as I started it that I shouldn't write it. And yet I couldn't write anything else. So slowly, methodically, I put myself in the place I feared more than anything. Cut off. Isolated. Denied all my cheats and hacks to not think about the pain I'd never told anyone about."

He slid a hand to Jacob's knee. "Except in that same place, I also found you. Someone I couldn't charm or win over with a glance, a wink, or a dance. Someone who liked and respected my work but didn't want a piece of me the way everyone else did. You were just so... different. But you saw me. Not the manic front I put out but the me who flounders sometimes, that still thinks about the time when I was ten and I had a fever but no one was home and I was convinced I would die abandoned. That feeling of wandering through empty spaces, crying out, but no one comes. Except you did." He ran a hand through his hair and realized he was shaking. "Now you tell me I did that for you. My stories, born out of my own isolation and loneliness, reached you in yours. You've let me come into your space and struggle to heal myself. You've seen me stripped down, but you want me anyway." He shook his head. "You think I don't want you for that?"

"You won't stay here, and I will."

"You won't let me date you, but you want me to marry you?"

Jacob shoved at him, but not very hard. He looked tired. And very sad.

Rasul poured them both more to drink.

Jacob sipped at his, but mostly he rolled the glass against his cheek with one hand, petting Mr. Nancy with the other. Rasul hadn't even seen the cat come onto the table, but there he was now, fluffy and sweet.

"I hope you understand," Rasul said at last, "that someone who fears abandonment as much as I do isn't going to have a relationship with you and then just wave goodbye and disappear when my teaching tenure is up."

Jacob nodded. "It's not about that as much as I pretend it is. I'm afraid of change. I wasn't counting on my dreams becoming reality."

Rasul stared straight ahead, arrested. "Okay, go ahead and hate me because this is mercenary as hell... but I think you just solved my midpoint plot crisis before I even got there."

God bless him, but Jacob laughed. Softly, but a laugh was a laugh. "I could never hate you."

Rasul captured Jacob's hand, drew it to his lips for a soft kiss. "Don't you understand? I feel the same way."

Jacob sagged against him—the distance was a bit of a stretch, and Rasul scooted closer so he could feel Jacob's head on his shoulder.

"You weren't supposed to be like this," Jacob whispered.

Unable to help himself, Rasul kissed the top of Jacob's head. "How was I supposed to be?"

"Ephemeral. Impossible. A dream I could keep in my heart. A man in the mists I could imagine to be whoever I wanted him to be, whatever I needed. A mystery who spoke to me in riddles every few years. The mist that leads me on, and on."

Funny, Rasul could relate. In a way he hadn't realized until now, the longing for Jacob had fueled him through the drafting of this book. The desire to *be* that man, to forge a maze in those mists, to push past the weights in his heart so he could make Jacob smile.

What if we can both have our dreams of each other?

Shutting his eyes, he drew Jacob closer into his side. *I love you, Jacob. I'm going to make this work. I don't know how yet, but I'm going to find a way for us to get to the happy ever after.*

He sat there with the man he loved, stroking him, until Jacob fell asleep. Then, sidestepping curious cats, he tucked Jacob into bed, locked the apartment door, and made himself a bed on the floor beneath the heavily ticking clock. As it lured him into his own sleep, he dreamed of the universes he created, pushing them on and on, determined not to stop until he found the one where the two of them could be together.

JACOB WOKE to the soft sound of rain outside his window and the smell of cool air and worms.

His head weighed a ton and his mouth felt as if the worms had crawled around in there, but the soothing sound of the weather outside was a balm to his queasy stomach. He hadn't remembered opening a window the night before. Though to be honest, the whole of the previous evening was slightly hazy. He'd gone to meet Gus and Matt, and then….

His eyes flew open as memory settled in, jagged and discordant. Stumbling up his stairs, finding Rasul there. Sitting at the kitchen table, drinking scotch, talking….

"Oh God." Jacob sat bolt upright, then clutched at his head. "*Oh God.*"

Stumbling to the bathroom on autopilot, he scrambled to piece the previous evening together in his mind. Jesus, what had he told Rasul? He had this bad, bad feeling he'd confessed everything. He was pretty sure he'd told him about the damn cardigans, for crying out loud.

Whimpering, Jacob rested his forehead against the mirror. Then he washed his face, brushed his teeth, used the toilet, and got ready to face the music.

The tick of the clock drew his attention, and his heart leapt out of his throat as he noted the time. *Ten thirty?* He was late opening the store! Had he forgotten to set an alarm? He ran a hand through his hair as he tried to decide what to do.

That was when he saw the cat bowls, which were half-full. He frowned at them. They shouldn't have any food in them if he'd gone this long without feeding the cats. In fact, all three animals should have woken him up in protest. They were his eternal backup alarm.

On the kitchen table was a piece of paper held in place by a small ceramic figurine, the type that looked as if it might decorate the dirt in a potted plant. It was a gray castle turret wrapped with blooming vines.

Holding it in his hand, Jacob read the note.

> *I let you sleep in. Don't worry about the store—*
> *Gina set me up and I'm running it for you. There's some*
> *oatmeal in the oven, and tea and toast are ready for you*
> *to start on the counter. Take your time and enjoy the*
> *morning.*
> *I went to the floral shop down the street to leave*
> *you a flower with your breakfast, but then I worried what*
> *mess the cats would make. I decided to give you a castle*
> *instead.*
> *R*

A glance at the counter revealed a mug with teabag dangling over the side and, yes, two pieces of bread standing up in the toaster, waiting to be plunged. The electric kettle was filled and ready to go, and steel-cut oatmeal rested in a bowl in the oven, set to warm.

Jacob set the castle back on the table and readied his breakfast. He had his tablet in front of him as he ate, but mostly his gaze was drawn to the turret. He thought about it the entire time he showered as well.

His heart pounded as he made his way down the stairs. By this time it was a quarter past eleven. The shop was quiet, the usual blanket of silence that came at midday. Jacob wove his way through the stacks as silently as he could, stopping when he had a clear view of the front desk.

Rasul was there, sitting on a stool and reading a book.

He had on his glasses again, his chin-length curls drawn into a casual ponytail at the back of his crown. Whatever he was reading had him entirely engrossed.

He was so handsome. So vibrant even in stillness.

He made you breakfast and gave you a castle, then arranged to run your shop so you could sleep in.

How was Jacob supposed to resist that?

Gathering his courage, Jacob stepped forward.

It took Rasul a moment to notice his presence, but when he did he smiled, closing the book and rising. "Hey there, sleepyhead. Feeling okay this morning?"

Why did such an innocuous question make Jacob feel so fluttery? "A bit of a headache, but breakfast helped. Thank you for that." He felt a blush creep up his neck. "And the castle."

Rasul's smile and wink made Jacob's knees weak. He'd never survive this.

Rasul settled onto the stool again and gazed out across the shop. "It was really busy this morning, but it's finally quieted down now that book club has gone. There were a few moms and their kids and some grandparents upstairs, but not anymore."

Jacob leaned against the wall. "It's usually quiet at this time, but it'll pick up around lunch and again midafternoon."

"What do you do when it's only you here?"

"Sometimes I do financial things or place orders, but often I simply sit. The books are comforting company."

"Agreed." Rasul threaded his hands behind his head. "I'm a little jealous. I think every author dreams of running a bookshop someday. I know it's not all communing with books and chatting with customers, but dang."

"I've worked hard to make it feel like an essential part of the community. Hosting events, helping organizations with their special orders. All the Main Street businesses do that, but some of us are making a concerted effort to connect with the changes of the century. We can't compete with big corporations or The Online Store That Will Not Be Named when it comes to discounting, but we've worked hard to instill in people the idea that you pay for more than just the item. Which admittedly means I have to show up at as many local events as possible and make sure I take out ads in the paper and the high school yearbook, any and everything to keep Moore Books in the public's consciousness. I keep the exterior in shape and the space clean and attractive too. It helps quite a bit."

"It's an amazing space. I put it in the book. The dimension where—" He stopped, then smiled ruefully as he lowered his hands. "Well, I should probably keep that secret so you can enjoy the story. You *will* beta read it for me, right?"

Jacob had been doing so well, but that question made him shut his eyes and draw a careful breath.

When he opened his eyes, Rasul stood in front of him, vibrant and focused.

"Jacob." Rasul didn't touch him, but Jacob felt caressed somehow, as if each word were Rasul divesting him of his armor. "I'm moved by what you said about me, how you put me on a pedestal and used that to get yourself through some tough times. But I'm not a god. I'm a real person who makes a lot of mistakes."

He leaned in close enough that Jacob could feel his breath.

"I want to share those mistakes with you."

Forget armor. Rasul was shedding his clothes from his body now, leaving him naked. Jacob stared at the bony edges of Rasul's clavicle.

Thought about licking it.

Helpless, he lifted his gaze to Rasul's eyes and held his breath. Was it his imagination, or was Rasul moving closer? Oh God, were they going to kiss, right here in his shop?

Please, yes.

Hypnotized, Jacob held still as Rasul leaned in, holding Jacob firmly in place with his gaze.

The chime of the door startled Jacob, but Rasul didn't move, only put a hand gently to the wall beside Jacob's head.

"Hellooo," a cheerful elderly woman's voice rang out.

Rasul's hand stroked Jacob's cheek. Then he pushed away and turned toward the front of the store. "Be right there," he called to the customer before moving around the counter as, behind him, Jacob slid quietly to the floor.

Something told him Rasul had just shown him what he was like when he flirted in earnest. Jacob knew if this were true, he wouldn't last more than ten minutes under such an assault.

Chapter Nine

RASUL WAS keenly aware the tables had been turned in his relationship with Jacob, and he couldn't be happier.

Initially he'd intended to bring up their scotch-fueled table confessions and politely receive permission to proceed, but one glance at his would-be lover made it clear the last thing Jacob was ready to do was talk about his feelings, so Rasul changed his strategy of engagement. Jacob didn't want to look at the sun directly? Rasul could work with that. It had been a long time since he'd started a relationship with a slow and steady approach, but he still knew the moves.

He loved the way every glance, every touch, every exchange felt different now. Before, he'd constantly dialed himself back in deference to Jacob's wall, but now that he was on the other side, he didn't attack the way he knew Jacob both longed for and feared. Now that he could swoop the man up anytime he wanted, he was going to milk this courtship—a real one this time—for all he could.

The near-kiss behind the checkout counter, thrilling as it had been, wasn't his best move. He kept a clear berth from Jacob after that as they worked together until Gina came for her afternoon shift. When Jacob hinted Rasul should maybe go write, he instead declared he was going home to get a shower before class. There was zero chance of him making any words today.

His class picked up on his good mood right away, though. They teased him, and he let them, derailing their lessons a bit to tell stories from book tour days and answering questions about the publishing process. He redirected to the other published authors in the room, especially Meg, who brought some much-needed levity to their dreams.

"But seriously, what good thing happened to you?" Ben asked, grinning as if he already knew.

"Let's just say I'm enjoying my relationship and leave it at that," Rasul replied.

When he got home, he opened his laptop and did a quick check through social media, though he didn't post—couldn't, obviously, on Instagram. Two days ago he *had* posted on Twitter, apologizing for disappearing without notice and saying that he was on hiatus to finish his novel, and now his notifications overflowed with people encouraging him. There were also several Adinastans asking why he'd abandoned her, but there were even more people asking about his new relationship, wondering if that had worked out.

There was also a DM from Adina on Twitter.

Hey baby. Glad work's going well for you. Wish I could say the same, but you know. Still think about you a lot. We make a great team. I mean, I know that relationship you say you're in right now is fake.

His gut churning, he immediately called Elizabeth, even though it was late.

"This is unexpected," she said by way of greeting. "What's up?"

When he read her the message from Adina, she sobered.

"What does she mean, she knows your relationship is fake?"

"I don't know," Rasul replied, and he meant it. "It's not fake." *Not anymore, anyway.*

"That woman makes me nervous. Screenshot that and send it to me, then block her."

Rasul's gut twisted. "Seriously? Block her?"

She sighed. "Well, maybe not, you're right. Jesus, she's work. Okay, what about this. Because I'm all about protecting this momentum you have going. Would you allow me to manage your Twitter and Instagram for a while? Let me have the password so I can monitor it for you, including these DMs?"

God, that felt highly, highly intimate. "Um, there are some risqué DMs in our history."

"I assumed. Look, I had straight sex once. It wasn't great, but it didn't traumatize me. I promise I won't judge you. I may scan through it just to see if there's a pattern or warning sign you're missing, but I promise I'm doing all this to help you. I want you to finish this book for your own sake as much as mine. And I want you to keep dating this

Jacob guy. You're so much calmer and focused since you started seeing him. Don't let Adina derail you."

In the end he agreed to give her the passwords, so long as she swore not to change them. It made him super nervous, but it also relieved him. If he were to trust anyone with his account, it was Elizabeth.

After that, he didn't go online at all, only to do research and check his mail, which he did with less and less frequency, except for his school account. It was weird, but also good. It also left him with even more time to read, but also time to ruminate on how best to move forward with his relationship with Jacob, which despite their mutual admission of feelings had remained in the same place as it had the night they drank scotch together.

One Wednesday afternoon, instead of going over to Jacob's to work, he trudged through the cold afternoon drizzle to the store just past Moore Books: Engleton's Fine Clothing. He had to pass the bookstore on the way, though, and he saw the blond employee in the window arranging things. She ducked away again at the sight of him.

Seriously, what was with that kid?

Rasul hadn't been in the clothing shop before, but he regretted the lapse the second he stepped inside. It was elegant and soothing, full of wood paneling that seemed to be real wood, and carefully arranged displays that made him consider purchasing a breezy button-down even though his current wardrobe was nothing but ragged knit T-shirts and pullovers. They had those too, without the ragged part, of course, and Rasul was browsing the henleys and sweaters when Matt Engleton approached him with a polite, professional smile.

"Mr. Youssef. What a pleasure. How can we help you today?"

Rasul raised his eyebrows and was about to make a joke regarding Matt's formality, since they'd met several times now and Matt had always called him Rasul, but then he spied the elderly balding man peering through the curtained door behind the register, regarding Matt and Rasul with intense interest.

Twenty bucks said that was Daddy Engleton. Or, honestly, it might be Grandpa.

Rasul filed away his ribbing and matched Matt's tone. "It's getting colder faster than I anticipated, and I realized today I just don't have winter clothing enough for Copper Point. The perils of living in Los Angeles."

"You've certainly come to the right place." He raked Rasul's body with a professional gaze. "Hmm. I'd say you were a 16 neck, 34 sleeve, 43 chest? And…." He tipped his head to the side. "32 waist, 30 inseam? How close am I?"

"Frighteningly."

Matt winked at him. "Favorite colors?"

"Whatever looks good." He couldn't bring himself to say *whatever Jacob would like.*

"I think this burgundy sweater would do nicely, and this oatmeal-colored henley in a waffle pattern. Shall I start a fitting room for you?"

"Please."

Rasul wasn't exactly a clotheshorse, but he enjoyed the luxurious experience of having Matt patiently wait on him, suggesting colors and styles, dismissing one outfit but offering a replacement. By the time he was done, he had almost three hundred dollars' worth of new duds, and he wasn't even sorry.

"The only thing is, now my junky tennis shoes are going to show up your great clothes," he remarked ruefully as Matt rang him up.

Matt didn't miss a beat. "Paris Shoe Company is next door." He passed Rasul a card from beside the register. "One of the original Copper Point stores, run by the descendants of the original family."

Rasul took the card. "Paris, huh?"

"Copper Point was originally settled by French traders, including the Blanchetts, no relation to Cate. I believe there was a time some of their shoes came directly from Paris, hence the name. Italy and of course Asia are far more represented now."

"I'll check them out." Rasul glanced at the curtain behind Matt. It was unmanned, but just in case, he lowered his voice. "Any chance I could take you out for coffee later? You and maybe Gus as well? But not Jacob."

Matt regarded him carefully. "If you take us out for coffee, we're going to get a text from Jacob before we so much as place our order asking what's going on. Even as off the grid as he is, people will text him to let him know. If your goal is to talk to the two of us in private, I'll arrange something more subdued." He glanced at his watch. "Gus will be a bit slammed until six thirty. I'll see when he can steal some time and let you know, but I'm betting it will be seven. We'll meet here. Come to the back door and knock."

"This feels very *Spy vs. Spy*."

Matt raised his eyebrows. "That's… an incredibly old reference."

"I'm a bit retro." He gathered up his bags. "Thanks for helping me shop, and thanks for arranging the meeting. I'll go check out Paris now."

He was just checking out another hundred dollars' worth of purchases next door when his phone made its discordant clang to let him know he had a text. It was from Matt.

7 pm, back door of Engleton's. Don't drive. Bring snacks. Gus says they should be homemade.

Shaking his head, he punched back a laborious *ok thnks* and gathered his haul to take it back to his apartment.

He still hated his living quarters, but he'd grown accustomed to them as much as he suspected he ever would. Christopher, the math professor, had pointed out the best way to get rid of cooking smells was to infuse the place with his own, and thus Rasul had begun the marathon cooking adventures that had occupied his first month, sometimes in the middle of the night. His favorite thing to make right now was kimchee, because the smell lingered so long after. Indian food was another usual for the same reason, and of course Syrian. He cooked some of his grandmother's greatest hits, kawaj and tabbouleh and, one Sunday when he was particularly lonesome and frustrated, mujaddara. He'd fed quite a bit of the leftovers to Jacob, who he'd learned would eat just about any food but resisted cooking any of it. Now that he was courting the man in earnest, he planned a far more aggressive culinary assault.

Right now, though, he needed a better lay of the land.

At six thirty he got dressed in one of the new outfits and his new pair of shoes, packed up his latest culinary adventure, and set out for Engleton's. It was raining again, this time with a little more emphasis, but he still walked, huddling under an umbrella as he made his way down the street, passing the now familiar shops and somewhat familiar people. He was still a minor celebrity in town, but people seemed to have gotten used to him, and only regarded him with mild curiosity, as if at any moment he might do a trick and entertain them. When he got closer to the community center and library, there were more children, and several of them waved at him. He recognized a few from the bookshop, some of them having been patrons that very morning.

He wondered if he could do something at the library, something low-key. The librarian had approached him the first week he was in town, but he hadn't wanted to draw more attention to himself then. Maybe he could lead a book club? Though if he did that, he should probably do it at the bookstore. Or should he? He'd ask Jacob.

His musings took him all the way to the clothing store, and as directed, he went around the back, shaking out his umbrella as he stood under the awning.

Gus answered his knock, his gaze falling immediately to the bag in his hand. "So you *did* bring snacks. And you made them?"

Rasul passed him the bag. "I had some time, yeah, so I made maneesh and baba ganoush."

Gus made appreciative noises as he stuck his head deeper into the paper sack. "Mmm. You could give up the author gig and open a Middle Eastern restaurant. We'd make sure it was a success."

He followed Gus into a small hallway leading into a storeroom full of hanging clothing and unopened boxes. "Funny, I never cooked much before I came here. I was always on the go. I'm into it, though, especially trying to recreate my grandmother's recipes."

"Well, we fully support you and volunteer as taste testers."

Matt was already seated at a table in the middle of the storeroom, pouring out coffee from a carafe. "Come on in." He nodded at a Keurig in the corner. "That's my dad's. Gus won't let me touch it and brought us coffee from his shop."

"Sounds good to me." Rasul set his offerings on the table and took a cup from Matt.

"I've been trying to figure out how to ask this," Gus said as he took a seat, "but I've never figured out a good way to do it, so I apologize if I mangle it. I know your family has been in the States for some time, but… do you have family still in Syria? Are they in any trouble? Ever since you came, I hear reports from there on the news and feel a bit more ill than usual."

It had been a while since Rasul had been asked this, though he got it often in Copper Point. He took a sip of the coffee. "Some distant relations. We went there a few times when I was in high school. My dad did what he could to get people out, but with the immigration restrictions…." He shrugged against the hollow pit in his stomach. "We've lost contact with most of them. A few made it to Turkey, but they're in camps. Or, they were. It's been a while since I've heard anything."

Gus grimaced. "I'm sorry."

Rasul packed his complicated feelings about his distant family and his father's homeland away and rested his hands on the table. "So. I wanted to pick your brains about the best way to court Jacob, for real." When they shared a heavy glance and raised their eyebrows, Rasul added, "I was still at his place when he came home the night he got drunk with you. He... got chatty. We both did, to be honest."

Matt shook his head as he pulled the plastic wrap off the baba ganoush. "I *knew* we should have walked him all the way up."

Rasul cracked open the container holding the maneesh and pushed it toward Matt and Gus. "But now I know how he really feels, and I think he's open to us getting closer, if I'm mindful of how I go. I wanted to know if there was anything I should be careful of, or bear in mind, and if you guys had any information that would help me out."

Gus and Matt didn't say anything at first, only dragged their maneesh through the baba ganoush and regarded one another solemnly while they chewed.

"This was a tactical error," Gus said at last, "to ask him to bring food when we knew we'd have to sit in judgment."

"But can anyone who brings food like this be all bad, truly?" Matt licked some errant baba ganoush off his fingers and leaned back in his chair. "Here's the thing. We like you, more than we expected. But Jacob is...." He rubbed his cheek. "Not fragile, exactly, but he's self-protective for a reason. When he was younger, he was a lot more adventurous. If you'd have come here when he was in high school, he'd have pursued you, or even if you'd met while he was in college."

It was difficult to picture. "Did his parents' deaths affect him that much?"

"They tipped him over the edge," Matt said. He consulted Gus with a glance again, Gus shrugged, and Matt dove in. "His job already wasn't going well, and he'd had a few overly complicated romantic relationships. His parents were worried about him and kept trying to get him to come home because they worried he was dangerously depressed, which I think he was. They wanted him to talk to someone and look into medication. I know this because they were friends with my family. Jacob's a little older than me, but we hung out even when we were younger. I idolized him in middle school and would hang on him when he would come back from college. But his parents were always talking about him, and they worried out loud constantly when they came over to the store while he was in

Chicago. They were our accountants. Anyway, they were going to drive to Chicago and address things in person, but the snowstorm first delayed them, then took their lives."

Gus sighed. "I didn't meet him before, since I've only lived here from college on, but everything people told me confirms this. I didn't know him while I was in undergrad, not until I started making a project of the coffee shop I'd eventually own. When I first met him, he was a shell of a human. I tried to lure him into the shop a lot and engage him, but it was hard. I think it's mostly that he lost so much that he treasured all at once, at the same time he was questioning his occupation and plan for the future. Obviously he's a lot better now, but…." Gus looked helplessly at Matt, who shrugged. Gus grimaced and continued. "It's a little complicated that you're here. You have no idea how weird it is for him that his favorite author exists in Copper Point at all, let alone that said author is trying to date him. On the one hand, we're excited for him and for you. On the other, we're afraid he's going to break again."

Matt cut Rasul off as he started to speak. "Look, I know what you're going to say. You're thinking, so he had an author crush on me, maybe even a celebrity crush. But now we've gotten to know one another, so it's fine. Right?" When Rasul nodded, Matt snorted. "*Wrong*. That man carried your books around like they were Bibles and he was the head priest. Your stories were *the* reason he crawled out of the pit, but there was a long time he was pretty unsteady even with that. It was like he hinged his whole sanity around that point. Over the years he's evened out, and he looks back at those first days with embarrassment, but they still happened."

"I think he worries his feelings for you aren't real, that it's impossible for him to untangle the you in his head from the you in front of him," Gus said. "He got upset, not excited, when he found out you were coming. I think he was fully cognizant both that he had kind of a weird place for you in his psyche but also that it was super important to him."

"Granted," Matt added, "he's come around since getting to know you. He does genuinely like you."

None of this was exactly news to Rasul, but he'd never had it all laid out like this before. He sat back in his chair and contemplated the tabletop. "So what you're saying is that I need to… what? Convince him this is real? That I'm not a figment of his imagination?"

Gus shook his head. "No. He gets that. We're not saying he's still where he was right after his parents died or before he opened the bookstore."

"But you do, basically, take him back to where he was at that time, just by existing," Matt finished. "Not completely. But enough that he's at a kind of war with himself. Personally, I think it's good for him. He's been walled off too much for too long. And in a way, only you could have broken him out of his shell for good."

"Don't toy with him, though," Gus added. "We're not saying you have to relocate to Copper Point, but don't view this as a fling. If you do, it'd be better to stick to friendship, or your fake dating or whatever."

"I don't view this as a fling." Rasul frowned at the tabletop. "This is important for me too. I'm learning a lot about myself by being here. And he's the only reason I'm going to finish this book."

"My advice," Matt said, "is to go slow. I know you probably think about this as glacially paced already, but his getting drunk the other night is the first time he's really allowed himself to consider this potentially possible. Or more to the point, he had to get drunk to let himself go there. We've been hoping he'd date someone for a while, but nobody ever would have guessed *you* would be who he'd end up with."

Rasul felt more out to sea by the minute. "I honestly only came here to get some direction. This is… a lot."

Gus tilted his head. "That's what we've been trying to tell you. Being with Jacob, truly being with him, especially you being with him, is a lot. Normally we wouldn't get this involved in a friend's love life. We want this to work for both of you, but we also don't want him to lose the ground he's gained."

"Like I said. Go slow." Matt patted his shoulder. "I know that's not usually how you operate, but give it a shot. You said Jacob's been good for you. Maybe this will be too."

Rasul rubbed his cheek. "I'm just afraid I'll fuck it up. And fuck him up in the process."

"Don't worry." Gus sipped his coffee, meeting Rasul's gaze over the rim. "We'll be watching to make sure you don't."

JACOB WASN'T precisely sure what he'd expected after Rasul nearly kissed him behind the cash register, but it certainly wasn't that he'd disappear for nearly two weeks.

He didn't disappear *precisely*. He still came by, though not as often, and when he did, he went straight to Jacob's kitchen, put on headphones, and entered a zone not even a fresh cup of tea beside him could jolt him from. On the days he didn't show, he uncharacteristically didn't text or call to apologize for not coming.

It worried Jacob. It also made him distracted, which meant when the time came to finally decide whether he was going put his name in for chamber president, he said yes out of some weird panic response. He couldn't even be bothered by Les Clark's outraged fury and the silent promise in his eyes that he would take Jacob down at all costs. He was too busy wondering what was going on with Rasul.

His restlessness must have showed, because one day Jodie came up to him while they were working and asked, "Is something going on? Did something happen?"

Caught off guard at being addressed so bluntly by the young girl who rarely remembered to greet him or tell him she was leaving, Jacob paused stacking the new releases. "Ah, I'm fine, thank you. Why do you ask?"

She fidgeted. "No reason. Just… wondering."

Obviously something was going on, but teen girls had always been a mystery to Jacob, on every level. He tried to brush away the awkwardness with a breezy smile. "Everything good with you? How are classes?"

She shrugged. "Fine. Grandpa is making me take precalculus and I don't want to, but other than that I'm okay."

Since Jodie's grandfather was Les Clark, he thought it might be best if he didn't make any judgments there and sent her back to work.

He didn't stop worrying about what Rasul's silence meant, and when he couldn't take it anymore, Jacob sent Rasul an email. It felt like a strange thing to do, but it was cruel to ask him to respond on that keypad.

> *I noticed you haven't been by as much. Is everything all right?*

He resisted the urge to add, *Did I do anything to upset you?*

Jacob had deliberately done this during the time he knew Rasul kept aside for wrestling with his inbox, so he received a reply fairly quickly.

*All good. Was thinking about some things, then
started writing and hit a real groove all the way to the
midpoint. Kind of superstitious about the midpoint. Don't
want to break it. Can we make a date for next week? I
should be through the worst of it by then. I mean a real
date, not one for show.*

Oh. Jacob touched his lips as he read the email again. Well, that
was a decent explanation. And a bit exciting. He was doing that well?
An actual date. He drew in a breath, let it out, and replied.

*I'm glad to hear the story is coming along. Can I
bring you over some food? Maybe some little meals you
can heat up easily? I won't stay and bother you. I just
worry about you not eating. Also, yes, I'd love a date.
Saturday?*

Another reply.

*Food would be welcomed, but isn't required. I don't
want to put you out. I just wish this place had DoorDash.
Saturday sounds perfect.*

Jacob had meant to leave it at that, but couldn't resist one more
exchange.

*I'm surprised you're writing in your apartment.
Didn't you say you hated it there?*

This reply took slightly longer. It was so old-school, sitting there
waiting for an email reply. He should have suggested they log in to
desktop chat.

*This probably sounds weird, but being in a different
space is giving me what I need. I don't have much to do
there and don't particularly like it, so I focus on getting*

the words out. Also, I made a few modifications. I miss the bookshop, though.

Jacob did *not* tell him the bookshop, and its owner, missed him too.

He loved the idea of being meal delivery for Rasul. He wasn't sure what this DoorDash thing was, so he looked it up. It certainly did sound handy, and also something that would never come somewhere as small as Copper Point. He could be a personal DoorDash, however, which worked out because despite how much he loved the idea of bringing food to Rasul, he still hated cooking more than the bare minimum.

So he made some trips around town, worked his charm and set up his plans, then did a swing through the grocery store before heading over to Rasul's place. He caught him just after he finished his office hours.

"Hey." Rasul's smile was soft and inviting as he leaned on the doorframe. Then he stepped back as he saw the bags in Jacob's hands. "Wow. Come on in."

"I brought you a few things because I assume your fridge is bare, as are your cupboards." After toeing out of his shoes and draping his jacket over a chair, Jacob carried the bags to the counter. "When you get writing, I've noticed you forget other things, or at least resent doing them."

"Guilty." Rasul poked into the bags. "Ooh, Cheetos."

"I have another something for you." Jacob withdrew a small collection of cardstock from one of the bags and presented it to Rasul, who read it with a slight frown.

"Rasul Youssef's Personal Order and Delivery Service?"

"Yes." Jacob pointed to a card. "If a restaurant is on there, it means I set up an account with them and they're in touch with my network of people willing—and safe—to make a delivery. You can square up with the businesses later, and I'm paying the delivery people. It's not an app on your phone, but it is one phone call away to delivery."

Rasul's mouth had fallen open as he flipped through the cards, each one for a different restaurant. "This is amazing. These are all the best restaurants in town." He gasped and looked up at Jacob. "This is the secret Taiwanese menu at China Garden!"

"I know how much you liked it when QUAG met there."

"This is so great. *Thank you.*"

He leaned forward and brushed a kiss on Jacob's cheek.

Jacob's whole body tingled, and he couldn't help touching the space where Rasul's lips had been. "I don't want to keep you, because I know you need to get back to work. But between what I brought and the restaurants on call, you should be set for a week at least."

Rasul took a step closer. "I intend to see you sooner than that, you know."

Jacob blushed. He tried not to withdraw or be ridiculously demure, but he felt flustered. He stepped farther into the apartment instead. "This isn't half as bad as you make it out to be."

Rasul huffed. "The kitchen is so damn dark. No natural light whatsoever. Plus it's too quiet."

Jacob drifted to the window, peered outside to the small, badly maintained courtyard below. "Where do you write when you work here?"

"My bedroom mostly. That room I don't mind so much." He grabbed Jacob's hand and tugged him through the living room. "Here, I'll show you."

Jacob's pulse fluttered—it didn't matter how he chided himself for being ridiculous, it still happened. He gasped when they went through the door. "Oh—wow, this is amazing!"

Letting go of Jacob, Rasul stood in the middle of the room, or at least up against the side of the bed, arms extended and a grin on his face. The glow of thousands of string lights filled the walls, part of the ceiling, and spilled onto the floor. In several spaces, there was dark gauzy fabric behind the lights, making it feel as if….

Well, as if Jacob had stepped beyond a veil and into the stars.

Rasul beamed at the space he'd created. "Christopher helped me rig it. Gorgeous, right? It puts me in the mood when I feel like I'm losing the threads of the story. Which is sadly much easier than I'd like."

The door was open behind Jacob, and he couldn't decide if he wanted to rush out of it or close it tightly and meld into the space. He was highly conscious of Rasul's bed, half-made and littered with pillows. The room smelled like him, like the sweatshirts he often left behind when he worked and which Jacob would steal whiffs of as he hung them politely on the back of Rasul's usual chair.

If you shut the door, he'll make love to you right now.

Jacob took a half step backward, making himself a doorstop. "It's lovely. I'm glad to hear writing is going so well."

"Yeah." Rasul put his hands in his pockets and rocked on his heels. "I worry a lot that it'll evaporate. For a while there, I'd open the document thrilled at how much progress I was making, eager to push out more. Then I realized how far I was and started dreading each day would be the one when I realized it was nothing but ash."

"I'm sure it's not ash."

More fidgeting. Now it was Rasul who couldn't look at Jacob. "It's so close to home. I feel exposed but also worry it's too ridiculous."

"Can you show your agent and have her reassure you?"

"Oh, she's seen sections of it, and she likes it. But...."

Oh—Rasul was blushing.

Rasul lifted his gaze to Jacob's. "I want *you* to like it."

Thump. Thump. Thump. Jacob put his hand over his heart, trying to quiet it. "I...." He couldn't say anything more.

"There's so much of you in this book. So much *for* you." Rasul gestured to the lights around them. "When you read my work, I want you to feel like this room makes me feel as I write. Soft and safe, slightly breathless, hopeful."

Knees. Where were Jacob's knees? "I... I feel that way about your work already."

Rasul shook his head, a flare of passion kindling in his gaze. "I want you to feel it *more*. I want this book to blow my other two away—for *you*."

Jacob gave up. He leaned into the doorway to keep himself upright.

Rasul didn't move, but he somehow crowded Jacob all the same. His gaze was so intense. "I want to press you against the door and kiss you until you're boneless. I want to push you into this bed and undo you until we're both weak and spent." His gaze softened. "You're not ready, and to be honest, the pining and tension is fueling the book. When it's done, though... when it's done, I want you to read it. And I want to make love to you."

Jacob's fingers curled against the wall, the wood of the frame. He couldn't answer. He could barely breathe.

Rasul's smile made Jacob's blood fizzle. "I'm going to go back to work now. And I'll use your delivery service. Next week, when I feel more stable about this, I'll call you and we'll go on a date. You think about where you'd like to go. In the meantime...."

He crossed to the dresser, opened the top drawer, and withdrew something small. When he held it out, Jacob saw it was a key.

"I have a key to your place. You should have one to mine." Rasul held the tip of the key by his fingertips and extended it toward Jacob. "Feel free to use it anytime."

Why was Jacob so turned-on by a damn key? He swallowed against his dry throat, then swallowed again. "Y-you're working."

The smolder in Rasul's gaze could have lit a blaze in a rainstorm. "If you use this to let yourself into my bedroom, I won't be working for very long. And I won't mind."

Jacob shouldn't take the key. He knew this. He should make a polite refusal, give a smile, and depart. Under no circumstances should he take the key from Rasul. He absolutely should never use it.

Shaking, Jacob took two steps forward, feeling as if he were in a dream. For a second, when he closed his fingers on the metal, he swore he felt a jolt of electricity, a sharp current connecting the two of them, running through every inch of his body.

Shut the door and you can stay. Shut the door, and he'll pull you into his arms.

Jacob drew back, stumbling, then hurried out of the room, through the house to the door, swiping up his jacket and shoes on his way out. Once he was down the stairs in the foyer, he dropped his shoes and wrangled his feet into them.

With a shaking breath, he tucked the key into his pocket and left the building.

Chapter Ten

VEIL OF Stars was either the best thing Rasul had ever written, or the worst, and not knowing which it was drove him up the wall.

He didn't remember feeling this way about his first two novels, or any of the short fiction he'd managed to churn out while he spun his wheels. The first one had been... well, lightning, really. His father had nagged him the whole time he'd been writing, telling him how novels never made any money and no one would read it. He'd written *The Sword Dancer's Daughter* full of defiance and a determination to make his dad eat it even as Rasul battled a crippling depression telling him he and everything he did was garbage. The book hadn't been garbage. People had read it, and there'd been that movie option too. No movie was ever made, but still. He'd been paid, enough to feel smug.

Book two had been slightly different. There was a lot of expectation on him, and weird jealousy from people he didn't even know, everyone ready to watch him fall on his face. So he'd made sure he didn't fall. And this was enough, apparently, for everyone to leave him alone. The movie for *Carnivale* was indeed in the works. His dad bragged about him now. His mother gave his books to her friends. The critics eagerly awaited his next offering, certain it would be a hit.

That, for some reason, was when Rasul had pancaked, and he hadn't been able to recover. Not until now.

Not until Jacob.

The day before Jacob had shown up with meals on wheels, Rasul had decided. He didn't care what else happened with the story, but Jacob was going to like it. Every critic could laugh at it, his publisher could throw it out the window—none of it mattered, so long as Jacob thought it was good. This mantra had carried him over a dangerous impasse, and after he'd seen the way Jacob melted inside his bedroom, clearly longing to come inside, equally terrified and needing to stay away—that had sealed the deal. He *would* please Jacob with this story. Maybe he wouldn't win his heart and get him into bed, but piercing him with story would be enough.

It wouldn't. He wanted Jacob more every day. But that was fine. It made him work harder.

The protagonist, Adam Hasan, was a pretty serious self-insert, but it was his adolescent self-insert, so no one would know except his dad, who might actually not see it anyway because he didn't read Rasul's stuff. He wouldn't continue past the first kiss, at least.

It was a steamy kiss. He'd felt surprisingly self-conscious and had stalled himself for a day worrying he was going to get that worst sex scene award, so in a panic he'd rifled through the romance section of the bookstore and done some homework. He'd emerged hours later full of sober reflection, then had read some more.

He was pretty sure he was writing a romance novel, surprisingly enough. A young adult romance novel. He wasn't sure what Elizabeth would think of that, but she didn't matter. Only Jacob did.

Would Jacob like it if Rasul wrote a romance novel? Rasul knew he liked them. He'd seen some in the living room in Jacob's apartment. Obviously he'd read those immediately.

Anyway, it was a romance novel now, and Jacob would love it. Rasul was confident in that most times, especially when he sat inside the veil and blasted music through his headphones to set a mood. Today, the day he was supposed to meet Jacob for a date, the song was Styx's "Come Sail Away." He had it on repeat and at full blast, and he bobbed and swayed to the beat as he wrote, singing along with and banging his head to the chorus.

It got really cheesy, because the song influenced the plot, and Adam and Milo were sailing through a technicolor trail that in Rasul's head looked like the sky in *The NeverEnding Story*. He didn't care. It was a great scene.

Adam and Milo looked a lot like him and Jacob, but absolutely nobody would ever know that.

Rasul was whirring along and belting quite definitely off-key when the door to his bedroom cracked open. Looking uncertain, Jacob stuck his head in.

Heart skipping a beat, Rasul tugged down his headphones and grinned. "Hey."

Jacob's cheeks stained with a blush. "You said to just come in. I heard you singing." He frowned at the headphones. "That's *loud*."

"Keeps me in the zone." Rasul hit Pause on the keyboard. "You ready to go?"

"I can read in the living room if you want to write some more."

"I won't get another word out of myself if I know you're in the other room and I could be off having fun." He closed the laptop. "Let's go."

He tugged the bedsheets haphazardly back into place and brushed hands over himself, realizing he probably should have changed. He'd originally intended to organize the date and make it wonderful, but book brain had taken over, so when Jacob said he'd plan something, he'd gone with it. If there had been details about the outing, though, he'd missed them. He glanced at Jacob, who had on a coat and therefore gave no silent hints.

"What you're wearing is fine," Jacob said. "I thought we'd take a walk around the lighthouse."

"There's a lighthouse?" Rasul started to take the scrunchie out of his hair, then paused when he saw the look on Jacob's face. "What?"

Jacob immediately averted his gaze. "Nothing."

"That didn't look like nothing. Do I look weird?" He stepped past Jacob to get to the bathroom, examining himself in the mirror. "Am I too messy? Should I shower?"

"No." Jacob sighed, folding his arms over his chest. "I like your hair pulled back like that, that's all I was thinking." His arms sagged a little as he added, "And when you wear your glasses."

Rasul tilted his head and looked at himself again. He indeed had his hair up and was wearing glasses. "I thought I looked like a sleazy hipster."

"You don't."

"Well, I'll leave them both, then."

Jacob had his car out front, and when they climbed in, Rasul spied a picnic basket in the back seat. An actual picnic basket.

"It's probably too cold for a picnic," Jacob said as they pulled away from the curb. He glanced at Rasul's head. "I should have had you bring a hat."

"Don't have one."

"Well, we'll have to swing by Walmart and pick one up. It gets cold by the bay."

Rasul clutched at his heart. "Wait a minute. We're stopping at a *corporate store?*"

"There's no helping it. Engleton's only has driving caps, which don't seem like they'd suit you. There will be some handmade winter gear at the holiday bazaar in a few weeks, but that doesn't do us any good today."

"What's the holiday bazaar?"

"Kind of like a farmer's market, but without fruit or vegetables. Area crafters sell goods on Saturdays in the community center. The Main Street businesses offer good sales at the same time and hold events. People come from quite a ways a way to participate in it as well as shop Main Street. The library also hosts a used book sale the Saturday after Thanksgiving."

"Isn't that competition for you?"

Jacob shook his head. "I'd never survive without the library. In fact, I donate pretty heavily to the sale."

"Why do you say you wouldn't survive without the library?"

"Because people who read do it a lot, and sadly most don't have that much money. Libraries nurture readers, teach them to read more broadly and give them ideas. I'm for the next book in the series, when you can't stand to wait, or to pick up your own copy for your shelf. Also, my books are given as gifts. In my store and at the library I have a wish list depository and keep up the database, so if someone's grandmother wants to buy them a book, they know exactly what to get."

Rasul whistled low. "That's brilliant."

"Gus thought of it. He's good with ideas like that. I keep stock at his place too, and if anyone buys a book with me, they get a free drink coupon punch on their card."

"Main Street takes care of its own."

Jacob nodded. "We try."

Rasul enjoyed, just a little, watching Jacob actively dislike the discount store. Their trip to the winter hats and gloves took them past the book section, which was mostly a sad rack of a narrow selection of best sellers.

Jacob curled up his nose at it. "Look at this. Half of these books have been out for years, but they don't have yours, and you're in town. I'm sure the buyer doesn't even know, or care. Also their idea of diversity is laughable. And yet this book"—he picked up a copy of the number-one best seller, according to their rack—"is priced so low they're not making any money on it. Its whole purpose is to keep people out of my store and bring them here so that they buy televisions and toasters too. But even those only make them a fraction of what the old appliance store made before it had to close. They only get away with this because they trade in inhuman volume."

Never mind, this wasn't fun anymore. Rasul tugged gently at Jacob's arm. "Come on. Let's buy this hat and gloves and go see the lighthouse. As soon as the bazaar opens, I'll go buy hats, scarves, and gloves from every vendor."

It took Jacob a bit to calm down, but once they pulled off the highway and started to trek up the hill, he relaxed and went into story mode. "The lighthouse hasn't been used in years, but it's a historical site, so we keep it up. When the copper trade was in full swing, Copper Point was a busy port. The lighthouse isn't needed anymore with the lights barges have, but it looks nice on the clifftop."

It *was* quite pretty, gleaming white brick against the early November sun. Almost like the turret of a castle. "Weird how you can't see it from town."

"It's just far enough away. The copper mines were farther north of town, and the ports are of course nowhere near the city, since we sit on a high cliff ourselves."

"Why *did* they build the town so high up? I was surprised I didn't see a bay full of sailboats."

"The port is over by the country club. However, there aren't as many boats as you might be thinking of. Lake Superior is cold and can be incredibly dangerous. If you want picturesque moments on the water, go over to Door County and Lake Michigan. The water is cold there too, unfortunately."

"I like the cold." Rasul threaded his fingers behind his head and looked out the window. "Before I came here, I was in LA. Too hot, too dry."

Jacob glanced over at him. "You don't miss California? The parties?"

Rasul snorted. "I hated the parties."

"Yet you went all the time."

Rasul couldn't decide if he was flattered or mortified. Both, maybe. "I couldn't stand to be alone with myself, facing how badly I was failing."

"Do you feel like you're failing now?"

Unexpectedly, Rasul's heart seized. He let out a ragged breath to relax the muscles in his chest. "No. I feel like I've stumbled into the most magical place in the world."

Jacob laughed. "Copper Point? Really?"

It's not Copper Point that draws me, not the most. Rasul ran a hand through his hair. "I like it here. Teaching is going better than I thought it would. The people are great, at the university and in town in general."

The man who owns the bookstore, in particular.

Jacob nodded. "You haven't talked about teaching as much lately. I worried you didn't like it."

"Oh no, it's great. It's not what I expected, but it's fun. I like watching people find their feet. The fanfic writers are my favorite. They're so… pure. They just want to eat, breathe, and sleep the characters that started out as someone else's and then became their own." He rested his arm on the window. "I kind of want to do something for my students when we finish the second semester—they're all staying on for round two. Have them do a short story anthology or something. You can print all kinds of stuff on demand for cheap nowadays."

"If you do, I'll host an event for them in the store. Let them have a signing."

Rasul beamed. "You would? That'd be amazing."

"Of course. It's what we do."

It was, Rasul realized. Jacob, Gus, Matt—even Christopher and Ram—they all took care of one another. That was what Rasul loved about this place too.

Mostly, though, Copper Point was Jacob. It would always be Jacob, and the story he helped Rasul create.

It was windy when they got out of the car, making Rasul extra glad they'd stopped for a hat and pair of gloves. The lighthouse was a self-guided tour, with warning signs about the stairs. By the time they got to the top, Rasul's legs were jelly. The view was worth it, however.

"This is amazing." He gripped the iron rail and stared out across the bay toward the place where it spilled into mist.

"It's a popular confession point for high schoolers and kids at the college. Which I never understood. As soon as you pulled off onto this road or even headed in this direction, wouldn't you know?"

Rasul scoffed. "The anticipation is only part of the experience. Walking up the stairs, heart pounding, knowing what you were about to hear…. Good place for a first kiss too. That's worth hiking for." He rested his elbows on the rail and let his gaze unfocus, writing brain taking over. "Except if I were writing it, I'd build up the anticipation and then have something go haywire. Or I'd have the wrong love interest bring them up here, and it would be a breakup instead of a proposal. Talk about getting somebody to hate a character." He winced and rubbed his cheek. "Sorry, lousy side effect of dating a writer."

"I don't mind. It's interesting." Jacob was leaning on the rail too, inches from Rasul. He stared easily over the water, as if he were incredibly comfortable.

Suddenly Rasul wanted to make sure Jacob *wasn't* comfortable. He should be sweating the same way Rasul was.

Turning to face Jacob, Rasul ran a gloved finger down his boyfriend's arm. "Maybe *we* should have our first kiss here."

Mmm, but it was delicious the way Jacob leapt back. "I—I thought you said—your book—"

"I said I'd wait until I finished to take you to bed." Rasul took a slow, predatory step toward Jacob, who backed up again. "Too cold to have sex up here, but a kiss would warm me right up."

"Wait, that's not why—" Jacob almost tripped over his feet in his haste to get further away.

Rasul swept in and caught him. He felt Jacob trembling as he righted him. "Don't want a kiss from me?"

"That's not—I don't—" With a shuddering sigh, Jacob closed his eyes. "You're doing this on purpose, sending me to pieces."

"Mmm-hmm. Because you're so delicious when you're a mess." Jacob's eyes flared open, and Rasul laughed. "But you're also delightful when ferocious. You're perfect, full stop, Jacob Moore. Let me kiss you. Please."

Jacob let out a shaking breath. His gaze fell on Rasul's lips.

The wind whipped around them, but Rasul was full of warmth. For the first time in a long, long time, the universe felt right and good, and he didn't want this moment to end.

Sliding a hand behind Jacob's head, Rasul pulled himself forward and kissed him.

It wasn't the kiss he'd anticipated giving him. It was soft and sweet, almost hesitant. For all Jacob's outward panic, it was Rasul's soul that screamed in terror, afraid to leap, afraid to dream. This man had changed everything, and with the snap of his fingers, he could do it again. It would be so easy, so terrifyingly easy, for Rasul to find himself more alone than ever.

But he wasn't alone right now. Oh, he absolutely wasn't alone.

Letting out a breath, he tilted his head and opened his mouth over Jacob's.

Jacob startled, hesitated, then kissed him with all the passion Rasul had seen banked in his eyes.

They clutched at each other, grabbing jackets, tugging at hats. Rasul's glasses bumped Jacob's face, but he kept going, extricating his hands from his gloves so he could feel the faint trail of stubble along Jacob's cheek, down his neck.

When they ran out of air, they pressed their foreheads together and held on to each other's heads.

"Your hat went over the side, I think," Jacob said at last.

"Wasn't that great of a hat anyway." Rasul couldn't stop stroking Jacob's cheeks with his thumbs.

Jacob let his hands slip to Rasul's neck. "I was going to suggest we take the picnic to my apartment, but that seems like a bad idea now."

Oh, it seemed like an incredible idea. But Rasul could be patient. "We can eat in the car." When Jacob gave him a look, he laughed. "The front seat, you dirty-minded man." He pressed a kiss to Jacob's nose. "Then take me back. I want to go finish this story, so I can show it to you, and so...."

He dragged his thumb over Jacob's lips.

Jacob shut his eyes, and Rasul almost said screw it, and took him back to the apartment then and there. But then Jacob grabbed his hand and tugged him toward the stairs. "Your ears are red. We need to get inside."

Sighing, Rasul followed.

But as they neared the bottom, Jacob stopped and said, without turning around, "The first time will be at your apartment. In your bedroom. With the lights."

If they'd still been at the top of the lighthouse, Rasul would have leapt off the edge and flown, joyfully, into the milky November sun. "That can be arranged."

TOWARD THE end of November, Jacob started having a recurring dream that he was back in high school.

Sometimes there were mundane bits where he wandered the halls, but he always ended up at a school dance. He'd gone intermittently to dances in real life, mostly hanging out with his friends, all of whom had moved away after college. They were all back now in this dream, plus people who hadn't lived in Copper Point in high school, like Gus and Jack Wu, and Matt, who had been much younger than him. There were also people who had been years ahead of him, like Simon, Owen, and Jared. They danced together for fast songs, but when a slow dance came on, all the men who were partnered in real life went out together, plus Matt and Gus. That tracked, as they'd dated briefly when they were both in college. The end result was that Jacob was left alone, the wallflower holding a glass of punch and pretending not to care that he was by himself. Sometimes the cats showed up, Mr. Nancy winding around his feet, Susan sitting on the punch table judging everyone, Moriarty tripping people.

Always at some point Air Supply would start to play, specifically "The One That You Love." Then a very adult, very sexy Rasul would part the crowd and move forward, hand extended to Jacob, asking him to dance.

Usually this was when Jacob woke up, but sometimes he ran out of the gymnasium and into fog that never ended. He didn't have the dream often, but it was regular enough that when he heard an Air Supply song come over the radio in the grocery store, he twitched. He also started acting awkward around Rasul, which wasn't fair, but he couldn't help it.

Jacob knew the dreams were caused by stress, a lot of it brought on because of Clark's constant digs. They were subtle, but they were a regular drumbeat, and they ate at him. Just as he had with every other candidate for the chamber, Clark ragged on Jacob's business sense during meetings and to every member, stopping by their businesses to tell them why Jacob was so dangerous. Clark criticized Jacob's choices, his methodologies, his dangerous ways. The attacks held no water with Jacob's friends, but the real dangers were the neutral parties like James Petersen, who ran Petersen Home Furnishings. Petersen liked Jacob well enough, but his business was threatened every time another online retailer made it easier to shop elsewhere cheaper. It wasn't so much that he believed Jacob was a threat as he worried Clark was right, that the only way to be safe was to never change.

Jacob worried he should have had more of a campaign. Well, he *knew* he should have had one. He kept thinking of what Rasul had said on their first date, about how he should let someone else do it if he didn't want to. But he'd put his name in now. Wasn't he letting everyone down if he didn't commit? Probably.

So he tried counter-messaging, visiting the members too, listening to their concerns. He didn't promise them he could fix everything, but he did offer some tips when he had them, and he never got upset if they said they weren't sure those ideas would work. Maybe *he* wouldn't work.

"You're doing better than you think," Rebecca told him after a hospital board meeting when he mentioned his potential failure as a candidate. "Besides, Julian and I are working behind the scenes."

That gave Jacob some hope, but he kept having nightmares.

Then, three days before Thanksgiving, he didn't simply dream that he ran away from Rasul through the fog. He darted out of the gym and into the living room of his parents' house, arriving in time to see them heading out the door to the garage, waving at him and telling him they were running an errand and would be back soon.

He woke still shouting at them not to go, tears streaming down his face.

As he shook off the tendrils of the nightmare, he took in the details of his room: his bed, the dresser, the three cats sitting in a concerned circle around him. Shaking, he got up to get a glass of water.

He had the glass half full before he dropped it in the sink and collapsed against the counter, sobbing.

In the dream, he'd *known* they were departing for what would be their last ride. They wore the clothes they'd worn that day, the ones from the pictures of the event they'd been at. The ones that had been incinerated somewhere in one of the hospitals, too torn and bloody to save. He'd had variations of this dream about three years after their death, right before he'd started the bookstore. There was no way he could handle it if that dream came back. He'd rather go to the school dance naked and have Rasul laugh at him as he walked off with a troupe of models.

Rasul.

He had his phone in his hand before he realized it, had started dialing faster than he could check the time. His gaze fell on the clock, though, as Rasul picked up: 2:30 a.m. He winced.

"Hello?" Rasul's voice was only slightly rough.

"I'm sorry." Jacob shut his eyes, focused on slow breathing, but his voice was still shaky. "I shouldn't have called."

"Jacob?" Rasul became instantly clear and alert. "What happened? What's wrong?"

He meant to say *It's stupid*, but instead he whispered, "Nightmare. Parents."

"Oh, baby. Hold on. I'll be right over."

"No, no." Jacob collapsed into the sofa and shut his eyes. "I only… needed to hear your voice."

"Well, you can hear it as much as you want." There was shuffling in the background, something closing. "I need a break anyway. I think I'm producing swill at this point."

"You're still working at this hour?"

"I want to finish. And not only because I want to have a sleepover." He sighed, and Jacob could imagine him running a hand through his hair. "I went back and added a plot thread. I had a big eureka last night, which is good, but I had to retrofit things. Except I worry I'm breaking it."

"Surely you should sleep and start fresh."

"Probably? But I get into these grooves, like a trance, and I know if I stop, I'll lose it. Except there's always a point where it tips over and I'm practically writing in a made-up language. Creation rides a fine line."

"You're so much happier, though, than when you first came. You almost resented writing, but now you're doing a lot better, at least it seems like you are."

"No, you're right. A lot of it is because I chucked all my expectations out the window. I don't care what anybody thinks about this, except that I want to love it." There was a slight pause, and his voice softened. "And I want *you* to love it. That's what I'm the most worried about."

For the first time since he'd woken up, Jacob felt warm. His hand moved to his chest of its own accord. "I'm absolutely sure I will."

"No." Rasul was emphatic. "I want you to *love* it. I want it to burn you inside like it does me. I want you to feel in your bones that this was written precisely for you, because it was. It is."

Forget warm, Jacob was steaming. He fanned his face. "Um, wow."

"Not a joke, Jacob. There's so much of me in this book. So much of *us*. Not just our relationship, but us individually. I can't wait for you to see it. I want you to read Milo and not only recognize yourself but feel empowered. I want you to see parts of yourself you didn't know you had. I want you to find the ones you forgot."

Jacob couldn't have been more affected by Rasul's words even if he'd said them at the nape of his neck. The image made Jacob's knees wobble, and he went back to the sink, trying again for a glass of water. "Nobody I've ever met is as passionate as you. Nobody's ever been able to make me *feel* passion the way you do. You undo me in ways I didn't even know to plan to guard against."

There was a pause, and it went on long enough Jacob stopped with the glass of water halfway to his mouth.

"Rasul?" he said, suddenly worried.

Now Rasul sounded ragged. "Um, well." His voice cracked. "So, I was about to walk up your stairs, but now I'm trying to decide if that's a good idea."

The glass clanged in the sink as Jacob rushed across the living room, heart pounding, and unlocked the door.

At the bottom of the stairs was Rasul, standing in the fresh dusting of snow, wearing his brand-new bobble hat from the bazaar, phone to his ear as he gazed up at Jacob.

Jacob lowered his own phone, Air Supply blasting in his head.

"Come up," he told Rasul. "It's too cold to stand down there."

Rasul didn't move except to hang up his phone and put it in his pocket. "If I come up there, we both know what's going to happen."

Yes, Jacob absolutely did. "The first time is still inside the veil of stars."

God, but he loved the slowly dawning look of mischief on Rasul's face. "But there's a whole lot of other stuff we can do inside your apartment?"

Jacob motioned to him impatiently. "It's *freezing*, and I don't even have socks on."

"Then I'd better come warm you up."

They started kissing as soon as the door closed, Jacob cradling Rasul's head and holding his own lower body back while Rasul stepped out of his boots and tossed his coat aside. Then he pulled Jacob against him and went at him with a hunger that spun Jacob's head into the night sky.

"I'm so crazy about you." Rasul kissed his way along Jacob's jaw, threading his fingers into Jacob's hair. "You have no idea how much I want you. Let me show you." He nipped at Jacob's chin. "In fact, let's get in your car and go back to my place."

Jacob laughed and kissed him back, lingering. "You said it was good for your book to wait."

"I'm ridiculous. I don't know what I'm talking about." He ground a thick erection against Jacob's matching one. "I want to make love to you for six days. A month. A year. Ten years."

Jacob kissed him, long and slow, cooing into Rasul's mouth as cold hands slid beneath his waistband and cupped his ass. But when those hands slid to his hips and started to tug his pants down, Jacob pulled away and took Rasul's face in his hands.

"Look me in the eye and tell me this isn't going to break your spell."

Rasul did look him in the eye, so intently Jacob would have said yes to doing him on the stage at Founder's Day. Then Rasul sighed, shut his eyes, and sagged. "I can't do it. It sounds absolutely ridiculous and I want desperately to say it won't matter, but...."

Jacob kissed his hairline. "I can wait."

"I'm not sure *I* can." But he took a step back, clearly resigning himself. "I want to know if you have any other nightmares. I'll buzz over and kiss them away."

Jacob nodded, heart fluttering happily. "I promise I'll tell you."

"Also, I feel silly for asking so late, and I'm sure you already have plans, but what are you doing for Thanksgiving? Christmas?"

"If you're offering to cook for me, I'm coming to your place."

"Mmm, no, let's do it here. You don't have plans?"

Jacob made a mental note to call up Gus and Matt to cancel. "No plans."

"Christmas either?"

Gina would understand. "Nope, nothing."

Rasul raised his eyebrow, but he grinned. "You're telling me stories, but I suppose turnabout's fair play."

Jacob tweaked his nose. "Go home and get some sleep."

"Screw that, I'm making coffee and starting another chapter."

Jacob waved him away, then leaned against the door after he'd locked it, smiling like a giddy schoolboy for several minutes.

When he went back to sleep, he dreamed again. But this time, when Rasul asked him to dance, Jacob stepped out boldly into his arms.

Chapter Eleven

Rasul did well until Elizabeth told him he had a publication date.

"You told me we'd set one when I finished," he protested, fighting a sudden rush of bile in his throat.

"You said you were *practically* finished. I've stayed in contact with your publisher, and they let me know when there are gaps you could fill and still get decent press. There's one coming up now. It'll mean a rush editing job, and they'll be squeaking and calling in favors to get it to reviewers on time, but they're counting on the fact that everyone and their pet rock wants to read this. So your turn-in date is January 15. They wanted January 1, but I talked them into midmonth."

No question, Rasul was going to throw up after this phone call. "*It's December 10.*"

"So you've got a month and five days. You can do it."

"You want me to finish drafting, *revise*, everything in a month?"

"I do. Don't let this panic you. You can do this. You're *doing* this. Everyone is so impressed, Rasul. In fact, I'm mailing you your phone back."

"*Don't.*" Rasul shuddered. "Not until I turn the book in. The due date is bad enough. The phone would ruin everything."

Elizabeth whistled low. "You've really changed. All right, no phone until I get a manuscript."

Rasul leaned his forehead against his kitchen wall. "What happens if I miss the deadline?"

"We're not going to think about that."

He let out a breath. "Anything from Adina?"

"We're not discussing that."

"*Elizabeth.*"

"There's nothing you need to know. Do not let your head go there. Protect this book at all costs."

He did his best. He kept his head down, did his work, taught his class. His students, always in tune with his emotions, picked up on his tension. Meg, as usual, was the first one to speak up. "Professor Youssef? Are you all right? You look upset."

Four months ago he'd have lied, smiled, and given a breezy dismissal. He didn't have it in him today. "Just got some news that shook me a bit, is all."

Ron put down his pencil and regarded Rasul with concern. "What happened?"

Again. He should have dismissed this, but for whatever reason, he couldn't. "It's… well, I was going to lie and say it wasn't a big deal, but it is. My agent got a due date for my novel, and it's next month. I'm still trying to absorb it."

Stacy's eyes went wide. "So it'll be out soon?"

Rasul shook his head. "No, this is the date I need to turn it in by. It'll be out about a year from now. Slightly less, actually. Which isn't usual, but they're rushing it for me."

Ron's jaw fell. "That's *rushing*?"

Meg looked confused. "But I could put something up on Amazon *tomorrow*."

"Can't you just drop a book like Beyoncé?"

Rasul realized they'd never talked about publishing timetables before. He settled onto his stool and wiped his beard as he tried to think of where to start. "Well, if this book hadn't been sold years ago and if I hadn't been paid everything but the second half of the advance, which I get when I turn it in, yeah, I could drop it like Beyoncé. But I wouldn't get the advance reviews from big magazines and newspapers, and the marketing and publishing team and my personal publicist couldn't nurture buzz. If I weren't established already, this timeline would be too tight. They're counting on the fact that everyone will want to see what I've been doing all this time."

Tina looked so confused. "But we'd all read it now if it came out."

"*You* would, yes. But it takes time to get the word out in a big way. Usually with publishing, as an author you're always working two years ahead. By the time the book comes out, you're neck deep in the next thing." He paused as the thought dawned on him. "I think that's part of where I went astray with this book. *Carnivale* was so engrossing that I couldn't get traction on book three. To be honest, I don't like promoting my work. I get it's my job, but I'd rather work on the next thing in peace."

Stacy, one of the fanfic writers, laughed. "But you're so *good* at giving interviews. I've watched them all online a thousand times."

The others agreed enthusiastically.

Rasul felt like big pieces of awareness were dropping on him. "I didn't start writing, though, so I could be famous. I wrote because I had a story I wanted to tell. Because I love the process of creating. But all that attention pulled my focus. I think it messed with my head too. Once I got hooked, I couldn't stop, even though it wasn't making me happy."

Ron beamed. "The cotton-candy theory of parties. I love that."

"Yeah, but it's really everything. Attention is food for the moment, but once people pull away, you're left there feeling isolated, and you need another hit. It's less cotton candy and more heroin." He had to stop a minute and realize how much the past few months had been a detox.

Maybe he *never* wanted his phone back.

"But don't you need to keep up a social media presence?" Meg asked. "That's what everything I've read about marketing for authors has said."

Rasul thought of his online accounts, dusty and neglected, and how much lighter he felt because of it. "If you feel motivated by them, then go for it. But if they're a drain on your creativity, what's the point?"

Stacy looked thoughtful. "I do have a hard time writing if I leave Twitter open. I always want to check it when I'm stuck."

"Instagram is my crack," someone else said.

Rasul knew they'd never get to the official lesson today. Maybe this was the lesson they all needed, especially him. "You have to remember why you're writing. Everyone will have a different answer, but you have to have a lighthouse. *Your* lighthouse. Don't look at someone else's. If you write because it brings you joy, if you don't care about those big reviewers or those flashy release parties, then don't worry about it. Do what works for you."

"Is that what you do?" Ron asked.

Rasul drew a long breath, then let it out. "I'm trying."

They talked about publishing for the entire two-hour class, and when it was done, he felt good, but raw. Opening his phone, he texted Jacob.

Rough day. Can I see you?

The reply came back immediately. *Sure. I'm at Café Sól having a Mini Main Street meeting. Want to meet me there, or should I come to you?*

The thought of sitting at Gus's table with a cup of vacuum coffee and a cluster of empathetic friends eased his whole soul. *I'll be right over.*

WHEN RASUL entered a room, Jacob's whole universe shifted.

Gus had been pointing this out even before Rasul texted, and he and Matt had pointed to Jacob's reaction to the messages as proof of their point. Jacob had to acknowledge they were right. Rasul had affected Jacob since the man had appeared in his store. He'd been in a kind of denial about it ever since that day, pretending if he hung back, he wouldn't be too involved. But ever since the day at the lighthouse, he'd known the truth. Rasul had been his north star since his parents died, and that wasn't likely to change. If anything, Rasul being physically in his life made that light shine brighter. He'd kept him at arm's length thinking that would keep him safe, but in hindsight, he'd been lost at first contact.

As Rasul entered the back room at Gus's shop, though, crisp with cold and bright with terror as he explained he'd been given a due date he wasn't ready for—as Jacob listened and nodded along with Gus and Matt's encouragement—Jacob acknowledged this was the way things were now. If Rasul left his life, either the books would remain as his light, or he'd have to find a new guidepost. But for the first time, he realized he could handle that. He didn't want it, but ironically, because of Rasul, he *could* face that future.

Rasul tilted his head and waved a hand in front of Jacob's face. "Hello. Am I boring you?"

Jacob snapped out of his reverie. "No, sorry. Just thinking."

Rasul clasped his hand under the table and faced the others. "Anyway, enough of my whining. What were you guys talking about before I showed up?"

Before Jacob could panic, Gus put his chin in his hand. "We were debating which Disney hero we most identified with."

Rasul leaned back in his chair. "Ah. Well, that's easy. I'm Aladdin. And that's *not* because he's Arab. He's a lying sack of crap bullshitting his way through the world, smiling so nobody notices. Who were you guys?"

Jacob had been indexing the Disney heroes he knew. "Belle, I guess. Because of the bookshop."

Rasul snorted. "Please. You're Moana all the way."

Jacob's eyebrows lifted as he turned to him. "How in the world am I Moana?"

Rasul ticked the reasons off on his fingers. "You dreamed of leaving your home, you left, you figured out where your heart really was, you came back, and you led your village out of the dark and into the future. *Obviously* you're Moana."

Matt put his chin in his hand. "I'm jealous. You guys get the good ones. I'm just the mice from *Cinderella*, sewing clothes."

Gus boffed him playfully in his shoulder. "Get off. You're Shang all the way."

Matt straightened, blushing a little. "Really? You think so?"

Rasul grinned. "I agree completely."

Jacob loved this game. "Who are you, Gus?"

"I'm clearly Meg." He sipped his coffee with an arch look.

Matt rubbed his hands together. "Let's do the rest of the QUAG gang."

They all had a good time assigning roles to their friends—Owen was immediately dubbed the Beast, and Erin was Belle. Jared was Anna from *Frozen*, and Nick was Hercules. Simon was Ariel. They struggled with Jack until Rasul declared him to be Jim Hawkins. When everyone else didn't know who that was and said they hadn't seen *Treasure Planet*, Rasul threw up his hands and insisted they have a movie night as soon as he turned in his book.

"Oh, hey, being here with the three of you reminds me." Rasul turned to Jacob. "How's your candidacy going? Is that codger still bothering you?"

Jacob sighed. "Yes, but I'm trying to hold my own. There's not much to do but keep showing up places, trying not to look bothered."

Gus waved a finger at him. "Not true. The chamber ball is coming up. You can make a killer raffle basket for the auction."

Rasul shook his head. "You guys are always having parties in this town. Is there dancing at this one too?"

"*Always* dancing." Gus laughed. "Though I doubt anything will ever top your show at the university gala last year."

Matt waggled his eyebrows at Gus. "Maybe you'll take Ben to the ball this year?"

Gus swatted him on the shoulder. "Don't even dare give him that idea."

Matt turned a twinkling gaze to Jacob. "Any chance you'll let me start you a custom suit this time?"

Jacob started to decline, but Rasul elbowed him gently. "You've got to let him. Matt's a genius, and he'll set you up right."

Jacob frowned. "But he wants to make it flashy, I just know it."

Instead of ribbing Jacob as expected, Matt frowned back, looking affronted. "Hey. I know who you are, what you like, what you don't. I wouldn't put you in something that would make you uncomfortable."

Gus nodded. "I agree. Besides, he'll consult you on the way. Let him do this."

Why everyone suddenly wanted Jacob to have a suit, he couldn't begin to guess. "It's too expensive a gift, especially for something I'd rarely wear."

"Oh, you'll wear it." Matt's eyes sparkled, and Jacob realized there was no escaping now.

He sighed. "Fine."

"And you won't pay for it either," Matt added. When Jacob started to sputter, Matt held up his hand. "No arguments. It'll be your Christmas present."

"Christmas *and* birthday present." Jacob folded his arms over his chest and stared Matt down.

"I can work with that." Matt sighed. "Honestly, with the way everything is going, I'm going to need that much time."

"Certainly no need to rush." Jacob turned to the others. "Can we please talk about something else now?"

They planned their respective business baskets for a little while, but eventually they declared it was late and everyone took their leave. As Matt and Rasul chatted near the door, Gus pulled Jacob back.

"Hey, I was meaning to tell you. You might want to go pop onto the Instagram of that model he used to date. She's posting some interesting stuff." When Jacob cut a glance to Rasul, Gus shook his head. "No. Don't get him involved yet. I don't want to harsh his groove. But maybe log in sometime and check. I'm probably overthinking things, but I wanted to give somebody a heads-up."

"Got it," Jacob said.

Rasul didn't have the haunted look he'd had when he arrived anymore, and as Jacob bid him goodbye, Rasul assured him with a peck on his cheek that he was great now and was hurrying home to get some writing in before he had to go to bed.

When Jacob got home, he didn't go to bed, either. After feeding the cats, he curled up on the couch with his iPad and purchased *Moana*.

He'd seen the movie when it first came out, going with Matt and Gus because, as they'd lamented, the Lin-Manuel Miranda–penned songs in it were as close as they were going to get to *Hamilton*. Never had it occurred to Jacob to identify with the heroine, however, not on the level Rasul suggested. So he revisited the tale with new eyes that night before he went to bed.

It was a great film, and the music, especially the Miranda-penned songs, were amazing. To his astonishment, he was able to see why Rasul compared him to Moana. He *had* left his island wanting to see the world. He *had* decided home was better, but that perhaps home could be slightly more open-minded. Even his loss was represented, in several ways. And he did relate to the idea that he could only venture forward with the backing of his people. The ones he got along with, and the ones he struggled to accept.

What got him, as always, was when Moana gave Te Fiti her heart back.

He'd wept in the theater without knowing why, but revisiting the scene now, it resonated all the way into his core, into his own heart. Because despite what Rasul had said, *Jacob* had been Te Fiti. It was Rasul, through his work, who had walked boldly up to him and shown him who he was, reminded him that *only he* defined who he was. That despite loss and devastation, he could make himself okay.

At the same time, he did understand that now, for Rasul, the roles had reversed. Except the metaphor was so much stronger this time. Like Te Fiti to Moana, Rasul had been the one to show Jacob what strength meant. Now it was Jacob's privilege to hold up a mirror for his hero, his friend, his lover.

To hand him back his heart. To help him heal himself so he could go back to healing everyone who read his work.

Would it hurt if Rasul left Copper Point once his tenure was up, if at best Jacob received the occasional email? Yes. It absolutely would. But he wouldn't say no to this relationship, not anymore, not ever again.

Because Rasul wasn't a god. He was a man who got lost the same as Jacob did.

It would be his honor, Jacob thought, to show him the way home. Wherever that home might be.

Chapter Twelve

BY CHRISTMAS, Rasul lost all sense of time and space.

His class on break, his office hours suspended, with Jacob and practically the whole town teaming up to stock his fridge and even, to his chagrin and humility, doing his laundry, Rasul practically lived in his manuscript. The fact that he wrote about two people manipulating time and space didn't help him either. Several times he'd worked so long his wrists and forearms screamed, and he had to go to the Chinese masseuses out in the strip mall to regain functionality, and even while they worked on him, his mind raced ahead to fill in the spaces in the story still needing attention. On the rare occasions he spent time with other humans in a conversational setting, he fell asleep midsentence regularly. Jacob and the others took to not only bringing over food but seeing that he ate it, and despite the bitter December cold, Jacob frequently walked Rasul's zombified self along the greenbelt to give him a moment's grounding in reality.

Christmas was a kind of dream, Jacob taking over the meal despite Rasul's original promise to do the cooking. They snuggled together in Jacob's living room after, a holiday movie playing that didn't remotely register with Rasul because his brain wouldn't stop writing.

"I worry about you," Jacob said, massaging Rasul's weary fingers and wrist. "I think you might be working too hard."

"Probably. But I want to finish." He let his body go slack against Jacob, shifting to provide his other hand for treatment. "I want you to read it. I want to turn it in. I want to feel like I can still do this."

"Is it okay for me to ask how close you are to the end?"

"Normally, no. Right now, it's okay." Rasul shut his eyes as Jacob's ministrations hit just the right spot. "I'm in the middle of the dark moment. I'd have been all the way to the end by now if I'd let myself revise after, but I'm super invested in handing it to you as fast as possible before I get too invested in big edits. So I keep going over old sections, adding things, moving them, expanding. There are only about eight scenes ahead of me, but it's going slower because of the way I'm drafting and editing at the same time."

"I'll forever have a new appreciation for how hard authors work after this."

Rasul shrugged. "I don't think it's always like this. It wasn't like this the last two times for me. The stakes are just so high."

He thought about those stakes all the time. He stayed up late that night once Jacob had gone to bed, stopping work on the scene he'd been on to go back to the midsection, the opening, several big reveals, scraping over every detail as if it might be the one that redeemed him, that took him to a new place.

If I get this done, he kept telling himself, *everything is going to change.* He couldn't articulate what that change would be. He only knew in his soul that his whole life would pivot around this point and take him to a new dimension.

Maybe it was because this was his first queer main character, a character with his own ethnic identity. A character who yearned the way he did, who got lost the way he did, who screwed up the way he did. Several delirious nights as he got too lost in the dimension-creating storyline, he became convinced writing this novel would heal all the hurts of his youth.

Because he was putting them all in. Coded, remixed so he had to draw on the distilled nature of them, not the fine details, but he included them all. His confusion and sorrow over his parents' disinterest in his life. His frustration as a teenager of not understanding what his identity was—was he Syrian? Brazilian? American? All three? Did it matter that to a lot of people, he passed for white? Was it okay that he buried parts of himself to fit in? Was it bad that he partied and lied to everyone, including himself, about who he was, just for a moment's peace?

Above all, though, he soaked himself in the central, vibrating question: What would have happened if, when he was smiling and pretending he wasn't cracking and hollow inside, someone like Jacob had appeared before him and led him to a place of peace? What would have changed if he'd accepted that hand?

He had an index card taped to the top of his laptop that read, in black Sharpie, WHAT IS HAPPINESS? Whenever he was stuck, he stared at it.

Whenever it was late at night and he was alone inside the veil of stars, he answered it, usually out loud.

"Happiness is knowing peace within myself."

He gave that peace to Adam as best he could. He empowered Adam and Milo both, but to Adam in particular, he paved a way to understanding and accepting himself and his path. Showing him how to find the way through to the light, which came from his own heart.

I'm okay. I've always been okay. I can be okay whenever I want, no matter what happens.

He wrote a love scene for the boys. He knew his editors wouldn't like it, that they'd say young adult novels shouldn't have sex, people underage, etc. Thinking of Judy Blume and *Forever*, he didn't just ignore his editor's anticipated objections, he wrote the sex in a way that would make it absolutely impossible to remove. In some kind of strange move by the universe, his thermostat broke the night he wrote that scene, sending his apartment above eighty degrees. He wrote the scene naked with ethereal Middle Eastern vocals blasting in his headphones, a towel draped over the wrist pad of his laptop to catch the sweat. He made the characters sweat too, giving them the intense, passionate union he knew they deserved. He made Adam say to Milo everything he longed to say to Jacob.

Everything he fully intended to say.

He wept several times while he wrote, sometimes at points that made sense, sometimes in some kind of release-valve catharsis that didn't come from the scene but from the act of finishing the story itself. Well before he wrote the final chapter, he understood fully that he *was* completing this. That no matter what his editors, his agent, the literary world thought about it, this was the book he'd needed to write. That for him, it was already exactly what it needed to be.

He knew, in his bones, that it was exactly what Jacob needed it to be too.

It was two in the afternoon on December 31 that he wrote the last words of the final scene. It felt so... random, so off script, but that's when it came. Had it been the middle of the night, he'd have gone out into the snowy street and shouted, but it was midday and people were bustling about, getting ready for New Year's Eve parties. He thought about doing it anyway. He thought about renting one of those trucks with a megaphone and announcing it to the town.

He thought about calling Jacob, and he almost did. But then he stopped.

No. I'm going to see him in person. I'm going to do this right.

He made a frantic call to Evan Clare, who enthusiastically met him at the college and approved his three-hundred-and-fifty-page double-spaced, single-sided printout. He went to the florist, the chocolatier, and even the thrift shop. He packed up the things he needed at home, made a call to Gina, and when she arrived, loaded himself and a bulging suitcase into her car.

He sweated a little as he sat in the parking lot behind the bookstore long after she went inside, shutting his eyes and giving himself one last pep talk. Then he grabbed everything and went in through the front door.

He looked past the customers to the man behind the counter. The man in the soft blue cardigan patiently going over his sales figures. The man who looked up at him, surprised, then smiled with warmth behind those brown eyes.

Heart galloping, Rasul strode up the counter, plunked down the box. Waited.

As he watched Jacob open the lid, face lighting up with surprise and joy at what he saw inside—a printed manuscript surrounded by a chain of flowers and battery-operated lights and weighed down by a box of gourmet chocolate—Rasul felt the universe opening up for him the way it had for Adam. Ever-changing, always racing, but anchored in every way around the central point of this man.

He let out a breath as his heart sighed and settled, finally, into place.

JACOB'S ENTIRE nervous system began to hum as he realized what was in the box in front of him. Heart beating in what felt like triplicate, the world narrowing, he met Rasul's wild gaze. "This is…?"

Rasul nodded. "Finished. A bit rough still, but… yeah. Finished."

Jacob ran his hand over the title page. *VEIL OF STARS by Rasul Youssef.* In the upper right corner it said *80,000 words.*

The flowers that surrounded it were white, and they glowed slightly. He realized there were tiny battery-powered lights embedded within them.

Rasul rubbed the back of his head. "The lights and… everything is a little cheesy, but… well."

Jacob ran his hand over the box of chocolates—all his favorites—the flowers, the manuscript heading. "Backlit flowers, chocolates, and the first look at my favorite author's manuscript. Are you flirting with me, Rasul Youssef?"

"God yes."

There were customers in the shop, but Jacob didn't care about them, not now. His whole world was the box in front of him. "I wish I could start reading right away."

"You can." Rasul jerked his head toward the door where Gina stood waiting. "I called Gina, and she's going to come help me close up. I'll work the register. You go upstairs and start reading. I'll get things to make dinner."

"Are you sure?" Jacob couldn't look away from the manuscript.

"Completely and utterly. I'm barely going to be able to breathe until you finish. Please start reading right now."

Jacob would, gladly. But first….

He went around the counter, kissed Rasul softly on the cheek, and drew him into his arms. "I'm so proud of you."

Rasul clutched at his back. "You haven't read it yet. It might suck. You might be completely disappointed in me."

"Impossible. But even if I were, that doesn't matter. You finished it. You worked so hard. You did a good job."

"Thank you." Rasul shivered as Jacob kissed, then licked his neck. "Go read."

Jacob all but ran to the door leading to the apartment, pressing the box to his chest as he fumbled with the key. He took the stairs two at a time, or as best he could manage, sailing over the waiting Moriarty. He trembled as he put water on for tea, as he arranged a reading nest for himself on the couch. Once his tea was ready, he tucked himself in, drew a breath, and pulled aside the cover page.

The sheet of paper beneath it had two lines.

> *For Jacob*
> *who showed me what lay beyond the veil*

Beneath that was Rasul's scrawled signature, complete with a rough and endearing heart.

Jacob put a hand over his mouth and stared at the paper for several seconds, his eyes filling with tears. Then, with a sigh, he wiped them away with a tissue, the box of which he'd strategically placed on the tea tray beside him.

"Making me cry even before page one," he murmured and flipped the page again.

He started reading.

When he'd first picked up Rasul's book in the hospital gift shop, Jacob had been taken aback by the power of Rasul's narrative style, the way it pulled the reader hard and fast into the fictional world, the way it made everything around the reader bloom in a rich, breathless fashion. Critics praised him for this skill too, and it was considered his signature. In those first two books, he'd written in an engaging but omnipotent third-person past.

Veil of Stars was written in stark, immediate first-person present.

He still drew Jacob in like he'd been sucked through a black hole into another world, but the point of view he'd chosen made Jacob feel as if these were *his* hands, as if these nervous gulps for air came from his own lungs.

I walk through the gauntlet of a thousand friends, smiling as I receive their greetings and praise, knowing I'm utterly alone.

The surrealist bent Rasul was known for began right away, as the hero, Adam Hasan, described what had first been a metaphorical but had become a physical veil between him and the world around him. The more Adam pushed himself to pretend it wasn't there, the thicker it became. Adam spoke of the invisible barrier between him and the world cavalierly, but at the same time, it was clear the veil bothered him. His panic and despair bled through his dismissals.

But then Milo Bloom appeared.

Jacob knew instantly Adam had a crush on Milo, but for the entire first few chapters, Adam made a point of denying it, taking intense pains to insist he focused on him only because he stood out among the crowd, that somehow he seemed to pierce the veil. A shame, Adam lamented, because Milo *wasn't* his friend, just someone he knew. Yet of course he knew so much more about this boy than anyone else at his school.

As he turned page after page, stacking the read pieces of paper beside him on the tray, Jacob descended further and further into the imaginary world. As Adam's reality shifted and swirled around him,

Jacob quickly lost his sense of time and place, real and imagined, along with the protagonist. The only constant was that no matter how the universe shifted around him, Milo was always there somewhere, was always a focal point, and Adam couldn't shake the feeling that if he only made contact with Milo, the universe would right again. The two traveled back in time, into alternate dimensions, into the future. Sometimes their schoolmates and families came along and sometimes didn't, but always, Milo was there.

When Jacob got to the part where Adam began to suspect Milo was *aware* he was traveling through space and time, a touch on his shoulder made him surface from the story. Blinking, struggling to focus, he looked up to see Rasul standing beside him with a tray of food.

"It's past seven. Time to eat." Rasul set the tray on the ottoman, shifted the pile of read manuscript pages to the floor, and moved the tray closer to Jacob.

Jacob glanced worriedly at the papers that had been set aside. "Don't step on them."

Rasul looked amused. "I can print you three hundred more just like them."

"No, you can't. This is the one you printed for me and surrounded with lights and flowers and weighed down with chocolate."

Rasul nudged the box, the ribbon still around it. "You haven't even eaten the chocolate."

Jacob lifted his chin. "I didn't want to get the pages dirty."

Rasul put his hands on his hips. "You're not even halfway through. You're going to have to stop and eat."

Though Jacob would have protested more, he smelled the fragrant stew and fresh bread from the tray beside him. "Fine. I'll eat while I read."

Rasul bit his lip. "Is it okay?"

Jacob gave him a long look. "I'm unwilling to put it down long enough to put food in my body, and you dare ask that question?"

Rasul sighed and turned away. "Read faster, then."

"You can't bully me into rushing this. I've waited forever for this book."

Rasul made *yeah, yeah* motions with his hand and retreated to the kitchen.

For a few moments Jacob was aware of the tick of the clock, the clink of dishes and water in the sink, Rasul humming softly to himself as he worked, and then the world fell away as Jacob melted back into the story. He cradled the bowl of stew against his body, warming his hands as he ate the food and ingested each page.

It was an unconventional, drawn-out courtship, Jacob realized as Adam and Milo started working together, neither of them confirming they were from a different dimension but both, it seemed, highly suspecting it. Adam admitted, at least to himself, that he was in love with Milo, and he sometimes dared to dream Milo might feel the same way. He worried a lot, though, that he was projecting onto him, that perhaps Milo wasn't even there with him.

At ten, with half the box of chocolates gone and several pots of tea having sent him to the bathroom multiple times (he took manuscript pages with him), Jacob hit the middle of the book, where Adam's longing for Milo sent them both into a tiny pocket universe, a craggy and ethereal lighthouse surrounded by a veil of stars. On the deck of that space, Adam spoke to Milo, admitting that he was aware of everything happening, that he remembered every jump, and that he was sure he'd somehow been accidentally been manipulating the universe and its dimensions. He also learned that Milo thought *he* was the one manipulating everything.

The two of them teamed up to try to solve the mystery of what was happening to them, learning the lighthouse was the central point from which all their manipulated universes converged, and with effort they could choose which one to leap to next. But when they found the one they were fairly sure led back to their own timeline and dimension, Adam panicked, not wanting to go back to the world where he wasn't with Milo. His reluctance destroyed their jump and sent them into alternate worlds where they weren't together, and the only way to make it back to the lighthouse was to admit to the void how he felt about Milo, for Milo to shout it back. When they arrived at the lighthouse again, they were awkward around each other for a few seconds, then gave up, kissed passionately, and fell from the ledge into a universe of softness and wonder.

Rasul had written sex in his other novels, but it had been just that, a manipulation of bodies or a descent into pleasure. It had never been a union like this, a personal, meaningful connection, an exploration of each other. It touched Jacob, made him nostalgic, and aroused him.

Eventually, the boys acknowledged they should go back to their world. Though they vowed to stay together, Milo worried aloud that perhaps none of this was real either. That Adam was a figment of his imagination. That Adam, or he, would forget upon reentry. Adam tried to dismiss this playfully, but it worried him too. What would happen if they went back and nothing had changed?

They make love one last time, not exactly a goodbye but something like it, a grounding in case the worst happened. In case they got lost in other dimensions this time and couldn't find each other again. In case they both forgot. As they leapt through the veil for the last time, they held hands until the pressure tugged them apart.

As Adam fell, he felt the magic that had pulled him into this universe twist and fade away, rendering him a normal seventeen-year-old boy. He started to doubt his adventures had happened. He doubted if Milo had ever been there at all. When he woke, he was in his bed, his mother fussing about him having a fever.

He anguished as his memories of the veil begin to fade, but he held on to the memory of the stars, insisting they remained even only as a vague, distant field inside his mind. When he finally went back to school, his stomach churning with nerves, he did his best to prepare for the fact that Milo might not recognize him, might not care. He held tight to the feeling, real or imagined, that they'd had a connection, and told himself even if he was the only one who still possessed it, it would be enough. He acknowledged he was the one who put himself behind the veil, that even if he had to build it all over again, he *could* do it, that even if he could never connect with Milo in this reality, he could connect with someone else this way. That no matter who he found or who he lost, he could always find a way to be okay, starting with loving himself.

Jacob had to stop and blow his nose and hold tissues to his eyes.

Then he read to the end of the story. He read how Adam walked through the crush of people, pushed aside the veil, went straight up to Milo, and said hello.

Milo turned, smiled, and Adam felt the rush of the universes surrounding them, lifting them up, carrying them forward into new adventures.

In the margins of the last page, filling every available inch of space, was Rasul's handwriting, the same thing over and over and over.

I love you. I love you. I love you. I love you. I love you.

The paper crinkled in Jacob's hand as his vision blurred, until he couldn't stand it anymore. Putting the page down in his lap, he covered his eyes with his palms and sobbed. And sobbed. And sobbed.

I love you. I love you. I love you. I love you. I love you.

Still wiping his eyes, he displaced the cats from his legs and stumbled through the apartment, but he couldn't find Rasul anywhere. For a second he felt a flare of despair and betrayal—he'd said he wouldn't leave—but then Jacob remembered there was another floor to the building.

Trembling, he crept down the stairs and into the bookstore.

It was full of stars.

The netting and lights from Rasul's apartment were here now, making a tunnel through the stacks to an open area in the back, where Rasul sat in an easy chair, wearing his glasses and reading. He glanced up as Jacob approached.

He looked hopeful, but mostly terrified.

Jacob froze, too many competing emotions inside him to allow a reaction. He wanted to be cool like Milo and smile, to mirror the end of the novel. He wanted to sob and ask Rasul how he dared to do such a thing, to reach all the way inside him and pull him inside out, to mimic *I Capture the Castle* in subtle and overt ways. He wanted to thank him. He wanted to drag him into his arms and make love to him.

He wanted to tug him into their own magical universe and never, ever leave.

In the end, all he could do was whisper a ragged "Rasul," and sag against the nearest bookshelf, draped in acres of tulle and dotted with lights.

Putting aside his book, Rasul rose, crossed to Jacob, and pulled him into an embrace.

Their kiss was wild, drugging, a desperate attempt to convey emotions that would not fit into words. At some point one of them tugged at the tulle, they slipped, and then they were rolling around on the floor, literally wrapped in a veil of stars.

"I love you," Rasul whispered in the nook beneath Jacob's ear, along his jaw. "I love you more than anyone or anything."

"I love you more." Jacob curled into him, the lasts walls of resistance, futile as they were, crumbling inside him. "Your book is wonderful. Perfect. I never wanted it to end."

"It's for you. Every word. I don't care if anyone else likes it or not. Only that you do. It's yours."

"Everyone will love it. It's your best work by leaps and bounds." He clutched at Rasul's shoulder, the back of his head. "If I could have found a book like that when I was seventeen...."

"I know. I know." He kissed Jacob's cheek, his chin, sucked on his bottom lip. "I want to make love to you. Right here in the middle of your bookstore, surrounded by lights and tulle with my book still burning your brain."

Jacob wrapped his arms, his legs, his soul around Rasul. "Yes."

Their kiss was full of fire and passion, but it was a conflagration springing from months of stoked kindling and well-tended embers. Not a flash but a crest, an unstoppable force that ignited something deep within Jacob. It cracked open the part of him he'd kept shuttered away, the part of him that had decided years ago to draw him to the side, to keep him quiet, to create a veneer of safety out of the fact that he was only partially living. Freed, Jacob unfurled, a sail catching the wind from their joined blaze, lifting him out of the shadows, sending him directly into the flames.

Gripping Rasul's hair, he kissed him hard and deep, as if he could take the marrow from him. Tongues and teeth clashed, hands grabbed and tugged as they tried to climb inside one another. Clothes came away, skin scraped against skin. Jacob shivered as his fingers brushed Rasul's nipple, delighted as, when he made another pass to stroke it, Rasul was the one trembling.

He'd never dared to dream of something like this. Not with Rasul, not with anyone.

He wouldn't ever stop dreaming again.

Rasul practically purred as Jacob pushed him onto his back and straddled him. "I knew you had this in you. This fire. I saw it at the gala. I couldn't get it out of my mind."

"I'm going to fuck you, Rasul Youssef," Jacob declared as he parted his lover's legs and settled between them. "I'm going to claim every inch of your body and turn you so inside out you can't speak. We'll have to sleep in the stacks, because neither one of us is going to be able to walk."

Rasul's gaze was soft, unfocused, wild with lust and love. "Get to it, then."

Jacob did. He licked his way down Rasul's body, across his chest, nipping at the curling hair there, sucking at the quavering skin of his belly. Whenever Rasul tugged at him, trying to urge him on, Jacob gently pushed his hands away.

"You won't rush me." He dragged his nose down the side of the vee leading to Rasul's groin, his bobbing cock. "This time it's going to be about you. About pleasuring you. No performing for your partner like you usually do. No worrying about me. My pleasure tonight is seeing to yours. Just the way you've always wished it would happen."

Rasul gasped, his hands clutching weakly at Jacob's head. "How—?"

"It was a hunch before, but when I read the sex scene, I knew." Jacob pushed Rasul's knees back and kissed the inside of each thigh lovingly, as if he had an eternity to shower them with attention. "The longing Adam had as he reached for Milo, the way his whole soul let go when Milo took charge. Plus it just makes sense. Everyone thinks you're some legendary lover. Everyone's trying to use you. I never will, Rasul. I swear to you, I never, ever will."

Rasul put a hand over his eyes, but he couldn't hold back the quiet sob.

Jacob lifted his head to kiss Rasul's abdomen once more. "Let go. You've done so much. For yourself, for me, for so many people. Relax and enjoy this. I think we've both earned it."

Rasul did relax, at least until the blowjob Jacob gave him sent him writhing. Jacob drew their lovemaking out as long as he could, stoking Rasul's arousal only to cool him down with kisses against the back sides of his knees, to flip him onto his stomach and kiss the globes of his ass before parting them and making him howl with want. By the time he was actually ready to fuck him, Rasul was a limp noodle Jacob had to hold up and arrange into position.

"You're my everything," Jacob whispered to him as he drove inside, as Rasul clung weakly to his shoulders, head tipped back as he let Jacob ride him. "My whole world."

As they crashed back to earth, with the veil of stars twinkling beneath their bodies, Jacob pressed a kiss to Rasul's ear.

"I love you, Rasul."

Rasul buried his face in Jacob's neck. "I love you too."

Chapter Thirteen

THEY CRAWLED up the stairs to Jacob's bed around four in the morning. Or rather, Jacob hauled Rasul and his bandy-legged ass up the stairs. He was still weak in the knees at nine when his bladder insisted he waddle to the bathroom, and as he fell back into the mattress, snuggling against Jacob's warm back, he reveled in the sensation of a well-used backside.

It had been a long, long time since he'd been fucked like that. Not just the epic edging but the demand he surrender in every way. Absolutely nobody, though, had ever ordered him to quit trying to please them and simply let himself be done.

Sweet God Almighty, but he could get used to that.

He really, really wanted to get used to that.

When he next woke, it was one in the afternoon, his stomach was eating itself, and Jacob sat in the bed beside him.

Reading the manuscript.

"Again?" Rasul pushed himself groggily onto an elbow and leaned against his lover.

"Yes, again." Jacob laid the page he'd been reading neatly on the pile on the other side of him. "I always read your books several times in a row before I even begin to let myself think too much about them. Why you think this one would be any different is beyond me."

Rasul kissed Jacob's elbow, then nestled his head against his hip. "Is it weird this time, because you know me?"

"It's different for a lot of reasons. Part of my brain is still processing that I fucked you on a visible representation of the story in the middle of the stacks. Right next to the romance section. Did you do that on purpose?"

Rasul had, but he'd never admit it. "It was closest to the door."

Jacob ruffled Rasul's hair idly. "You worked very hard on the story, and it shows. Have you sent it to your agent yet?"

"No." He found Jacob's hand and tangled their fingers together. "I wanted you to read it first, to give me feedback."

"My feedback is that it's excellent."

"It has some rough spots. I think I could tie a few things together better. It doesn't vibrate right yet in my head. I was hoping I could ask you about some of it."

"Of course you can."

Rasul did. He started while they lay there in bed, until his stomach gurgles grew loud enough Jacob insisted they relocate to the kitchen. Once there, he tried to make breakfast, but Jacob waved him into a chair. "I can cook you some oatmeal. Unless you'd rather have lunch, since it's afternoon? Also, tea or coffee?"

"Oatmeal and coffee sound perfect, thank you. Can I have raisins and brown sugar? In the oatmeal."

"Of course."

While Jacob cooked and brewed coffee, Rasul continued to voice his concerns over the draft. Sometimes Jacob interjected questions or remarks, but mostly he listened. As Rasul had anticipated, Jacob had good judgment. He didn't hesitate to point out if something that bothered Rasul hadn't seemed an issue to him, and on a few notable occasions he turned around and quietly threatened Rasul if he changed a particular part. Other times he either agreed with Rasul's assessment that something could be revisited, and twice Jacob suggested places to look at again himself.

"This is an interesting exercise," Jacob said. "I honestly enjoyed it as it was, but I can see how editing shapes a story into exactly what you need it to be. Or perhaps the more appropriate phrase is what you *want* it to be."

Rasul nodded as he took another hearty swig of coffee. "Especially with how they all got their hands on this one when I was initially creating it, I want to keep it safe until I'm sure it's right—to me. I anticipate them balking at the sex scene."

"Why on earth would they do that? It's amazing. It illustrates so much about what each of them needs, and shows them giving it to one another. It's practically essential to believing the ending will be a happy one."

"Thank you." He clutched at his mug. "They'd want to cut it because marketing likes to err on the side of safe. The problem is they're underage."

"They're seventeen. Heavens, even in Copper Point *I'd* had sex by then. Is it because it's two men?"

"Probably in part? People have random moral boundaries regarding sex in media, especially in the United States." He scratched his head. "I thought about setting it with them in college, but it's absolutely not the same. It's that sense of being not quite hatched, still in your family's cradle, but biologically and mentally a functional adult. Honestly, I don't think it's a young adult novel, not in the sense people usually mean. It's a novel for adults who had a messed-up teenage experience and want to rewrite it."

"No, it's for a certain kind of teen too. Someone tuned in to that sense of being on the cusp, who understands all your universal metaphors in a way only they can. An adult reading sees those time and place shifts as a way of going back to their own experience, their wish for better outcomes even as they acknowledge their path had to be their path. For a teen, they represent possible futures, safe ways of exploring. This is going to blow people out of the water." He shrugged. "And probably upset some people too. But how is that different from your first two books?"

"Yeah, the blowback on *Carnivale* was rough." He scratched his chin, thinking. "You know, I can't get over how much calmer and freer I am when I'm not on social media. I also know more people here than I ever did in LA. Some of that is the function of geography, I'm sure, but I also attribute it to having to actually go talk to people with my face."

"You'll want to go back at least in part once you're done drafting. You like to be on the pulse of things."

A subtle thread of tension in Jacob's tone made Rasul glance up, and he saw the answering lines on Jacob's face. Something about *you'll want to go back* had extra meaning.

Oh. Rasul's coffee turned into sludge in his stomach. Jacob was talking about social media, but he was thinking about Rasul leaving Copper Point.

It was the first crack in their harmonious bubble. Rasul had been so focused on simply finishing, on shedding the albatross of failure from his neck. Of going to bed with Jacob, of sharing his story. The future hadn't seemed to contain anything else.

It was here now. He needed new goals, but he didn't have any.

Clearly the future had never been far from Jacob's mind.

Rasul clutched at his mug. "I don't want to go back to who I was before I came here."

"You *are* the person you were before you came here. You can't change who you are."

"I can get my shit together." Moriarty was huddled on the chair next to him, and Rasul absently stroked the cat's head. "I think this book rattled me so hard in part because I've been trying to have a conversation with myself for a long time, and now I've had it. I didn't want to be scared anymore. Not so much that I had to stay on the run from invisible demons. And as for social media and staying on the pulse of things—you're right, I enjoy it to a point. But I don't want it to be something I let consume me ever again the way it did. There were too many days I didn't open Instagram or Twitter, curious to see what was happening in the world. I opened the apps braced for battle. How is that helpful? I mean, at least Adina has gotten over me, but there will always be an Adina."

"Oh, Adina isn't over you."

Rasul had been focusing on the cat, but with that remark, his head whipped up. So did his heart rate. "What are you talking about?"

Gaze averted, Jacob sipped his coffee. "I… might have opened a personal Instagram to keep tabs on what was going on."

Jacob had the same badass look he'd worn when he was fucking Rasul the night before. If what he was saying hadn't been so unsettling, Rasul would have played footsie under the table and tried to coax him back to bed. He couldn't ignore this, though. "What's going on? What happened?"

"Word has gotten out, probably through your agent or editor or someone, that you were close to finishing your book. A lot of people are talking about it, including Adina. She's sort of been hinting for a while, but two days ago she out-and-out said you've worked out your differences and are back together. She's so proud of you, she says."

Rasul couldn't believe this. "Why in the world would she do that? Never mind. I know why. But…. Jesus, you and I did that whole thing where we had the fake relationship. And now the real one."

He remembered that DM she sent, saying she knew he wasn't really dating, and went cold.

"The funny thing is," Jacob said, "we documented our relationship better when it was fake. Perhaps that's it."

Rasul didn't think so. "I worry there's someone here feeding her information." He told Jacob about the DM, about giving his accounts to Elizabeth to monitor.

Jacob looked pensive. "It's possible we have a mole here somewhere, but it doesn't completely hold up. We *are* dating. We've been serious about each other... well, honestly, I think I was from the start, only in denial."

"Me too. But not in denial."

Jacob took his hand. "My point is, that shows. If we'd legitimately been faking our relationship, people would have wondered about it. So if there's someone who is telling her we're not dating, they're either very poorly informed or have their own agenda." He tapped his finger on the top of the table. "I still think the problem is there's nothing showing we're dating as far as the world is concerned. A few people here took some updates as intended at first, but since we haven't gone on public dates in a while and you've been working hard for some time, not really leaving the house, there's nothing more for people to post. And online a few people tried to say they thought we were still together. A few of them are local, in fact—at the college, where they're not as plugged in to what's going on in Copper Point proper. But every time someone tries to counter the narrative Adina is pushing, they get attacked."

Rasul ran a hand through his hair. "God, she must really be struggling in her efforts to get noticed if she's recycling our relationship like this."

"Or she honestly has feelings for you."

Rasul considered Jacob's point. "I suppose? Possibly? But I really don't think so. She has a lot of drive, but she also likes shortcuts. It's why her career isn't doing well. She'll work harder to pull one over on people or arrange a side hustle than she will on actively trying to put herself forward in a way that would help her. I think she gets too angry with how rough the business is and convinces herself she deserves better and this justifies whatever means she wants to use."

"Why exactly did you date her again?"

"I never dated her like you're thinking. It was more that we got together on the regular, which is a kind of dating, but we didn't have long deep talks or anything. We partied and we fucked. I hooked up with her because she's hot and because she can be charming and intriguing when she's not manically chasing her doomed career. Also at the time I was even more messed up than she was. Misery loves company, and she felt like a way out. Or a faster way down the drain. Depended on the day."

Jacob humphed and set down his cup.

Rasul studied the man in front of him, thinking about how much he cared for him, thinking for the first time what a future with him would be like. Never had he so much as considered staying in Copper Point, but it dawned on him that staying with Jacob meant remaining here. Jacob had roots, and that was part of what attracted Rasul to him. You didn't take Moana off her island. You learned to live on the island.

Right now, though, his Moana was jealous and annoyed. He wanted to fix that. "I can log on to my Insta on your phone and snap a picture of us, right now. That would solve the whole thing."

Jacob pursed his lips. "I admit this isn't my area of expertise. But I think they're in a frenzy and this will only become food. They seem attached to the narrative of you back with Adina, and injecting facts and logic only makes them furious. For you to appear after a long absence and suddenly post a photo, then vanish again? I suspect they'll think it's fake."

Rasul sighed. "You're probably right, dammit."

"If *I* posted one, tagged your account, and started updating more regularly with photos of you, *that* might work."

Rasul sat upright. "Holy hell, baby, I don't think you understand the kind of trolling you're going to get if you do that."

"No, I do. I've been reading the comments on Adina's page, and yours. Honestly, I'm amazed you wrote anything at all with that filling your head."

"You read that stuff and you want to voluntarily step into it?"

"I can turn off notifications and not read the comments."

"That's a lot easier said than done."

"You're right. I suspect I would learn a lot from this exercise. But I think that's part of why I want to do this."

The quietly fierce expression was back. Rasul's libido pushed aside his worries for his partner and purred at the idea of being protected. He also could read the subtext again, both in what Jacob said and how he said it.

I intend to keep you, if I can.

Rasul reached up to stroke Jacob's cheek. "I'll send your account information to Elizabeth, and I'll have her find someone to monitor the comments for threats and report them immediately. Actually, send the information for the bookstore's Instagram too, and warn Gina. Before you post anything, let me log on and follow you. I would strongly advise you to not read the comments anymore. Not on my page, not on Adina's, not on yours."

"I'll probably read a few, but I promise not to get involved."

Rasul squeezed Jacob's hand. "I'm telling you. Stay out of them. Nothing good will come of it."

Jacob withdrew his phone from its charger at the other end of the table with his free hand, pushed at the screen a bit with his thumb, and passed it over to Rasul. "Go ahead and log in."

Rasul did, surprised at the unsettled feeling in his stomach. He wanted to believe it was because he worried for Jacob, who couldn't possibly be ready for trolls, but if he were honest, it was just the idea of getting back into such a negative space, even if it was to friend Jacob.

You can't change who you are.

Was this who he was, though? As Rasul moved through his account, trying not to read things and feeling queasy at the number of notifications for comments and DMs, he struggled to connect this feeling to an important part of him. He hadn't been on social media because he enjoyed it. Maybe Twitter before it became a hellscape cascade of the dismal world news and a sea of trolls, maybe Instagram when he was in the heyday of promotion and he hadn't yet tried to start book three.

Well, no. It had been rough as soon as the backlash for *Carnivale* started. And Twitter had always been pretty fraught too.

Had he *ever* been happy online? What had he been chasing? Why would he go back to that?

"My username is *castlecaptured*," Jacob said, breaking Rasul's spell.

Shaking his head to clear it, Rasul entered the name. There were five posts. One of each cat, a nicely stylized picture of a cup of tea next to books, and a shot of the bay. Each one tugged at his heart.

Maybe he hadn't wondered about the future because there wasn't anything to think about. It was already decided.

He friended Jacob, logged out, and passed the phone back.

When Jacob held up the phone for a selfie, Rasul looked into the screen and felt his heart click into place. Everything he wanted was right there. The apartment. The cats. The clock. His lover.

His heart.

Before Jacob snapped the photo, he turned his head and kissed him on the cheek, a soft sigh escaping from the bottom of his soul.

Jacob smiled as he showed Rasul the result. "That's nice."

It wasn't just nice. It was perfect. Rasul leaned on Jacob's shoulder, his soul quieting again. "Email it to me, will you? I'm going to make it my desktop."

"I will, but let me take another one in landscape so it'll fit better."

They posed for several pictures, laughing and mugging for the camera. Rasul requested every single one of them, even as he made Jacob promise to take a thousand more.

THROUGHOUT JANUARY and February, Jacob battled the trolls on his Instagram.

It was by turns a fascinating and horrifying experience. He failed utterly in not reading the comments, but he did limit his logins to once or twice a day, not allowing any notifications on his lock screen or on top of the app itself on his home screen. He also, at Gus's suggestion, didn't ever respond to anyone.

Gus and Matt had both followed him immediately to get in on the fun, and of course Jared was an early follower too. Soon everyone on QUAG followed him, and they frequently brought up the drama when he ran into them around town. Before long, almost everyone in town who used the app followed him.

Gina didn't like it. The trolls quickly got annoyed that Jacob wouldn't take their bait, so they shifted to trying to get a reaction out of the store, and that drew Gina into the mess. Jacob had to take over the store's account because it was too much for her, though even he had to take notice when the commenters began leaving negative Yelp and Google reviews.

"I don't understand how people can talk like that," Gina said. "You'd be arrested if you behaved like that to someone's face."

It unsettled Jacob, but he was determined not to let it get to them. "I'm not responding to them anywhere." Jacob calmly sipped his coffee at the front desk as he flipped through a newspaper. "They have to find an outlet, so they keep trying for things that might reach me. This will blow over when I don't respond."

"But you're posting, so isn't that a response? Anyway, I don't like them attacking the store. It's not good for business."

"Most people around here aren't finding us because of those search engines, and we've actually quadrupled our Instagram followers since I posted that first photo of Rasul." But that online stain did concern him. Still, wouldn't it be worse if he backed out now?

Of course, Les Clark had a field day. Now he not only berated Jacob at meetings and questioned his judgment to every voting member, he also wrote opinion pieces in the paper, warning these unstable outside influences would doom the town. It seemed like hyperbole—until Engleton's and Café Sól saw negative comments on their online reviews.

Now Jacob was alarmed, and Matt and Gus were the ones trying to downplay what this meant.

"My dad was upset, but he just called our lawyer," Matt said. They were at an MMS meeting in the back of the coffee shop. "I don't know if he'll get anywhere with Google or Yelp, but if it's possible to do so, he'll get it done. He was never going to vote for you anyway, so he's not a loss."

"The college kids are really into the feud," Gus said with a smile. "Honestly, I think my business has picked up because of it. The kids who come to the store have started commenting back, and several have snapped photos of the two of you to prove their point. It's a war now. Copper Point versus the Adinastans."

Matt raised an eyebrow. "Are you serious? That's what they call themselves?"

Gus shrugged. "C-list celebrity, C-list fans."

Rasul was oblivious to all of this. He was too absorbed first in his edits, then in a barrage of advance magazine interviews, all of course he had to juggle against teaching. Most of Jacob's taunt photos were of Rasul working, though they did manage to sneak away one afternoon to get a pic at the lighthouse. Rasul said he needed to go for research, but it was also a nice day out, for the time of year. Jacob didn't bring up the online struggles. He figured if Rasul didn't mention them, that meant he didn't want to know.

Meanwhile, Jacob continued to run his bookstore, arrange for the care and feeding of his boyfriend, and check in with his haters. The bookstore's business was up, significantly in fact, and Rasul was so blitzed at the end of every day that Jacob practically poured him into bed. This left him a lot of time in the evenings to check on things online. He frequently startled the cats as he talked back out loud to comments from users named *adina4life33* and *WeLoveAdinaAndRasul*. The user who really made him angry, though, was *truthseeker98*. They were the ones who had all the Copper Point photos and who seemed to possibly be feeding new shots to Adina for her deepfake videos and photos. This meant someone was in his town, in his *store*, spying on him. It made him crazy.

He tried to console himself by saying the Adinastans obviously had no life and were incredibly sad creatures he shouldn't let bother him. He enjoyed their torment as they argued over whether Jacob was a liar or if he could somehow possibly be legit. Jacob observed them like a colony of insects from far away, and he swore he could see the patterns, could know everything about them sight unseen. There were factions, and ringleaders. They were invested in the story Adina had created, each for their own reasons. When he began looking at their pages, despite what they shouted at him, it was difficult to take them too seriously. They didn't have a lot of agency in their own lives. Most of them had more than one passionate online following, and they were consistently angry everywhere they went. Some of them posted all day long and in the middle of the night. It would have been one thing if they'd been enjoying themselves, but they were clearly miserable.

Especially truthseeker98. It was probably some twenty-year-old who'd dropped out of school and wanted to be an online influencer the same as Adina.

Adina herself was something else. While Jacob had a complicated set of feelings for her followers, the woman who had started all this he had no patience for. She was manipulative and self-involved, and while she might have her own reasons for pursuing Rasul, she had no right. Also, she was lying.

Not just lying, but *fabricating*. She'd taken to posting videos of her own that were so convincing they gave Jacob momentary pause. He was aware photo and video editing had gotten intense, but this was… this was something else. If you wanted to believe Adina's story, it would be easy with her fakes.

Why? He desperately wanted to ask her. *Why are you doing this? What could this possibly get you? You aren't dating him. He won't come back to you, especially because of this. What in the world are you doing?*

Gus wasn't surprised by her efforts. "People get caught up in alternate realities online. I think it's the illusion of control. Commanding the crowd like that is a heady experience. I remember in college I went with a boyfriend to a game, and this woman in the front of the stands started playing around, trying to get the crowd to mimic her. She got the whole section of the stands to respond. You could see the progression on her face. It was a lark at first, but she got caught up in the thrill of it. And people got caught up in following. She went on for a long time, and it was only some activity on the field that broke the spell. I think the internet is the same thing, but there's a lot less to distract you if you're operating in a bubble. Plus you can't see people's faces, can't know who they are or even guess because you just don't have enough information. But you're sure you know them, because you fill in the blanks. It's an endless cycle. You can distort your reality to be whatever you want, and people will follow you because they want to feel the world is more understandable than it is."

Jacob frowned. "I don't like it."

"Of course you don't. You don't like it when it happens here in town either. Les Clark and his iron hold on the chamber of commerce is the same thing, his determination that people and businesses should behave a certain way, that progress should only happen under his terms. He just wants to control people, and people want something comforting to follow." He winked. "That's what I love about *you*. You look like someone decent and dependable, and you are. But you're also a disrupter. You say, calmly, 'Follow me into a new future. It'll be fine.' And it's easy to believe. You could run for mayor if you wanted."

Jacob shuddered. "I don't want to be mayor." He considered what Gus had said. "You really think I'm like that, do you? Someone people can follow?"

"Of course. Matt and I do. A lot of people agree. That's why we're supporting you for chamber president. I don't think you're going to win this online battle, however."

That got up Jacob's nose. "Why not? *She* can't possibly win this."

"Why couldn't she? She's a master of her arena. You don't just leap into a war and win because you're using logic. She's got moves you don't even understand. But that's fine. You don't really want to win there anyway."

"But I *do*. I don't want them saying untrue things about Rasul."

"For Pete's sake. The whole internet is going to say untrue things about him forever. You can't possibly stop them all. But why bother? All that matters is what's in front of you. You have him. You have Copper Point. He's finished his novel. You're both going to live happily ever after. Do you need anything else, really? Do you honestly need to feel like the virtual world is yours too? Maybe you could get it for a short while, but you'd have to go defend it. All the time. Is that where you want all your focus to be?"

It wasn't, but Jacob was still bothered by the idea that people would still be somewhere carrying on and there wasn't anything he could do about it. He didn't want Gus to be right, and he kept thinking that if he were clever, if he found the right angle, he could get them all to stop. But as time wore on, he saw no matter what he posted, no matter how he jabbed, it was food. He began to see if he did a video post where he inserted logic into the whole thing, it would enrage them. And amidst it all was his rival, Adina, egging the fans on. And the hated truthseeker98.

There was no way out either. Even if Jacob took a break from posting, the others kept going. It drove him crazy wondering what they were saying when he wasn't looking. But by the same token, the more he watched them post, the sicker he felt.

In a passive-aggressive, or perhaps simply an aggressive, move, Jacob started filming Rasul. He interviewed him while they walked along the greenbelt or while he lay on the couch with one of the cats. He took perverse pleasure in asking Rasul about a current event or some other time marker that made it difficult for people to accuse him of remixing old videos. He particularly enjoyed how annoyed these videos made truthseeker98.

"Careful," Matt warned him when he gleefully relayed one of Adina's retort videos one day to Gus and Matt, showing truthseeker98's furious comments. "You're poking a hornet's nest."

Jacob snorted. "What are they going to do, come up here and make a scene?"

Gus laughed. "Are you kidding? No. Never. That would end the ruse. These types are lions online and mice in real life."

That only proved Jacob's point. "Well, then what can they do? I mean, honestly, all we need is a video of Rasul denying her."

Matt shook his head. "It's all about spin. Adina can turn around and paint Rasul as a user, that he duped her. Unless he gets down and dirty and keeps going after it—but that plays into her hand too. She's only got this online attention. That she dredged this up when it was already over isn't a good sign. I'm not trying to call her a crazy ex-girlfriend, because that oversimplifies this—but she *is* a wounded animal in a lot of ways. She can keep finding things you care about and destroy them. And honestly, if she really has a mole here, *they're* the true danger."

Gus sobered. "You make a good point. Maybe you should set this aside, Jacob."

Jacob went cold. "What do you mean, danger? Like, physical danger?"

Matt shrugged. "Maybe. I don't know. But again, I'm going to encourage you to let her have this arena. You had your fun, but it's time to get back to your real life. Rasul's ignoring it. His agent is too. Have you talked to her?"

"No, I haven't."

"This might be a good time to change that. She's clearly been watching this go down." Matt grimaced. "But honestly, my advice is let it go. I don't like what this is doing to you."

Jacob came up sharp. "What do you mean? What is this doing to me?"

"You're looking down instead of up. You've been so focused on this you haven't done anything with the chamber election in weeks. Meanwhile Clark is showcasing this fight as a reason you aren't suited. You're proving his point by getting in the mud. What does it gain your store? What does it gain Copper Point? What, really, does it even give Rasul? His reputation? He's better if he leaves it alone. Why aren't you?"

"It's *wrong*," Jacob insisted.

Matt wouldn't let up. "This isn't like you, Jacob. Let it go."

Gus sighed. "I think he's right. I shouldn't have egged you on. Come on, let's plan our raffle baskets instead."

Jacob couldn't get his mind on the baskets. He was too busy worrying about what Matt and Gus said. Had he really gotten too caught up? Was it actually the better strategy to not engage? He couldn't deny the accusation that he'd neglected his campaign for chamber president. He'd already resigned himself to not winning.

Had he truly lost because he'd gone into the weeds for Rasul? Wasn't it *right* to fight for who you loved?

He was still surly when he got back to the apartment, where Rasul sat in his ponytail and glasses at the kitchen table as usual, a cat in his lap and two sitting nearby observing him as he typed. He glanced up at Jacob as he entered and smiled. "Hey, handsome. Good MMS meeting?" He got a better look at Jacob and closed his computer. "Not a good meeting. Sit down. Tell me about it."

Jacob displaced an angry Susan from her chair and regarded Rasul soberly. "I don't want to distract you from your work."

"What work? I mean, yeah, there's a lot going on, but marketing and promotion is nothing like drafting a book. Talk to me. Is this the Adina baiting you've been doing coming to bite you in the ass? I've been worried about it, but I didn't want to harsh your groove."

Jacob blinked. "You knew what I was doing?"

Rasul laughed. "Of course I did. I haven't logged on yet because I knew it would make me upset, but Elizabeth has given me summaries." He reached across the table and took Jacob's hand. "I appreciate you standing up for me. A lot. It's very sexy. But you don't need to do it. I don't care about any of that anymore. Let Adina be in an imaginary relationship with me. I'll take you to the red-carpet opening of *Carnivale* in film and the whole world will know she's lying."

So it was just as Matt had said. "I don't like that she thinks she owns you. That they *all* do."

"Honestly? Adina's got to know. This is desperation. Is it unhealthy? Yeah, and it makes me sad. And scared. There but for my retreat to Copper Point go I. I wouldn't have burned out that way, but I would have done a Rasul version of it. So, I mean, let her. I've got a finished book, a great future, and an amazing boyfriend. Elizabeth has been pleased at how your little war with Adina has drawn attention, actually. My agent gets asked questions, tells the truth, they believe her, and then she starts pitching interviews for the book. A few of them have asked me about it, and I do nothing but talk about you. This is *all* going to fall apart within months for her." He drew Jacob's hand to his lips and kissed it. "However, I don't want *you* to fall apart."

"I—I'm not—"

"You don't like being online. You said that before. I don't exactly think it's changed now. You're not talking about your campaign anymore, or things for the bookstore. You just look grim. I wanted to let you play this through and figure it out, but… I know the look on your face. You've let this get to you."

How could he deny it? Now he felt ashamed. "I'm sorry." His shoulders rolled forward. "Matt thinks I've neglected the chamber election. I think I've already lost."

"How soon is it?"

"May, which isn't that far away now, but—"

"But nothing. I think I've done enough self-promotion for a bit." Rasul waggled his eyebrows. "Forget winning the stan wars. Let's go make you king of the chamber of commerce."

Jacob blushed and smiled. "Fine." He nodded to the computer. "So the interviews have been good?"

"They have. We finished the final proofs of the book weeks ago now, and they rushed a few digital advance reader copies. Normally there wouldn't be any reviews until the summer, but Elizabeth says she thinks a few of them are going to rush to be the first. I don't think I'm that special, but I guess there's a lot of buzz. Also apparently your war with Adina has been enticing everyone. They want to see what my time in Siberia has done to my writing. I think Elizabeth wants you to go on tour with me."

It was the first time they'd mentioned the future, a time past the end of the school year. "Oh? Do you want me to come along?"

"I don't want to tour at all. But if I go, and if you'd come, yes, I'd love to have you there. To hold my damn hand. I can't believe I used to go after this stuff like a junkie. If I could, I'd do all the signings here."

"We can certainly talk about it."

"Speaking of talking about it." Rasul shifted in Jacob's arms and looked up at him, slightly apprehensive. "I, um, told Larson and Evan I want a permanent position."

Jacob's heart skipped several beats. "Oh?"

Rasul nodded. "Part-time only. But yeah. I want to keep teaching. I like it." He drew a breath. "And… I want to stay. If I can."

Jacob listened to the tick of the clock several seconds, memorizing the moment. "Of course you can stay."

Rasul sat up more. "I mean that I want to stay with you. In this apartment. I want to move in. Can I do that?"

Jacob couldn't stop his smile. "Yes. Yes, you can."

After that, Jacob lost all interest in baiting people on Instagram. He focused on moving Rasul's things over to his place, on renewing his campaign for president, not because he thought he would win but because it was still important to try to draw people toward the future. Even if Clark was president until he died, Jacob could still do good work.

He had even less thought for who was saying what online when Rasul started getting critical feedback for his book. An indie literary magazine did a feature, calling it groundbreaking. The magazine wouldn't be out for a few months, but Elizabeth had gotten an advance of the article copy. Several other journals planned features on *Veil of Stars*.

Rasul was also heavily involved in crafting the Moore Books raffle basket. It had several books in it, yes, including both Rasul's published works and a just-off-the-press advance review copy of *Veil of Stars*, so fresh it didn't even have a final cover. It also had a copy of *Moana* on Blu-ray, *I Capture the Castle* in paperback, and several of both Rasul and Jacob's favorite films and novels. There was also a tea set, Earl Grey tea, and an IOU for homemade hummus and pita made by Rasul.

Rasul was also already talking about his next book. It was untitled and still in the formative stage, but it involved a teenager from the Midwest discovering something mysterious in the lake outside of town. He hadn't brought it up to Elizabeth, he said, because he wasn't letting anyone else have it until he knew he could protect it properly.

Jacob began to think things were good and couldn't get better. Despite his resignation over the election, Rebecca still thought he had a shot. Rasul had moved in the last of his things, and they teased each other over whether or not they'd repeat their wild dancing at the chamber ball. (Rasul said yes, Jacob said no.) According to Elizabeth, the internet had calmed down. Jacob wouldn't know—he'd removed the app from his phone. But according to Rasul's agent, the book world salivated for Rasul's new title. They couldn't care less who he was dating.

Then, two days before the ball, Gus came bursting into the bookstore, face white, phone in his hand.

"Did you see it? No, look at you, so calm. You haven't seen it." He pulled something up on his phone and shoved it in Jacob's face.

Jacob braced himself for some wild new Adina Instagram post. Instead, the page Gus showed him was from one of the worst gossip sites on the internet. An all-caps, mega-point font headline read SHOCKING RASUL YOUSSEF/ADINA HANIN SEX TAPE REVEALED. Below it was a still from a video with parts of it pixilated out. Not Rasul's face, though, or Adina's. Those were clear as day.

Jacob gasped.

Jodie, who had been putting away books left out by patrons, turned to look at them.

Gus pulled the phone away. "It was posted thirty minutes ago. Everyone in the shop is talking about it."

Jacob felt sick. "Is it fake?"

"I mean, who knows? Maybe? Maybe not? You'd have to ask Rasul. Only he would know whether or not he made a sex tape."

Jodie dropped the book she was holding and covered her mouth.

Jacob pulled Gus into his office and shut the door. "This is going to destroy Rasul. He's worked so hard to get beyond his past, and now here it comes back to bite him. Right when he's doing all these interviews with big-time reviewers. He was on the phone with *The New York Times Review of Books* the other day. What if this makes them pull all their press?"

"I don't know. I honestly have no idea about any of this. And really, neither do you. Where's Rasul? I assume his agent has already called him?"

"Probably not—he's in a meeting at the college. It should be getting out soon, but he always shuts off his phone when he's on campus. The particular phone he has is difficult to silence, so he turns it off when he knows he can't answer it." Jacob's gut twisted. "Oh my God."

"Come on." Gus grabbed his hand. "We're going to find him."

"I can't leave the store! Only Jodie is here. What if this blows up and press comes to the store and mobs her?"

"Shut the place down! This is an emergency."

It took them a few minutes to chase everyone out, but then they were in Gus's car and racing to the university.

"I can't believe he doesn't have his phone on him," Gus grumbled as they headed for the parking lot. "He has his smartphone back from his agent. Why doesn't he use that?"

"He doesn't want to, he says. It's upstairs in his bedside drawer. He keeps talking about selling it." Jacob grabbed his coat and his keys. "If we'd been thinking, we'd have called Evan or Christopher or Ram to intercept him."

Gus blinked. "Damn, I didn't think of that."

"We're here now. But we can text them in case."

They both texted madly as they crossed campus, and Gus got the first answer. "Christopher said he just saw Rasul walk across campus toward the Scheman Building. That's where his class is."

"Damn it, there are two ways to get to that from the administration building."

"I know. You take the main path, and I'll go around the back in case he used the shortcut. One of us should be able to catch him."

Jacob didn't exactly run once Gus let him off, but he did proceed with purpose down the tree-lined walkway to the building where the humanities classes were held. Heart beating in his ears, he scanned the sidewalk, looking for the familiar head of curly hair and dark beard.

As he rounded the corner, there was Rasul, surrounded by a group of people, most of them with cameras. Two of them seemed to be professional news crews.

"Mr. Youssef, what comment do you have to make about the emergence of an alleged sex tape with you and your girlfriend Adina?"

Jacob stopped walking, heart sinking. It was too late. He was already too late. Though clearly he wouldn't have ever been able to stop this train in the first place.

As his gaze met Rasul's, his heart broke. Rasul looked blindsided. Sick. Humiliated.

Jacob hadn't been able to protect him at all. And he had the horrible, terrible premonition that he might well have made things worse.

Chapter Fourteen

ONE SECOND Rasul had been walking down the sidewalk, excitedly telling one of his students about the gift basket for Moore Books, and the next he was surrounded by reporters shoving cameras in his face and asking him to respond to the revelation of his sex tape.

Sex tape.

All he could do was stand there and blink, too stunned to respond.

Ben Vargas was with him. *Ben Vargas*, twenty-one years old with stars in his eyes because he thought Rasul was so amazing. So amazing he had five boom mics in his face and a horde of hungry paparazzi.

Sex tape. Oh God, he'd been dreading this. He thought he was in the clear. But now here it was.

Ben had been knocked away from him, but nobody cared. They just wanted a statement, a reaction, something to feed the machine. The machine he'd stoked by living the kind of life that *did* produce a sex tape. Only with Adina, but it could have been anyone, really. He'd been careless. Reckless.

Through a gap in the throng, he spied a familiar cardigan standing in the middle of the sidewalk.

Jacob. Jacob knew about the sex tape.

Shit. Shit, shit shit. The look on his lover's face cut Rasul up like he'd never known he could bleed.

Out of nowhere, Gus appeared, fighting his way through the crush until he reached Rasul, at which point he grabbed his arm and yanked him into the clear. As they approached the still-stunned Jacob, Gus grabbed him too, heading for the doors of the building.

"Come on," Gus said smartly as he herded them inside, the press and eager onlookers hot on their heels. "Both of you, up the stairs. There's a faculty lounge. All my money is on someone having called campus security as soon as this mess started, so we're going to count on that and find ourselves a safe place."

They made it into the lounge just as security showed up. As Gus locked the door, Rasul started for Jacob, saw his wooden expression, and sank into a chair instead.

Dusting his hands, Gus turned to face them. "Well. This is a fine mess we have here. What do we do now?"

Rasul couldn't look at Jacob. "It's my fault. All my fault." He brushed his sleeve over his lips absently, feeling slightly nauseous.

"What are you talking about?" Jacob's voice was soft and wounded. "It's my fault. I egged them on. I'm... so sorry."

Rasul looked up at him, confused.

"It's not the fault of either one of you," Gus said, sounding incredibly pissed, "unless one of you released that." He turned to Rasul. "Not that it matters, but is it real? Did Adina, or anyone, actually have a sex tape of you?"

Rasul felt shame to his bones. "Adina did. She filmed us a few times. It was hot in the moment."

He shouldn't have to feel shame. There was nothing wrong with having sex, or with filming it. Except... except he remembered how he'd felt that night. He'd gotten so drunk, so high, because he couldn't take the self-loathing. It was right before he broke up with her the last time, not counting his one relapse before coming to Copper Point. It wasn't about the sex, the filming, or the partner. It was how he'd felt inside while it happened.

Now it was all over the internet for everyone to see. He wanted to throw up.

"Well, it is what it is," Gus said, not sounding particularly bothered. "We'll get you through it, don't worry about that, Rasul. Probably you should call your agent. If you don't have a crisis manager, you should get one fast."

Rasul ran a shaking hand through his hair. "I... yeah." He looked up at Jacob, gut twisting. "I'm so sorry."

Jacob came closer, touched Rasul's shoulder. "No, Gus is right. It's not your fault. She had no right to share that, not for any reason, not without your consent."

It *was* his fault, though. He shouldn't have gotten back with Adina before he came to Copper Point. He should have stopped seeing her the first time when he'd known she was trouble. He should have logged on to

Instagram and declared he was with Jacob right away. Should have made it clearer, should have—

A soft touch on his cheek brought him back. Jacob was crouched in front of him. "Hey. It's *not your fault*."

"I don't know what to do," he whispered. And he didn't. He always knew what to do, always had a plan, was always dancing, always moving. But he'd stopped here. He'd rested. And now he wasn't ready. Not for this. Not now.

Not ever.

Gus nodded at the door. "I'll sneak out and get some intel. You two stay here."

Jacob locked the door after Gus left, then pulled up a chair in front of Rasul. He touched his knee. "Are you okay?"

The word *yes* was right there on the tip of Rasul's tongue, but then he got a better look at Jacob's quietly searching expression. He caved. "No."

Jacob averted his gaze. "I'm the one who's sorry. This is all my fault. I never should have goaded them."

"How is this your fault? She's my unstable ex."

"I don't think she's unstable. Calculating, yes. Manipulative and cruel, yes. But she knows what she's doing." Jacob pursed his lips. "It's like you said. She's desperate. She's like you were when you came here. For whatever reason, she's past caring about whether or not this hurts you. You're something she can use on the way to the place she thinks she should be."

Rasul sagged forward, bending in half over his legs. "I'm not ready for this. I could have weathered it before, but now… it's like I exorcised all of it in *Veil of Stars* and now I can't take it. I *don't* want all my next interviews to be about this."

Jacob stroked his back. "We'll take care of you. *I'll* take care of you."

Shutting his eyes, Rasul sank into the comfort of Jacob's touch.

Gus came back a few minutes later and spirited them out a back door and into Christopher's waiting car. There was press at the bookstore, but Owen was there too, as well as Nick, and Julian, glaring at everyone in Lawyer. It had been a four-alarm QUAG call, apparently, and everyone who could had responded.

He had five missed calls from Elizabeth when he turned on his phone, and he honestly thought he might start puking before he could talk to her, but she wasn't angry—not at him, anyway. Her main concern was keeping him from talking to the press.

"Don't give them any comment. I'm working on some things on my end—we have this covered. Don't confirm or deny anything. Don't even tell them no comment, simply avoid them at all costs, and don't say a single solitary word."

"I'm so sorry," he said for what felt like the hundredth time. It couldn't possibly be enough.

"I don't need an apology. I told you, I've got this. I think I'm onto something here. Just give me a few days."

Rasul was hardly going to argue with her, or with anyone. His class that night was canceled, and for days he barely left the apartment, skulking around with the cats and waiting for news and food to be delivered.

Jacob was a rock, getting grilled every day in the shop, but it was rough on him, Rasul knew. He'd stopped apologizing because Jacob had made him, but he hated how this grit from his past had cast a pall over everything.

Worst of all, Les Clark was having a field day, tarring Jacob in the paper and declaring his choice of company and his lifestyle a cancer on the town.

It wasn't bad enough he'd shot his own rising career in the foot. Now Rasul was dragging down the man he loved. It was his worst nightmare he didn't even know to fear come to life. And he had absolutely no idea how to get out of it.

JACOB DESPISED what the sex tape scandal did to Rasul.

They were prisoners in the apartment that first night. Though the police made regular patrols past their house, there was more press in town now, all of it tabloids looking for a scoop. Jacob was annoyed, both at the interruption and at his helplessness. The people of Copper Point were in much the same boat, Gus reported via text. The novelty of this much excitement had worn off quickly.

Rasul, however, remained quiet and withdrawn. If Jacob tried to talk to him, all Rasul did was apologize.

"Her actions have nothing to do with you," Jacob pointed out over and over again. "You're the one who was wronged here. I don't understand why you're not angrier than you are."

"I've known who she was since our first date. I mean, I didn't know she'd take it this far, but I sensed the potential. I think it was part of what attracted me. To be honest, more than once I've wondered if I chose to be with her *because* I knew she might do this or something like it."

Jacob glowered. "Oh, for heaven's sake, that's ridiculous."

"I mean, yeah, but I don't think you get how ridiculous I was being when I got with her. I was angry, overwhelmed, and I hate to admit it, but more than a bit entitled. I knocked around between angry people who expected the impossible from me, terrified I'd disappoint them and lose everything. So I just sort of spiraled." Rasul was wrapped in a blanket in the living room, rocking himself gently to the tick of the clock. "I was a heartbeat away from being the same kind of mess she is."

"But you're *not* a mess. You're doing well. You pulled yourself out of it. And you don't deserve being hurt like this, no matter how many mistakes you may or may not have made."

"I know." He didn't sound like he did, though.

Rasul canceled his classes for the rest of the week. "My students are hounded enough as it is, getting hammered with questions and combed for anything that might make a news story." Jacob hated to see it, not the least of all because this whole disaster gave Adina the limelight just like she wanted. All eyes were on her as she pretended to blush and demur and protest she never expected such an intimate moment to leak out, and at such an unfortunate time.

"She's trying to Kardashian this, and it makes me furious," Gus said at an MMS meeting—held at the bookstore after hours. It was too difficult for Jacob to go anywhere else.

"Rasul's had it color all his interviews, and there have been some calls for the cancellation of his book," Jacob said, grim. "Since the publisher has been referring to it as young adult, some say an author this scandalous shouldn't be writing for children."

"That's terrible." Matt pursed his lips. "But expected, unfortunately. God, why are people such assholes?"

Elizabeth called every day, keeping Rasul steady, a technique that only sort of worked. A week after the scandal hit, though, she called *Jacob*.

"Mr. Moore. A pleasure to meet you. I wish it were under more auspicious circumstances."

"Likewise." Jacob had taken the call in his office, and he leaned back in his chair. "How can I help you?"

"I'm chasing down something my investigator turned up. She thinks there's someone in Copper Point who helped Adina out. There's so much fresh footage in her doctored videos that there has to be an inside individual. Or maybe even two."

"I've thought that too—but wait, *two*?"

"Let me ask you this, Jacob. Is there someone in town who has it out for *you*? Someone who has intimate access, especially of your store?"

Jacob opened his mouth, then closed it. "I mean, there's this petty man who doesn't want me to be president of the chamber of commerce, but I hardly see how that could have anything to do with Adina. And he *never* comes in my store or is around us regularly in any way."

"Is there any connection between someone you *do* see regularly and this individual?"

He started to say no, then froze as the realization dawned. "Oh no. *No*. I don't want to believe that." He wiped at his face, lowering his voice as he glanced toward the office door. "Les Clark's granddaughter. She's one of my part-timers." He lowered his voice further. "She's working today." The simplicity of the betrayal—so obviously in front of his face this whole time—hit him in waves. "She was the one who caused the stir that first day when he was shopping. But I can't imagine she would goad anyone into releasing a sex tape. She's still in high school! She's about to graduate, and I heard she was planning to major in elementary education in college."

"High schoolers do worse than this on a daily basis. The real question is, would her grandfather set something like this up?"

"He might, if he were angry and spiteful enough. Which he is." Jacob felt ill. "So you're saying Rasul's nightmare is because of me?"

"I don't know anything yet except that you're not to blame any more than Rasul is, and I don't blame him at all. My God, you gave me my author back, *and* made him happier than I've ever seen him in his life. Plus your little passive-aggressive spat with Adina gave us the right kind of boost. I have no issues with you, nor with Rasul. But if this wise guy and his granddaughter did anything to my author, I'm going to take them down."

"I can't believe Jodie has any part in this."

"You'd be surprised what people will do to get what they want. Put money or fame on the table, and you see someone's true colors. As a literary agent, I've seen the worst of everyone. Authors who'll step on anyone to chase their dreams, believing everything is worth the price if it gets them enough control and power. Same for other agents, and some editors. Polite to each other in a professional setting, but always jockeying for an imaginary golden ring. What's a little destruction of someone's career when something you want lies in front of you? It's grim to learn how many people you thought were good will drag others through the muck to get what they want, how many humans see other people as tools and props instead of members of a community. But you have to acknowledge these people exist. If you don't, they'll knife you in the back every time."

Jacob stared at the wall behind his desk for a long time after he'd hung up with Elizabeth, trying to digest what she'd told him. He just couldn't believe Jodie would be a part of this. Yes, she was often silly, but most teenagers were. Even Les—would he honestly try to sabotage another man's career for a simple community leadership position? How did he even begin to approach either of them?

He needed help wrapping his head around this. Who could he talk to, though? Not Rasul, obviously. Gus and Matt would be happy to listen, but he wanted someone who would do more than listen. Someone who would dissect this even more than Elizabeth had and help him see what he needed to do—

He sat up sharply. Rebecca. She was probably working too, but her job was often flexible. Plus, she wouldn't lie to him. Much as Jacob wanted to hear Elizabeth was just a cynical literary agent, he needed to know if even a little bit of what she said applied here. Rebecca would know how to handle this, how to approach Jodie without stirring anything up unnecessarily.

He hurried to find his phone and sent her a text. She replied immediately, telling him she was free and looking for an excuse to stretch her legs. She'd be over in five.

Jacob met her at the door. She took one look at him and raised her eyebrow. "This is serious, isn't it."

Aware Jodie was somewhere in the stacks, Jacob only offered Rebecca a strained smile and escorted her to the office.

"So it's about Jodie," she said in a low voice as soon as he closed the door.

"Yes." Jacob indicated for her to take his chair and perched himself on a small ottoman littered with junk mail. Resting his elbows on his knees, he relayed his conversation with Elizabeth to Rebecca.

Rebecca's lips were thin through the story, and when Jacob finished, she said, "Oh yeah, I'm with the agent. She's your mole."

Jacob sank forward, his disbelief rolling the rest of the way over into disappointment and a nest of more complicated feelings. It did seem she was the most likely candidate, once he told the story out loud. "So what do I do? Just confront her? Her grandfather?"

"No, not without a plan. Let me put one of the interns on this, scouring social media and archives for threads to solidly link her before you say a word. Rasul's got a case here, if he wants it, of libel and harassment. Do you know if anyone doxed him?"

Jacob started to say no, then paused. "There was this one user I always thought might be local. Truthseeker98. At one point they took a photo of the exterior of the bookstore and used it as the image for a long post ranting about how this is where I lived and, according to them, made up my lies about my relationship with Rasul."

"Well, that's tougher because I'm pretty sure you've publicly stated in print that you live above the bookstore. If she said Rasul lived here, that'd be another story. But don't worry about it, because my team will find what we need. They always do." She stood and patted his shoulder as he rose as well. "Give me twenty-four hours and I'll know how to best approach Jodie and whether or not we should bring her grandfather in right away, or maybe skip to him entirely."

"Thanks." Wiping his hand over his face, Jacob swallowed a sigh and opened the door to his office.

Jodie, tears streaming down her face, stood with her head bowed on the other side.

Rebecca quietly caught Jacob's forearm, her entire being telegraphing *don't say a word* to him.

"I h-heard you through the door. I'm sorry." Jodie's voice was a whisper. "I'm so sorry."

Though Jacob remained frozen, Rebecca sprang into action. She glanced around as she gestured at him. "Go sweep the store, make sure it's empty. Jodie, you come sit over here with me."

Jacob's heart beat in his ears as he brushed through the stacks upstairs and down. His mind kept trying to race ahead to predict what was going to happen, but he couldn't do it. Once everything was clear, he locked the door and joined Rebecca and Jodie in the seating area. Jodie was seated in the straight-backed chair in front of the fireplace, and Rebecca sat to the side in the overstuffed chair, so Jacob defaulted to the love seat across from Jodie.

As soon as Jacob was settled, Rebecca leaned forward, all her focus on Jodie. "Tell us what you're sorry for, Jodie."

She'd been sniffling the whole time Jacob checked the store, but with this one question, she shifted to full-on sobbing. "I didn't mean to h-hurt anyone. I-I've been an Ad-dinastan for y-years. I w-wanted to be just l-like her. And I h-heard you and Mr. Youssef say it was a fake relationship."

Jacob sat up straighter. "You did?"

She nodded. "I thought it was unfair to her, so I told her. She—she was so nice to me. Asked if I could h-help, so I did." She wiped at her eyes.

"But Jodie, we *are* dating. We have been for a long time."

"*I know.*" She wiped at her nose with the back of her hand. Jacob passed her some tissues and she blew her nose before continuing. "I realized it and I didn't know what to do. I told myself it was okay, that he was cheating, because if I told the truth, people would stop paying attention to me."

Jacob stilled. *You threw hot coals at my lover's mental health and his career because those things are less important than a D-list celebrity noticing you?* God, this was as bad as Elizabeth had said. Maybe worse.

What's a little betrayal or destruction of someone's career when something you want lies in front of you?

Something cold and quiet formed in the pit of Jacob's stomach.

Jodie dabbed at her eyes, which were still full of tears. "You don't understand. It's so hard to get noticed these days, and scandals are the best way to change that. I was already thinking, though, that maybe things had gone too far. The problem was before I could get myself to stop, my g-grandpa saw me DMing Adina."

Still reeling from the casualness with which this girl—a girl he thought was so innocent—used another human being as a lever to get a few clicks, Jacob needed a second to realize Jodie was about to deliver the connection Rebecca had wanted to hunt down.

Rebecca, way ahead of him, pressed on. "And Les Clark told you to continue?"

Jodie nodded miserably. "I felt weird about it, but it was my grandpa. I didn't know what to do. I thought maybe it was going to die on its own. But I think he's been talking to her without me." She started sobbing again. "I d-didn't mean to make Mr. Y-Youssef so depressed. I just wanted the attention. She said she'd make me famous." The tears started up again. "I'm sorry I said those mean things to you, about Rasul, sorry for all of it. I know you're going to fire me now, and I deserve it. I deserve everything I'm going to get."

Jacob's fists clenched on his thighs. Oh, how nice of her to agree to being fired, and how adorable she thought this would be enough compensation. As if losing a job she didn't need was enough to make up for the devastation this meant to Rasul. As if she could truly sit there and meekly wait for her punishment instead of stepping forward to take care of this in any way. Couldn't she at least quit and keep him out of it?

Setting his jaw, he faced her with arms folded over his chest.

Rebecca, however, remained calm, sounding almost motherly. "Jodie. Look at me, please."

She did as Rebecca asked, wiping furiously at her eyes.

Rebecca smiled the kindest smile Jacob had ever seen. "Are you willing to fix the mess you've made?"

Jodie nodded vigorously, reaching out to catch Rebecca's hand. "Yes, I want to fix this. I'll do whatever it takes."

"Good." Rebecca patted Jodie's hand, then sat back. A tiny glint formed in her eye. "You're going to confess what you did, and what your grandfather did." When Jodie hesitated, Rebecca's gentle smile turned sharp. "Here's the thing, Jodie. You and your grandfather did significant damage to a man's life. It's a serious situation, with a lot of legal liability I don't think either you or Mr. Clark took fully into account. But honestly, at this point I should talk first to your parents and your grandfather. You're still seventeen, right?" As Jodie paled, Rebecca's teeth appeared in her smile. "Ah, that's right, it was your birthday last month. You're eighteen now."

Jodie pushed to her feet, shoulders and arms rigid as she did her best to loom over Rebecca and Jacob. "It was a mistake! I said I was sorry! I said you could fire me! Isn't that enough? What more do you want from me?"

Rebecca blinked at her as if she were quite surprised. "You said just a minute ago you'd do whatever it takes. We both heard you. Right, Jacob?"

"Yes." Jacob balled his fists against his thighs, attempting to marshal his rage. "You hurt the person I love, and you did it while I *paid you money*. You betrayed us in the place we felt the safest. At my business. In our home."

It galled him to see how Jodie's defenses only rose at this, tears absent as she grasped for excuses to justify herself. "People do this sort of thing online all the time. Everybody knows it's no big deal, and Rasul is a big enough celebrity he should expect it. Besides, he's always been a playboy. What does it matter? He practically asked for this."

The urge to slap her, shake her, do anything physical to try to push his rage onto her was so strong it almost choked him. She got to do all this to Rasul, but he couldn't do anything at all to her? Obviously violence wasn't the answer, but... *they didn't know*. None of them would ever understand the hell Rasul went through to make his stories, how much he cared about what his readers wanted, how much he just wanted to give people the story they needed that he could tell. Certainly neither Jodie nor her grandfather could comprehend how difficult it was to write about your own orientation, your own cultural landscape, when even your own publishing house wasn't in your corner to take the risk. No one would understand how far away Rasul was from their image of him, and nobody would give a damn to hear how much his cavalier ways had been a silent plea for help. He hadn't hurt *anyone*. All he did was accidentally present himself as a useful tool while clawing his way through misery.

It wasn't right for Jodie to even *think* she had the moral high ground here. But it was clear stories of Rasul's struggles wouldn't change her heart. She wasn't interested in Rasul.

The man Jacob loved so much.

With such a long, uncomfortable silence, Jodie began crack, and in her panic, she turned the waterworks back on. "I just want to forget this ever happened."

"That, I assure you, will be difficult." Rebecca leaned back in her chair, crossing her ankles as she gazed up at Jodie with a quiet smile that was polite and unmoved by her tears. "I think it best at this point for you to go home and wait for someone to contact you. Ask your parents for a lawyer. Though, I should say—" She winked as she waved her smartphone at Jodie. "Save yourself the stress of deleting your social media. I texted the team before we even sat down, and they let me know a few minutes ago they have all the archives they need."

Jodie looked like she was going to say something, then bolted out the door instead.

For several minutes neither of them said a word. Jacob struggled to breathe. After a few tight gasps as he tried for a deep inhale, Rebecca put her hand on his knee.

Jacob shut his eyes and hissed his remaining air through his nose. He inhaled, then shot the air out again.

His chest hurt. A small, hollow ache in the center that made him feel as if it was a black hole sucking his soul into it. So many emotions clanged inside him. He should probably do something about the rest of his staff, right? Make sure they weren't accomplices? How many other people who wandered his stacks, handled his money, smiled at his lover, were in truth only looking for a moment to take advantage? This really was his fault in the end. What a shameful job he'd done protecting Rasul. Shouldn't he have known better? Shouldn't he have seen?

In his shop. *In his shop* all this had happened.

Rebecca patted his knee and took his hand. "I'm going to help you. I *will* fix this for you. So stop beating yourself up."

God, that hole in Jacob's chest was going to kill him. "I can't wrap my head around why she did it."

"It doesn't matter. If she's broken the law, she's going to pay. Same with Clark. And trust me, I can always find a way to get my clients what they want."

Jacob looked up at her, desperate to find something to plug that hole inside him. But he didn't even know what to say anymore.

Rebecca winked at him. "It's going to be fine. Trust me. You're a good person, you believe in the existence of other good people, and it's one of the reasons I want you to be the president of the chamber of commerce. The reason I want you around in my life in general. You're one of the good ones. Me?" The glint returned to her eyes, and her smile grew knives. "I'm one of the bad ones. But I'm on your side, and I'll always be there." She rose, nodding at the back of the store. "Let's go find Rasul and make some plans."

It disturbed Jacob how calmly Rasul listened to the story—told by Rebecca because Jacob was still a little unsteady. This meant Jacob had nothing to do but watch Rasul's face as he took everything in. He looked mostly wooden, and tired, and only mildly surprised to hear it was Jodie who betrayed them.

When she finished, Rasul sat back. "My agent and my lawyer are going to go ham on this. Good thinking on those screen shots."

"Give them my contact information, and I'll set them up with whatever they want. Jacob, I'll be in touch with whatever I find, but I'm assuming there's already been a few calls from the Clark family lawyers." She looked pleased. "It's going to be fun, because everyone at that firm hates me." Rising, she smiled at them both. "I'll leave you two alone, then, and I'll be in touch. I'll see myself out."

Rasul shut his eyes and leaned his head back. Once Rebecca was gone, he wiped his hands over his face with a groan. "God, I really don't want to call Elizabeth and my lawyer right now, but I guess that's what I've got to do."

Jacob couldn't take it any longer. "You're a lot less angry than I thought."

Wearily, Rasul shrugged. "I mean, I *am* angry. A little rattled too, because I hadn't seen her coming. I really am rusty."

"Are you trying to tell me you're *used* to things like this?"

Rasul's laugh was dark, and exhausted. "I mean, I guess that's one way of looking at it. Everybody comes at me with a smile, effusing about how much they love me, but I usually assume they've got a knife behind their back, ready to carve out a slice of me for their own purposes."

"You shouldn't have to put up with that!"

"Hon, I don't know how to explain this to you—it's all I've ever known." Rasul's hollow gaze softened as he looked up at Jacob. "Until you." He laughed wryly. "If you ever pull out a knife, I'm just going to open my arms and accept it. You and Elizabeth are the two people I know in that category."

Jacob swallowed the bile in his throat and took Rasul's hand. "I will *never* betray you. If I don't like what you're doing, I'll get angry with you to your face. But I'll never betray you. Not a single time."

Rasul glanced away, but his rueful smile died quickly, and his shoulders sagged.

Wordlessly, Jacob pulled him into his arms and held him.

RASUL'S AGENT and attorney moved fast, and Rebecca kept their pace. Once they showered the Clark family lawyers and the relevant prosecutors with the documentation of Jodie and Les's crimes, Rebecca, Elizabeth, and the lawyer teamed up with Rasul's publicist and began a PR blitz. It started with an article on a midlevel news site, followed by remixes everywhere else, offering proof of the harassment of Rasul by Adina and Les in a coordinated attempt to defame and embarrass Rasul for their own ends.

Jacob watched everything unfold in awe. From the outside, everything appeared so organic and casual, but behind the scenes countless deals and called-in favors greased the wheels. It sobered him to realize much of the entertainment journalism he'd assumed was impartial happened because someone knew someone else and owed them a favor, or had a vested interest in getting on someone's good side. One afternoon Jacob was in the kitchen, making tea as Rasul and Elizabeth strategized, discussing who they should give exclusives to in exchange for favorable coverage. It all seemed so dirty to Jacob, but apparently it was just how the business worked.

More than once, he walked past the stacks and wondered about the grim stories that could be told about each title he had for sale. How many favors and deals been made for each launch? Which authors he'd assumed had achieved success had done so by merit, and which had ascended on the backs of other people? He was afraid to know the answer. He feared if he did, he'd never read another book again.

Once the actual articles began to appear, both locally in Copper Point and nationally, public sentiment quickly spun their way. Rasul and Jacob's team kept on the offensive, making screenshots of posts and direct messages available to any outlet who asked for them, and of course everyone took them. Then the machine took over on its own. Someone, somehow, had gotten ahold of Les's emails, which were horrifying. Les damned himself as a scheming homophobe who used his vulnerable granddaughter to achieve his own petty goals.

The PR team was impressive too. Jacob had wondered why Rasul didn't press charges regarding the sex tape at first, but Rebecca had understood right away. "The tape's existence isn't good for Rasul's image. They're going to try to imply, without actually saying so, that perhaps everything is fake, even the sex tape. They've done a good job framing the story with Rasul as the victim. If she had a better lawyer, or if Clark were smarter, they could have flipped the script on Rasul, making him the bad guy. Always move first if you can to claim the narrative, and shut up if someone else grabs it first." Rebecca smiled darkly. "Happily, none of the opposing parties are capable of doing anything but digging themselves deeper and helping our cause."

Jacob couldn't take this. "So we're just going to do the same thing they did?"

Rebecca threaded her fingers over her chest. "No, we're not. They broke laws and harmed people. We're just helping them bury themselves, and they've made it super easy. Besides, only a few people actually care about what rules were broken. They just want a good story. Everybody wants a motive, but motive doesn't matter."

He laughed. "Oh, come on, of course motive matters."

"Only on TV, honey. In the real world, if you hit my car, it doesn't matter why you did it. You still damaged my property, and someone needs to pay for it, and that someone won't be me. Slippery road? You're still at fault, failure to stop. Your rearview camera blinked out and you backed into me, or the sun hit your eyes and made it hard to drive? Still your fault. The law doesn't care why you broke it, only that you broke it. Public opinion isn't the law. It's entertainment. So always give them a good show."

Jacob felt queasy. "This is all so cynical and awful."

"Of course it is. That's why you pay me to be good at dealing with it. You and Rasul go breathe hope into the world, telling stories and distributing them to others. Leave the bottom feeders to us sharks."

So Jacob did. He focused on supporting Rasul and selling books and being present in his community while the articles and online battles raged and the lawyers clashed. Public opinion shifted their way, guided by the expert maneuverings of people whose job it was to convince people of whatever truth was on the table. The Clark family lawyers tried to do the same, but they weren't as good at their jobs. Eventually Les retired from the bank and stepped down from the chamber of commerce. Jodie elected to homeschool for the remainder of the year. Adina was torn to shreds. Her platforms demonetized her. The gossip mags she so longed to be included in only spoke of her as the worst jezebel, as walking poison. And as far as modeling agencies went, she was blacklisted for life.

Just like that, it was done.

Outside of their internal wounds, Jacob and Rasul had never been better received in Copper Point. Local opinion had never been exactly against Rasul, but now everyone embraced him as one of their own who had been deeply wronged, and he was showered in casseroles and baked goods accordingly. Jacob received more approval than sympathy, people stopping by and purchasing books before telling him how wonderful he was, encouraging him to run for whatever public office he could.

Jacob still felt unsettled by it all, and to his shame, eventually Rasul consoled *him*.

"I get how you feel. It still bothers me, yeah, but it used to really get me down. Because the whole thing is a waste." They were curled on the couch together, Rasul's head lying in Jacob's lap as he stared up at him. "In the end no one gets anything, and no one is happy. Because even if they successfully step on you and get somewhere, once you sip at the dark magic, you can't stop. If you've used one person, you'll use any person, any thing, any excuse to get what you want. And the truth of the matter is, we only survive with each other. Living for yourself alone means eventually you're completely alone."

"It's just so wrong," Jacob said, feeling foolish because it seemed a naïve plea, but he couldn't help it.

Rasul didn't judge him, only reached up to stroke his face. "I know. Because you're after justice. Me too, if I'm honest. I want the world to be better, want to believe it can be better. It's difficult to grasp that some people don't even want to discuss what's right and wrong. Only what's possible."

Jacob thought about what Rasul had said all night long, unable to sleep a wink. It was true, he did want justice. He *believed* in justice, that everyone would support it if they could see it clearly. He didn't like this idea that the world was full of mercenaries ready to sell the truth for a few dollars.

He didn't understand how Rasul could write such hopeful, wonderful stories in the face of that disappointment.

As even more time passed and the world wove Rasul and Jacob's drama into its fabric, Jacob couldn't shake the determination that this story needed a better climax. Something soothing, so he and Rasul could go on believing in things like hope and happy ever after. Something *pure*, not manipulated. A bit of joy, a fissure of light to propel them forward.

The idea came to him one morning when the cats got him out of bed at five, the thoughts rising out of the mists of his tea as he clamored for proper consciousness. It woke him up completely, bloomed as he stood under the shower, and swelled as he paced the living room, the steady *thunk, click* of the clock punctuating his steps. At seven he texted Matt and Gus, and at eight Matt called him.

"Is everything okay? Did something happen?"

"Mini Main Street, this afternoon, at your store." Jacob caught a glance at his reflection in the mirror by the door and touched the collar of his sweater. "We need to bump up the timeline on that suit you're making for me."

THE LAST few days of April and first week of May were quiet, giving Rasul a lot of time to think. Perhaps a bit more than he wanted.

He still had interview requests, but he'd put all of them off. His excuse was he had a lot going on with the end of the school year, that he had to help Jacob get ready for the chamber ball, but the truth was he didn't want to face awkward questions he didn't know the answer to.

In so many ways, he was falling into depression, the depression he'd known lurked for him ever since he first realized how difficult it would be for him to write *Veil of Stars*. He'd run from this mental state, fought it tooth and nail. He thought he'd escaped it by finishing and getting together with Jacob, but like a riptide, darkness pulled him back. It didn't matter that Elizabeth and Rebecca had solved the crisis. He was going to feel that sick sense of exposure for a long time.

Exposure coupled with shame that it had been a crisis of his own making.

He'd said as much one night to Jacob, and Jacob had been irate on his behalf, pointing out there were laws against using someone's private photos and videos against them without permission, especially to coerce or shame. While Rasul appreciated this defense very much, even needed to hear it several times a week, it left out the gritty mess he held tight in his hand. His own part in this. That he should have known better. He should have done better for himself.

Jacob stayed beside him through this low like a rock, bringing him takeout, soothing him with the same reassurances over and over. "You got here on the path you had to take. I'm never going to judge you for that, and I hope you don't judge yourself either. I am, however, very glad you came."

He tried not to judge himself. The weather was finally warming, and he became addicted to taking long walks down the greenbelt park behind the store. He wandered all the way to the southern end, where he could peer down at the craggy riot of clear water against the jagged rocks, and to the northern end, from which point he could see the lighthouse.

On the morning of the chamber ball, he went up the lighthouse again and stood alone at the breezy apex, letting his thoughts unfurl across the bay.

He liked to run from things. He knew that. It had been a good strategy for a long, long time, until it hadn't. He'd built a life for himself full of the things he felt he should like, things he believed, or hoped, could keep him safe. From what, he still couldn't articulate. Criticism? No. Judgment? Ha. No.

From loneliness, he acknowledged at last. From insignificance.

Well, he thought with a wry smile, there was nowhere to feel quite so lonely as by yourself at the top of a lighthouse. It wasn't terrifying, though. It made him sad, yes, and it let in all those feelings he'd tried so desperately to push aside. But he didn't need to run from them anymore. He didn't want to.

He wanted to stay in Copper Point, with his friends and the person he loved, and find out what came after you stopped being afraid.

When he got back to the bookstore, Matt and Gus loitered at the bottom of the stairs in evening wear, waiting for him.

Panicked, Rasul pulled out his phone and looked at the time. "Don't I still have several hours to get ready?"

Matt and Gus exchanged a knowing look.

"Technically. But not actually." Matt pushed off the railing and crossed to Rasul, taking his elbow. "Come on. You'll miss your fitting."

"Fitting? For what?"

Gus took Rasul's other elbow. "Your boyfriend has arranged some pampering for you before the event."

"Starting with a fitting for a customized suit."

Rasul kept looking from one to the other. "There's no way in hell you can make a bespoke suit in two hours."

Matt snorted. "No, there isn't. But we can do some fairly decent finishes on the one I ordered for you."

Engleton's was quiet as they entered, only one employee behind the counter and an older couple shopping near the front of the store. Gus took Rasul to the fitting area and chatted idly until Matt rolled out a clothing dummy. It was wearing a fetching royal blue suit with big white checks, a pale blue shirt, a cheeky paisley bow tie, and a felted burgundy vest. There were also a pair of burgundy wingtip shoes.

Rasul grinned as he touched the suit. "This is for me? Really?"

Matt looked a bit smug. "We all consulted on it. We were fairly sure you'd like it."

"I love it. I want to put it on right now."

"You will, but only for a fitting. Then I'll get to work while you continue your pampering journey."

Rasul hurried into the clothes, admiring himself in the mirror as Matt took his measurements. "Where's Jacob, anyway?"

"Chamber stuff," Gus offered, tugging at the hem of Rasul's jacket and smoothing the fabric over his shoulders critically. "Technically we should be helping, but we've been assigned Rasul duty. We don't mind."

Rasul lifted his arm at Matt's direction. "Do you think he regrets getting voted in as president?" It had been almost an afterthought, with him the only one running and Les Clark out of the picture completely.

"Probably a little," Matt said around the pins in his mouth. "Hold still."

"He'll be fine," Gus said. "He always grumbles a bit at changes initially. But he loves a challenge."

"Does he have help setting up and all that, though?" Rasul asked. "I had planned to offer my services."

"He'll have our heads if you show up a second before he asked us to bring you." Gus patted Rasul's shoulder. "Just relax and enjoy your boyfriend's bossy side."

Rasul had no objections when it was put like that.

He hated to leave his suit, but Matt had whisked it away for alterations, and Gus took Rasul on to his next stop, which turned out to be his favorite masseuse at the Chinese massage parlor. Gus waited in the lobby while Rasul had every bit of tension efficiently expelled from his body. He tried not to moan in ecstasy, but a few times he couldn't help it.

After Gus paid the bill there, Rasul was taken to an affable barber two blocks off University Avenue who gave him a cut and a beard trim and told Rasul how much he'd enjoyed his books. After this it was back to the bookstore apartment, where Gina waited, petting the cats.

"I'll leave you now," she said, heading down the stairs. "My job was just to set things up. I hope I did it right."

Rasul didn't know what she was talking about until he went into the bathroom, at which point he laughed, and wiped a few tears away. Green sheets were hung across the room, and a ridged baking dish sat in the bottom of steaming, scented water. Petals were strewn around the room and across the surface of the tub, and a note was propped up on the vanity.

I had them leave you a towel this time, Cassandra. See you soon.

The bath was wonderful—Rasul took the dish out and said a prayer of thanks the water contained no dye—and when he was done, he came out to find Gus and Matt waiting for him, as well as his suit.

By the time he was dressed and walking down the street to the community center flanked by his friends, Rasul couldn't deny he felt more than a bit better than when he'd been brooding alone atop the lighthouse. He was a sucker for being cared for. It was a nice evening too. He couldn't wait for Jacob to join him.

He'd half hoped he'd meet Jacob outside the community center, but apparently he was inside seeing to last-minute issues. So while they waited for the doors to open, he chatted with Gus, Matt, and other community members waiting outside. Several people complimented him on his suit, which he completely credited Matt for.

"Wait until you see Jacob," Matt said, and suddenly that was all Rasul could think about.

His heart beat triple time as he filed into the community center, trying to peer around the crush to find his boyfriend. There were just so many people.

Murmuring apologies, he slipped around a clutch of people talking instead of walking and ducked around a pillar and into—

Into a veil of stars.

He couldn't breathe.

The entire main room of the community center had been draped in netting, and inside it were thousands and thousands of tiny white lights. It was his novel come to life. Except the veil wasn't isolating. It overflowed with the people he'd come to know and love, the messy, wonderful members of the community he now called home.

In the center of it, standing in the middle of the dance floor watching him, was Jacob.

He was so handsome and dashing Rasul felt dizzy. *His* suit was absolutely bespoke—the burgundy felted wool of his vest was the whole of Jacob's outfit, except for the silky tan vest and tie. He had a blue checked pocket square, and his coffee-colored shoes gleamed in the sparkling light.

Smiling, he held out his hand to Rasul. "May I have this dance?"

Before Rasul could melt completely, music started from the far side of the room. He started laughing when he recognized it.

"You're a bad guy, huh?" he said as he let Jacob pull him into his embrace.

"The worst," Jacob promised against Rasul's ear.

This time Jacob didn't hesitate or blush as they ground against one another. They moved in perfect synchronization, wrapped up in one another as if they were the only people in the world. Rasul couldn't stop smiling, but with the way Jacob's heated gaze bored into him, he couldn't stop blushing either.

This is why it's okay for you to stop running. You can afford to feel all your feelings now, because this man will be there to fish you out if you slip into the sea.

Rasul drew Jacob's head closer and pressed a heated, brief kiss against his neck.

And I'll be there to catch you too.

When the music switched to Air Supply's "Even the Nights Are Better," Rasul wasn't surprised. He simply downshifted, following Jacob as he led Rasul into a soft sway. As the town looked on and more than a few people snapped pictures, Rasul spun around the room with the person he loved the most, singing softly along with the music.

When the song wound to a close, he felt something small and metal pressed into his hand. Jacob closed Rasul's hand over it and Rasul recognized what it was, his heart soaring into the sky.

"I love you, Rasul," Jacob said into his ear. "Marry me. Stay with me forever."

Unable to stop grinning, Rasul lifted the ring, pressed it to his lips, then caressed the side of Jacob's face with it.

"Yes," he said, then felt his soul fly as Jacob kissed him and the whole room cheered.

Author of over thirty novels, Midwest-native HEIDI CULLINAN writes positive-outcome romances for LGBT characters struggling against insurmountable odds because she believes there's no such thing as too much happy ever after. Heidi is a two-time RITA® finalist, and her books have been recommended by *Library Journal, USA Today, RT Magazine*, and *Publishers Weekly*. When Heidi isn't writing, she enjoys cooking, reading novels and manga, playing with her cats, and watching too much anime.

Visit Heidi's website at www.heidicullinan.com.
You can contact her at heidi@heidicullinan.com.